SECRET ORBIT

SECRET ORBIT

KEN EDWARDS

grand IOTA

Published by
grandIOTA

2 Shoreline, St Margaret's Rd, St Leonards TN37 6FB
&
37 Downsway, North Woodingdean, Brighton BN2 6BD

www.grandiota.co.uk

First edition 2022
Copyright © Ken Edwards, 2022
All rights reserved

Typesetting & book design by Reality Street
Cover and title page images & author photo by Elaine Edwards

A catalogue record for this book is available from the British Library

ISBN: 978-1-874400-86-8

Day 1

YOU WAKE IN what seems to be an abandoned factory. The pipework and ductwork is of an extraordinary beauty. There is no way out. This is the Holding Pen, whence no-one in reality, despite the stated protocols and procedures and mission statements established by the Management, ever escapes. But hang on a minute. You must have escaped, it's vivid in your memory; except it isn't, that's an illusion, because of course there is no longer any discernible electro-chemical activity in that skull of yours, because, frankly, you have the condition known as brain death. That is to say, your brain stem is no longer in meaningful connection with your spinal cord. That trumps everything. So to say "you wake" or that "you remember you awoke" is fanciful. But there you are.

The good news is that this is no abandoned factory after all; actually, it looks uncommonly like your own bed in your own bedroom in your own flat. Congratulations. You made it. What do you think of that?

Sorry, your response is inaudible.

No blood flow, no oxygen, that's bad. You can't think how bad. But to get out of the Holding Pen, that's a result. If indeed you did. The only thing is – can you turn off that damn TV, or even just turn the volume down? it goes on and on, at a level of banality that beggars belief, plumbing new depths just when you thought you'd got to the bottom – the only thing is – no, of course you can't, you are immobilised by this condition of yours, that is to say death, or more properly brain stem death, and it's no longer at all possible for that bony finger of yours, not a few hours ago so mobile, so expressive, as were all ten fingers-and-thumbs, to press the off button. A pity you didn't have it tuned to a more interesting channel to begin with, BBC4, for instance, all those fascinating documentaries, and the added blessing of off-air silence during most of the daylight hours. Well, it can't be helped now. The only thing is: how did it happen?

There is no answer.

A dog is having hysterics in the street below, and its owner is shouting at it. No, you can't hear that either. Nor even the hum of traffic. But you seem fresh. Quite cool. Well, on this first day of your death your body will be rapidly cooling to room temperature. The inexorable dance of entropy kicks in, now that the vital metabolic processes and enzymatic functions needed to maintain body temperature are no longer in operation. You're not looking too bad, tucked up in your duvet. Appearances can, however, be deceptive. The bacteria that before death were feeding happily on the contents of your intestine, as they have been throughout the eight decades and more of your life, are now just beginning the enormous task of digesting the intestine itself. You won't notice that yet. The streams in your blood vessels are becoming irregular and lumpy as red blood cells clump together. Once circulation of the blood has completely ceased, gravity will predominate; that is, your blood will tend to flow downward, accumulating in capillaries and small veins in the lower parts of your body. Soon your skin will take on a different hue, with a patchy mottling, as you lie there peacefully. Relax, this is quite natural.

Looking back on your life, do you have any unfulfilled goals?

What's that? You don't know? No, of course you don't. You were a young man first, and then you became middle-aged and then you became an old man. That's about it. That's the story, in a nutshell. Of course, it's understandable, you are no longer in a position to say anything meaningful about it. Whatever happened happened. There's no going back. Thank god, it may be said. The very last time you saw yourself was probably last night, in the bathroom mirror. There you were, your reflection anyway, with a delay of approximately six nanoseconds, in your cracked and foxed bathroom mirror. All you saw was an old man you didn't recognise, who used to come in every morning looking worse than before; but he was you, a representation of you anyway, this is all you know: you remembered you'd come in, you'd lather and scrape at your face, you'd comb the few strands left of your hair, you'd strain to shit.

You had a medical condition, several medical conditions, described by one of the doctors as "complex", but now it doesn't matter any more, so that's the good side. Also your worldly possessions, it doesn't matter about them, the burglar can take them now, you don't care, do you? If he's still plying his trade. Or BJ can take them, if he ever returns. The key is still under the mat, he knows that. Do you follow? You're not listening, of course. Because all that's left to you is the final darkness, and you welcome it – it's a relief, it's easeful, as the poet said. Comfy. No need to worry about the Management either, they do not have dominion over your estate, not any more. You used to always be aware of the Management watching you, didn't you, that's a fact, how they would see you come, see you go. How there's nothing they didn't notice. You came to realise that. How you had to keep vigilant. Even when you went to post a letter, or something like that, via the short cut through the park, which is merely a dog toilet now. Through the gate in the arrowhead railings, then on to the diagonal path. You remember when it was all daffodils in spring, lovely it was, the way the council kept it. A lovely aspect, this flat has, looking over the park in spring. A typical London park. That was when you had your people, when they were truly alive. The park: a dog toilet now. You had a medical condition, which is to say you couldn't walk very far, inasmuch as you got tired and all that, so you just used to go out to post a letter and come straight back. Or get the paper. What's in the paper? Nothing. Rubbish. But no need to worry about all that now.

The burglar – he paid you another visit the other night. When was that? Ooh, maybe months ago. It's hard to keep track. This time he's taken your medical records, just took them out of the file, can you believe that? Well there's nothing much left to take by now. It's unbelievable. You're an old man, what have you got? Nothing. Your people are all gone now, long gone. Though sometimes you see them when you wake up, right here in the flat, at two in the morning. But this burglar, oh, he's been in a dozen times if he's been once. First, the radio: that's gone. Then you had these tins, which you won in the raffle at the day centre, tins of food, you stored them around the flat. You had one here behind the sofa, and one on that shelf, just hidden from sight, and another, you forget where (this is speculation, of course). All gone! you wake up in the morning, they've all disappeared. The chap, he's been again and taken them, every single one. It doesn't bear thinking about. Well, never mind him. He's welcome to anything else if he wants to come back now. He'll get a shock too, when he sees you. That'll be funny. Remember what happened? There you were in bed, you woke up in the night because you heard someone buggering about within the flat, you threw your mug, which happened to be by your bedside, at him, but he was too quick for you, and the mug banged on the floor but didn't break. He ran into the spare room, you toddled after, and you were banging on the door shouting, but he'd locked himself in the room. It was two o'clock in the morning, something like that. Are you going to come out? you were shouting. Finally the door opened, but it wasn't him, it was not the burglar, he must have left when you weren't attending, or climbed out via the window. And instead there was your mother, right there in the doorway, who's been dead these sixty years, so it was very confusing, and she said, There there, it's all right, just like you remember her doing way back when you were very little. There there, don't be afraid, and all that. A sort of glow about her. You began weeping, but when you opened your eyes she wasn't there any more, of course.

You used to go down the High Street, but it's all changed. That department store, which we all remember, gone now, and the draper's too. An old-fashioned draper's shop like the one your mother used to work in, back on the island, which is where you were born. The butcher's used to have this effigy on the pavement in front of it in those days: fat smiling butcher in a straw hat with a blue ribbon round it and a blue tie and red and white striped apron, and he's grinning and has a ginger moustache and sideburns. As tall as you are and twice as wide. Was there for years. Now it says on the sign "Halal Butcher". And the chaps behind the counter, they don't look anything like him. Fair enough, it all changes. Now it's all shops selling strange vegetables, and artificial hair. And cheap stuff, electronic gizmos of all kinds. Everything for a pound. It used to be class. That's what you always said, didn't you? You talked to your mirror about it all the time, which is to say your image, which is to say your self. Antique furniture shops all in a row across the street, on the other side of the park, smelling of French polish, beautiful; not any more. And it changes too fast, and the street's just full of youngsters, all jabbering. That's what they do, the youngsters, they jabber at their electronic gizmos. It's not human speech, you can't understand it. It goes too fast. They're laughing but their eyes have no mirth for you. There's this young white woman with scraped-back hair enters the post office with a baby in a pushchair, as you're coming out with your pension; you hold open the heavy glass door for her, but she doesn't even look at you, it's like you're not there, like you don't exist. She has tattoos all up her arm.

Crossing the park in the mist in winter, coming home, it's hard to see anything, the cold grass just fades into bluish nothing on every side. The mist swirls up and the darkness comes up on all sides and just engulfs the whole thing. You're in the middle of the crossroads, in the part, I mean, where the paths cross, quite frosty. And you're hearing this call from somewhere, at first far off then coming closer, this man's voice calling, "'Itler! 'Itler!" There he is ahead of you, looming up out of the mist. And then again, "'Itler! 'Itler!" And now you realise he's calling his *dog*; well, your blood's boiling about it. Now you can just manage to make him out in the fog, he's a man of some bulk. He's going, "'Itler! 'Itler!" and the great brutish dog just leaping out of the distance and making a fuss. You want to say to him, You don't know what you're on about! You know what *he* did? You don't know anything about it! But of course, you never say anything. Not wise. That's the kind of world we're in now. Everybody's forgotten. That's what BJ used to say. Whatever happened to BJ?

Time for a rest from all that, anyway. Best out of it. But is there any way to turn off that great bright gaudy-colour TV, or at least turn the damn sound down? No, of course not.

Day 2

THE TELEVISION'S ALL you've got now. Your only companion during the second day of your lying in state. Even that's different. A completely different TV from the one you had. You remember? Again, it was some time ago, when you were still chugging along. It happens like this. One morning you get up, and you have a look, and what do you know, the burglar's been again. This time the television's gone. To be more precise, there's *another* television there, not yours. It looks different, you know that in your bones, although you'd be hard put to describe what exactly's different about it; and when you try switching it on with the remote gizmo, well, it doesn't work. So the burglar's substituted another television for yours. You know very well it makes no sense, but there you are, that's what he's done. So you can't watch it now. You meet the neighbour from downstairs on your way out, and you tell him about it; he offers to come up to your flat, and he looks around, and says, I'm sorry I can't see any signs of breaking and entering. Well, the reason for that obviously is the chap's got a key. Or he's sussed out that you keep the key under the mat. You tell him this. The neighbour doesn't seem convinced. Anyway, he figures out how to use the new TV and the remote control, and he shows you how, and so finally you can work it. You thank him profusely. I wouldn't advise you to keep the key under the mat, though, he says. A very kind young man, that neighbour, that's something to be grateful for. But he's moved away since, he no longer lives downstairs. There's nobody there now. (Wasn't it great, though, to be able to go through your own front door and into the hall and down the stairs, all under your own steam; to contemplate the damp stains on the stairwell wall with your very own eyes, to talk to another human being, however briefly, with your own mouth? Weren't those the great days?)

And remember how every Thursday the ambulance came to take you to the day centre? Well, that's what used to happen for a while. Before you got sent to the Holding Pen, that is. If that is what happened. We shall return to that topic by and by. As for the day centre, there's nothing much to the place, it's just filled with tedious old folk who have nothing to do but sit around. Sometimes they are induced to sing. The staff say to you, come on, you used to be a musician, didn't you, why not join in? But your heart's not in it, it doesn't have the *thing*. The thing that swings. You are promised home care. The nurse will come round every day to give you the injections. Fix you up, they say. There's a lot of paperwork. Reams and reams of it. White copies and pink copies and blue copies. Now can we double check, Mr [FORENAME] [SURNAME], they say, would you prefer to be called Mr [SURNAME] or would you prefer to be called [FORENAME]? I don't give a monkey's what you call me, as a matter of fact, is what you say, to tell the honest truth. Oh, Mr [SURNAME], you're so funny. But anyway, that didn't turn out as it should have. Government cuts. They couldn't send a nurse round after all, you'd have to do your own injections, but they could send a care assistant. But she's not allowed to give you the jabs.

Lots of problems with this flat. Water pouring down the walls because the Freeholder hasn't fixed the roof. But that was also Jackanapes upstairs letting the water run, of course. Tiles fall off the bathroom wall, parts of the wooden flooring begin to creak, you can hear the wind blowing planks off the roof onto the communal yard at the back, and even your teeth begin to dislodge. Fridge doesn't work properly. Where are you going to keep your insulin? Another nurse visits to sort it out. She's the honey-coloured one, smiling, big white teeth, reassures you, it's going to be OK. Pats you on the hand, and all that caper. It's all right, [FORE-NAME] (you're on first-name terms now), we'll sort it all out, don't you worry. She means well, you have to give her that. Toothache now, so they make an appointment for you with the dentist – it's OK, you can get there under your own steam, you tell them – who says you will need extractions. What you didn't expect was for him to yank the two upper right-hand-side back teeth out right there and then, but he did (one of which shattered and was displayed to you afterwards in bloody pieces). Ah, all your teeth going down like ninepins. The shape collapsed. The new teeth added to your plate, and now you have a mouth full of crockery.

Lots of problems, no more no more. Your day is done. Yes, the day is departing, and now the darkened air releases all the creatures in the park over the road from their labours. The birds, the squirrels, they flee to their nests and drays. Your memory was coming to an end before it all ended. The good ones the bad ones. Woe, woe and thrice woe. Those tiny creatures of your imagination have to keep well hidden (beneath the bedclothes) or those unseen glittery predators that abound in the night will swoop and swallow them up, rendering them unto invisibility. The planet is dark and desolate, with strange abandoned buildings everywhere. The desert speaks with a fine noise, a tune maybe you remembered, as long as you had memory. Which was not much longer. The noise clusters closely enough to empty itself, it lingers, thunderously. And people cluster with other people whose approval they crave, but they are all like refugees, marooned in that desert place.

Once, you were unconsciously conscripted into the role of a scapegoat: everyone hated you and it was your job to be hated. At last they could all see through the nice guy to your essential hatefulness. You may have screamed against your shunning, "By the way, I was once blue-eyed!", but it was of no avail; they turned away from you, disgusted all the more. Of course you know, and everybody knows, you were never blue-eyed, far from it, but irony has no purchase here, not among these people. Then it goes a stage further, and they can't even see you any more. You have entered the invisibility stage, which is even worse than being hated. So to remedy this you are induced to wear a magic skull-mask, covering your entire head, because this is the only way people can see you, although it has the unwanted side effect of rendering you hideous. That's no good, then. Upon removing your mask, you notice that most of your head has now become visible again, although there is still a blank where your right eye is. Perhaps things are getting better.

Once, a very long time ago, you used to drive a car to work, but something went wrong with the engine one day, you had to get out and seek help; but then you discovered you had nothing on but a sleeping bag wrapped around you, and moreover you couldn't remain upright any longer, you had to try to make progress by slithering along the ground in the sleeping bag, snakelike; finally, not even that was left to you, you were naked and had no possessions, though you needed money and identity documents. That was not a good memory. Bad memory. Definitely.

Earlier, bright sunshine suddenly turned to foreboding gloom; then the most ferocious hailstorm you ever witnessed hit the neighbourhood for about five minutes before abruptly stopping. The rattle against the windowpanes was loud and alarming. Within minutes the street and communal area at the back were converted into snowscapes, and when sunshine eventually returned there were still thick piles of hailstones the size of gobstoppers accumulated in shadowed areas. Crossing the park at dusk, on the way back from the dentist, the bluish glimmer of the turf all around you. Midway on the path, you pass two men in heavy coats. Then suddenly they are gone. In the distance, to your left, the moving lights of the traffic. There is scarcely anybody else about, the houses on the other side of the park seem uninhabited, even the birds have been silenced, the weather is greyly oppressive; for all you know everyone has been carried off by a plague or a silent invasion. This half-life, of course, is worse than death – stripped of all care for the exterior, oblivious of everything, having nothing and wanting nothing other than to hang on to this nothing. A claustrophobic labyrinth of personal memory leading to a dismal locked door behind which you can hear a doleful singing.

You are replete with all this.

You are absent from all this.

You've got pain all the way up your leg and sometimes even up to your head; the pills the doctor prescribed are not doing any good. You have nightmares – "really evil, but they're getting better", you told the doctor, which is also what you told the pleasant young man who lived downstairs for a while, who nodded sympathetically, and you told BJ when he was around – and sometimes you wake in the night and think your people are still alive – of course, they're all dead, you know that – and you go round the flat looking for them until you come to your senses again.

You remember that family who moved in downstairs, after the young man moved out? Well, it looks like *they've* gone – departed in the early hours, following a flurry of hoovering and dumping stuff in the rubbish and recycling area at the back of the block, which is a pitiful disgrace to behold, as you often said when it was within your powers to behold anything. Black plastic bags have been stacked beside the overflowing bins, some spilling their contents following nocturnal attacks by rodents or foxes, and items of crockery, plastic toys and other detritus are distributed loosely around. The loose items include a burnt-out pan, a reminder of that time when the family inadvertently left something cooking on the stove while they'd gone out and black, acrid smoke started billowing past your window, which confused you no end, but someone in the vicinity had the presence of mind to phone the fire brigade, who arrived with all due pomp and smashed their way through a front window to save the day. But they're gone for good, it seems, that family from hell, as the flat appears to be completely empty, judging from a view through the kitchen window (no longer available to you, unfortunately) – and no doubt soon a TO LET notice from the managing agent will appear out-side, taking its place among the thicket of no fewer than eight estate agents' placards that line the street right now. Upstairs was rumoured to have been sold after the departure of Jackanapes, but, though there have been signs of comings and goings, that too seems to be empty. So you have few neighbours at present. How does that feel? Peaceful?

You remember? … Sorry. Forgetting. It's too late for that.

Let's have a look at you.

You're not looking too good today. Just a little stiff. Well, that's what you are now, in common parlance: a stiff. This is what is known as *rigor mortis*, of course – it seems to be well set in. It will have started within three to four hours after your demise, but rest assured the phenomenon will disappear in three or four days. It will typically develop in your smaller muscles first – in the eyelids, face, lower jaw and neck – before moving on to your trunk and limbs.

What's happening at a smaller scale, at a microscopic scale, is that those busy little enzymes inside your cells are released as each cell dies. The enzymes break down the cell and its connections with other cells. Because oxygen isn't getting to your cells now, you see. The muscle proteins aren't working, so your muscles can't contract and relax as they used to do. There is no energy coming in. So your joints have become fixed. Never mind, just stay where you are, this phase will pass. Everything does.

Day 3

THAT FLAT ACROSS the hallway from yours: is there anyone *there* now? It seems ominously quiet. Used to be Mrs Somebody, a pleasant widow, who lived there, always a smile on her face, used to go off for weekends in Aldeburgh now and again to play golf with her gentleman friend. You never saw him. You could rely on Mrs Somebody, if she wasn't away playing golf, to take in a parcel for you, or a message. She had white hair with a purplish tinge in certain lights, and thick glasses; she'd open the door cautiously, then smile her smile, Good afternoon, Mr [SURNAME], she'd say, and how are you this afternoon? How lovely the daffodils are in the park, don't you think? she'd continue, expertly filling in the spaces made by your awkward silences. Ah, such a sad loss, Mrs Somebody.

After she passed away (and you didn't realise she had for quite a while), and after a long period of quiet, the flat was let. It turned out that before her demise she'd sold out at a cut price to the Freeholder, who was rapaciously buying up all the dwindling leases in the building that he could get his hands on. It was Jackanapes, more in touch than you with what was going on, who told you that. Anyway, that's the cue for a period of extreme disturbance, months and months of it. Maybe a year of it. Not a good year. You start with a resolution to no longer give way to your rage. Sadly, you do not achieve this. In fact, there are times during the year when your rage has increased exponentially.

One Sunday morning, your sleep is disrupted in the early

hours by shattering sounds from that flat, Mrs Somebody's flat as was, whoops and yells underpinned by a booming, repetitive bassline that shakes the bowels of the building, these sounds persisting until about five in the morning, when they suddenly cease. And then the same again on numerous other occasions, the booming and shuddering beginning around midnight and going on until first light, punctuated by the occasional scream, once the crash of shattering glass. Also comings and goings on the stairs outside, pounding of footsteps up and down, banging on the door of that flat across the landing, no longer Mrs Somebody's, sound of the door opening, of a tense conversation taking place. And even on the nights when whoever the people are who are dwelling there now are not holding parties, the comings and goings, the climbing up and clattering down the stairs continues from time to time, also arguments at the front door, people clamouring to be let in and others barring them entry, people conducting lengthy business deals on the landing itself, sometimes concluding peacefully at other times developing into prolonged arguments, on one occasion at least culminating in sounds indicating a degree of violence, or threatened violence. Sometimes you hear them laughing uproariously; once you heard a stentorian male voice proclaiming, ABANDON ship! followed by a torrent of titters and the occasional cheer. But who are these people? They may be vampires for all you know. Consider: you never see them in daylight, or hear more than faint rumblings within the flat during the course of the average day; but they seem to come to life as midnight approaches, and there you are again with the comings and goings and door bangings until the first glimmer of morning light. Your sleep is completely broken now; the dreams have returned, with an obsessive theme running through them, of rampant unease turning to disease, including swirling plagues of pathogens over a devastated landscape, across which you crawl, a dead man before your time, a scumbled and ashy monochrome landscape, across which you struggle towards the refuge of a forest of what look like spent sunflowers, a circle full of stars in your belly, trapped in the alchemical degree zero of burnt death from which ALL HOPE has been banished. Beyond the forest is a tall house where people are rumoured to keep giraffes, or rather, bizarre giraffe-like creatures, in captivity. But these alien hybrid creatures are now escaping from the house; you can see them hauling themselves expertly from the upper rooms where they were trapped, using the window as their means of exit, with their long legs instantly converting into the flexible limbs of gibbons, enabling them to reach down and support their bodies as they lower themselves to the ground. These giraffe-like beings who have escaped, it seems, are the ancestors of those comers and goers in the flat opposite; they can now be observed sitting around convivially in a fug of smoke, to a soundtrack of bass-heavy grime, exchanging money for pharmaceuticals, their long, slender legs now capped by naked human hands and feet. Sometimes they break into loud, forced laughter, throwing their heads back on their long necks. At second glance, in fact, they seem almost human.

If your brain cells were functioning properly, or at all, you might well remember happier times than these (and in any case happier times than now, when you lie inert in your bed, even more helpless than a baby). Times when your people were around, and you spent an evening with them, laughing and joking and sharing a meal; when you could exchange brief pleasantries on the landing with Mrs Somebody; when you walked down the canyon of a London street where the warehouses used to be, steel girders overhead dotted with pigeons roosting and flapping and strutting;

when one of the West Indian openers cracked the ball perfectly, apparently with hardly any force, and it flew immediately to the boundary; when a woman you hardly knew caressed the back of your hand with her fingers; when you used to laugh at absurdity; when you used to scrape at your dark and healthy face in the bathroom mirror, happily humming jazz standards to yourself the while; when it was so cold the butter, even though left out in the kitchen, was as hard as though it had just come straight from the fridge, and had to be chiselled out with a knife; when you could surreptitiously lick fragments of food lodged in the crevices of your dental plate (the very one that now sits in a glass of water at the bedside, waiting to be popped back into your mouth – something that will never happen again).

But now look at you. YOU are like a bag of cement, you are so cold and heavy. It's the third day of your confinement, but there is no prospect of a resurrection.

Your eyelids, nevertheless, remain open. You are staring with apparent intent at the ceiling, as the TV blares on in the background. But the spark has gone from your eyes. Tiny spots will have appeared on each cornea, yellow or yellowish-brown. Those eyes will not function again. You were always anxious about your eyesight, you will recall (or would recall if recall were available to you). You worried at one time about whether you had a detached retina, having experienced flashes, which someone told you was an indicative sign, and also an increased numbers of floaters when you closed your eyes, vast, moving entanglements of spiderwebs, clotted in places, webs that extended their filigree to the far reaches of the universe. But nothing came of that, the doctor dismissed your concerns, and you forgot about it, moving on to the next worry. Now worry is something you have been relieved of. That also is something positive, isn't it?

The doorbell goes. You don't stir, obviously. Pause. The

doorbell goes a second time. Silence. Long silence. The caller must have gone away.

The mornings are dark blue and require artificial light.

Another flashback. The doorbell goes.

Hello?

It's fa-fa.

There's a hell of a crackle in the intercom, always has been.

WHO?

Father Fuck (it sounds like).

What's it about?

Your parish (crackle). Come to pay a visit, Mr [SURNAME], if it's convenient.

Ah, please, no. That was your mistake. You knew it at the time, but foolishly didn't correct it. In one of the boxes below [FORENAME] [SURNAME], where you had to enter [RELIGION] you put Catholic when you meant to put no religion or not applicable or something like that – it was just habit, but you never got round to crossing it out, or maybe having made the error it seemed like making too much of it to actually cross it out, so it was left, and obviously the information got passed on, with consequences.

ENTER (you press the buzzer).

Father Fuck turns out to be ruddy-faced and clad in an anorak. He shakes hands but is obviously not one for dispensing smiles too readily. You offer him a cup of tea, which he refuses. So there he sits hunched up in the armchair you have offered him, the anorak bunched next to him – he is wearing a plum-coloured V-neck pullover and a black shirt with dog collar above that – listening to your story in response to his questions, and grunting non-committally from time to time.

The Christian window cleaner comes out of your toilet. You'd forgotten he was there. The Christian window cleaner is called Chris. He is a pleasant man with a crooked mouth, the right lip upturned. He sports a stained sweatshirt and a pair of old corduroy trousers, the little grooves of the corduroy flattened at the knees where there is the most wear. Remembering your manners, you introduce them: this is Chris, this is Father Fuck, hello, how do you do. The Christian window cleaner smiles his crooked smile. The Christian window cleaner has not actually been cleaning your windows on this occasion, but when he was doing so the other day, under licence from the Freeholder or his managing agents, he requested the use of your toilet, which he availed himself of, after which he reported that the toilet seat was broken, which you already knew, and said he could come back and fix it. He also noticed the hot tap was dripping, and offered to try to fix that too.

There seems a distinct lack of cordiality between Father Fuck and Chris, which is surprising at first, but it may be that their respective brands of Christianity are incompatible and they instinctively know that, or it may be that they are previously acquainted, have had some differences between them, and are hiding that information from you.

Chris says the toilet seat has been fixed; it was a simple matter. He will now turn his attention to the dripping tap.

You mention to the priest that it's one problem after another these days, and that you will be glad to be out of it.

What do you mean by that, Mr [SURNAME]?

That you are looking for the right doctor, you explain. One who will understand; who will slip you a Mickey Finn, as they used to say in the old films, or give you a shot of something that will ease the pain of living, on a permanent basis.

Father Fuck grumbles under his breath. You ought not to say such things, Mr [SURNAME], it ill becomes you.

You mention that you are ready to move on.

Ah yes, but you have a lot to be grateful for.

You do not reply to this.

God will take you when it's his will, proclaims Father Fuck, who is beginning to perspire. He could probably use a drink.

Are you sure you don't want a cup of tea?

No thanks, says Father Fuck.

And how will I know when it's God's will? you enquire.

The mind of God is not available for our inspection.

Chris the Christian window cleaner emerges from the kitchen. The main stopcock is jammed too tightly, he reports, and he does not have the tools with him to remedy this. Therefore the dripping tap cannot be fixed today. He could return another day, but not until next week because of previous commitments, or, he suggests, you might be well advised to call a proper plumber. You ask him how much you owe him for the toilet seat, but he refuses payment. It's my gift to you, he says, crookedly grinning. You offer a donation to the evangelical organisation he is involved with, about which he's previously spoken, which helps people in Africa – but he refuses that too.

Father Fuck sits there imperturbably. It is your impression he's been outmanoeuvred in the charitable stakes, and knows it.

The Christian window cleaner has gone. Father Fuck, getting to his feet and mopping his brow, says, Well, Mr [SURNAME], I had better be on my way. I have my parochial duties, you see. We are very understaffed these days, and I have a lot of visits to undertake before the close of play. It was nice meeting you.

No sooner is he out of the door than the bell goes again.

Who is it?

Sandra.

Which one is Sandra? You let her in, anyway. Ah, that

one. Bright as a button, she is.

Hello, nurse.

Oh, [FORENAME], I'm not a nurse. I'm the care assistant, remember?

That's right. You are beginning to recognise them by their uniform. The pale green, the blue, the white. This one pale green, with the CARE-PLC logo on the breast. She is consulting her notes.

Have you had your insulin injection yet, [FORENAME]?

You tell her that you can't remember.

Oh, dear, she says. Are you sure you can't?

Maybe, maybe not.

But I'm not allowed to dispense medicines, you see. Only the nurse can do that. I can only supervise you. It's all in the hands of the Management anyway. We're getting the assessor to see you tomorrow – we're not very clear what it is you want us to do for you!

Nor am I, you explain. In fact, you cannot remember having asked for services of any description.

She bustles around the kitchen, her ponytail bobbing merrily. Lovely, she is, with tiny bright eyes that dance, plump white throat, quite trim though a little thick around the waist. Have you had your lunch, [FORENAME]? No, you don't think so, you reply. There's some cheese in your fridge, she says. Would you like that? So before she leaves she has made you a cheese sandwich – about the only service that's been identified so far that she is qualified to undertake.

Before long she has disappeared, and it is as though no-one has ever been. Tiny particles of dust fall through the air. You remind yourself that, for now, whatever else is going on, much of it beyond you, you are still HERE.

Day 4

THE PRESENTER IS short in stature, wide of smile, wears a shiny suit. He appears against a glittery background, pixels fragmenting all around him, shocking pink and electric blue, in a hysterical frenzy that paradoxically seems simultaneously self-contained within its frame. The contestants are five in number, three women and two men, all maybe in their thirties, grinning, casually dressed, first-name badges pinned on their left breasts, self-consciously playing to the camera while self-consciously affecting not to. A sum of money – eight thousand pounds – flashes on screen. The question being put to the contestants is to name the ten most southerly English ceremonial counties. Some seem puzzled by the word "ceremonial". One of their number, male, is shown in close-up smirking knowingly. Each in turn has a go, but one by one they fail and are eliminated, leaving one survivor, female, named "Jo", who has some success but flunks at the final two counties, which are revealed to be East and West Sussex.

A different presenter now, younger, in an open-neck shirt, even whiter teeth. He appears before a digital representation of a fairground amusement arcade machine, dispensing tokens worth sums of money. The contestant is a teenage boy, a student, a little chubby, smiling earnestly. He deliberates ponderously before giving what he describes as an educated guess to a question to which there are three multiple-choice options as an answer: it's Winston Churchill, he has decided, not Clement Attlee or Neville

Chamberlain. He is only a callow youth, he doesn't know that he doesn't need to do that pompous deliberation thing; but he should become aware before he is any older that in the rotten heart of Old England the answer is *always* Winston Churchill. Anyway. Dramatic pause. Text lights up, flashes repeatedly. *Is* the right answer! exclaims the presenter, who tells the lad that his lecturers will be proud of him, that he has not let them down. Tokens pour into the electronic void, racking up eight, nine, ten thousand pounds in prize money. What will the young man do with the winnings? He is planning a round the world trip, and so this will come in very handy, he replies, beaming.

Now seven of the world's greatest magicians will assemble together to present a show beyond your wildest dreams ...

You're not watching any of this, are you?

There's a fly buzzing somewhere in the room.

... beyond the wildest dreams you might have were it within your capacity still to dream. There are immense joys or agonies, it's uncertain which is which, still in store for you, asserts the game show host, the Lord of Games himself, who now wears a caramel jacket that strobes uncontrollably, which announcement is received with hysterical approbation by the studio audience, which has clearly been well primed, and so it's on with the show, but first we cut away to these messages: an absurdly attired peer of the realm in a hot air balloon recommends a certain beverage; a former Premier League football club manager parodies himself in a domestic situation advocating god knows what; a beautifully svelte young woman with a hard stare in her gorgeous eyes morphs into various personae in succession wearing various costumes, slamming on the brakes of a posh car, vaulting into ... but it's on with the show and with the game, whose purpose is as yet unclear. The Master of

Ceremonies' smile infects in turn every one of the contestants, some of whom wear profuse costume jewellery, others tattoos, and ... but, oh, that smile, each of the girls tries it on one by one, it makes creaking noises as it moves from the one to the other, eliciting laughter from the studio audience as it goes, but it's an unsustainable smile, and sure enough it cracks the first face, which splits in two, the two halves of the contestant's face moving in opposite directions, which is hysterical, and now all the faces have been infected and are fragmenting all over the screen.

So they get down to business and go on to enter the first circle ... what's that noise? ... cue video of cartoon mice with distorted body parts ... much grunting and ululating ... captions flash ...

What's that noise? A sudden clangour, followed almost immediately by a thud-thud, but very soft, truly gossamer-soft – a noise off, barely that. Ah, of course, the postie's been again. He has the front door code, he can gain access to all the flat doors in each block. You're not expecting anything in the post, are you? No, of course not. The letterbox flap has juddered, something came through. Another item or two have been added to the growing mound of junk mail on your doormat. You'll never get to see what they are. No matter. You're not missing much.

There you lie, at peace, as they say. Or even in state – like Lenin, but without the benefit of balm – in the waxy light filtered through the half-angled slats of the venetian blind. You are wearing only a baggy T-shirt of an indeterminate colour, the duvet half pulled up, your mottled bony hands folded in front of you. In the corner, the gaudy moving lights of the interminable TV shows, the incessant clamour, though it does seem in some respects very far away. On the side table there are two items: the useless TV remote control, and the little tumbler in which your dental plate reposes, the water it has been submerged in slowly evapor-ating. Once in a while, the doorbell can be heard. Usually there is a pause, then it repeats once, then is heard no more. The visitor will have given up and gone away. Who could it be? Father Fuck? But will he not have been told by the Man-agement that you have been removed to the Holding Pen? BJ? No – he surely still knows the key is under the mat, and that he could gain access any time he wished. But he will be far away by now. Maybe the Christian window cleaner? What if he were to peer through the bedroom window? But he doesn't do that, he doesn't look through windows like George Formby to see what shocking things may be revealed, they don't these days, they have these immensely long poles they manipulate from the ground, steering the flow of water to drench the windows remotely; so there is no possibility of the Christian window cleaner looking into the bedroom, seeing you lying there, discovering the awful truth, alerting the Management.

The truth is you're beginning to smell now, just a little. It's been four days. The fly's still buzzing. Buzzes, then is silent. Buzzes again. Is that the same fly you heard before you closed your eyes? When the muscles of your eyelids were still functioning? But there's a stillness in the room now. You want to watch that fly. (We know that you can-not.) Bacteria have been breaking down your tissues and cells, releasing fluids into your body cavities. That's what's happening. They produce various gases which you might have found foul-smelling in the past, but they are very attractive to house flies and blowflies and other insects. You may not want to know this, but, unhindered by the natural defences of a living animal, which you no longer are, those flies are able to lay eggs on and around any wounds there may be on your body, and also in any natural body openings (your mouth, your nose, your eyes, your arsehole, your genitalia). It may be a particular concern in this respect that your mouth appears to remain half-open, as if you have been interrupted while about to make some remark, also that you do appear to have a small visible wound on your right arm that has not yet healed. So these eggs will inevitably hatch and move conveniently into your body quite soon. Egg, maggot (with easy access to food, that is to say, the remains of your good self), new fly. That's the order of things.

All the things that happened before the windows failed, before you could not see to see, all of this is of no matter now. These are the facts so far in the case of yourself, Mr [SURNAME]. Case closed.

No sound troubles you from the downstairs flat, nor from the flat across the landing that is no longer inhabited by Mrs Somebody, and apparently not any longer by the kids and drug peddlers who thereafter caused mayhem for a while. Yes, it would be very peaceful, if you could only ignore the TV clamour that cannot be turned off. Whatever happened to the automatic standby feature?

What do you reckon? Eh? Never mind.

Day 5

BUT WHAT ABOUT the flat upstairs, the top-floor flat? That too seems pretty quiet right now. No unexplained bumps on the floor (your ceiling, that is), no noises as of furniture being dragged across the room, no water streaming down the walls (thankfully), no muffled cries. That was the regime for a while. But now it's silent. It would appear no-one is living in *that* flat either at the present time. You will not be disturbed as you lie there in your bed, although it has of course to be admitted that nothing will disturb you in your present condition in any case, not a frying-pan fire, not a pipe bomb, not a nuclear meltdown.

Well, it was different when him upstairs, Jackanapes or whatever his name was, lived there. It was pretty lively. Your first close encounter with Jackanapes, whose life signs were audible for a while, before you even met him – the aforementioned bumps and scrapes upstairs, the muffled conversations, the muffled easy-listening music, Abba's greatest hits, sometimes at three in the morning, over a period of weeks – was not a happy one.

So how it happens is as follows: late in the evening of a day of muted light, where the rain and wind seem to bellow against the windows, seizing and driving leaves and other debris against the glass, just as you're about to give up on it all and go to bed it suddenly comes to your attention while you're brushing the remains of your teeth that a slow torrent is pouring down your bathroom wall. A palpable Niagara in the making, a moving sheen of wetness that has already begun to puddle on the bathroom floor, seeking in its sneaky watery way for a means to follow the pull of gravity further, for any crack or minute crevice that would enable it to continue its course through your floor and down to the flat below. This is not the creeping damp you are already so familiar with, this is orders of magnitude beyond that, this is cause for panic. The elements are proving more than invasive.

Out the door and up the stairs you nip – yes, you had some nip still at this stage – snap on the landing light, knock on the door of the flat above; you can hear some movement within but no response. No response, though you know he's in there, what in hell is going on? Bang on the door again, no response. Back downstairs. The water is still coming down inexorably, it has settled into channels now. You don't know what to do next, other than run up again through the sudden gloom of the stairwell, for the timer has timed out on the landing light, bang a third time. You hear a muffled cry within, but no visual sign of him, Jackanapes, though you know he's there.

Perhaps the roof has finally caved in, perhaps the weather is pouring through into the top-floor flat and has overwhelmed its occupant.

Next thing, you hear the doorbell. Yours most clearly, for your own door is ajar, but also the muffled echo of every other doorbell in the block, all going at once. You're halfway down the stairs when the landing light suddenly comes on again and here are the police, two young uniformed officers climbing the stairs; you meet midway, and then you hear Jackanapes' door open above you and himself peers out into the landing: What's going on? you can hear him cry.

Jackanapes is in striped pyjamas, more clearly defined than you have ever seen him, bleary of eye, bare of foot and rumpled of receding hair. So there is some confused interaction between you and him and the two police and him and you. Well, it turns out it was he who called the cops, who arrived with unaccustomed speed for this part of the city, and it turns out he has been frightened by your banging so incessantly and repeatedly on his front door after midnight, that's why he called them, and the police turn on you, and you explain about the flood, and only then does Jackanapes retreat into his flat to inspect his own bathroom, wherein you and the two arms (or four arms) of the law follow, to behold, when he snaps on the light, his bath absolutely brimming with greenish water that is folding incessantly over the edge, Niagara style indeed, and splashing continuously with a glitter onto the floor and presumably through onto your ceiling and down your walls, because he forgot, he now admits sheepishly, that he was running a bath, and fell asleep on his bed before thinking to turn the tap off, which he does forthwith. And you all stand there talking about it, Jackanapes in his pyjamas smiling and apologising repeatedly, the young cops wearily amused at the antics of the elderly, one of them talking police talk into the radio on his shoulder, and finally taking their leave, clumping down the stairs again in all their heavy gear. And now Jackanapes shakes your hand, apologising once more, issues an invitation to you for the following evening, when he says as it happens he will be celebrating his birthday in his flat in a modest way by entertaining a small party of guests, to whose company you will be graciously admitted.

So there you are again the following evening. Jackanapes, this time properly dressed, thinning hair combed over, beard trimmed, exuding the faintest aroma of cologne, opens the door, welcomes you in a nonchalant sort of way. He ushers you in. There are only three other people present, disposed within the living room, the direct analogue of yours, with its view over the park except one storey higher.

He introduces you to a very ancient lady with white hair, sitting in an armchair with her left leg in plaster: his mother. She gives you a watery smile and nods her head up and down. Also in the party, sitting on hardback chairs with wine glasses in their hands, are two men of middle age: one black, stockily built, in a T-shirt over which he wears a hoodie jacket, on his feet the snowiest, whitest trainers you've ever seen; the other dark-complexioned but with pale eyes, goatee beard, in a dark suit and tie. He mentions their names as he introduces you, which you immediately forget. The first he describes as "my business associate" (the man in the hoodie bows curtly), the second (whom you think he said was Italian) as "my legal adviser" (a polite smile and a nod from the man in the suit). He offers you a generous glass of white wine, which you accept with both hands, anxious lest it brim over.

Jackanapes is very much the master of ceremonies, and indeed commands ninety per cent of the conversation. He apologises first for the unfortunate absence of Irina from the gathering this evening. You venture to enquire who Irina might be. Ah, says Jackanapes, with considerable effusiveness, of course, of course, I should have said, well there she is! and he points to a framed photo on the sideboard of a handsomely appointed young woman with severely styled dark hair and piercing eyes; there she is, he repeats, but sadly not here in person tonight, she can't be here because she has to be at a high-level medical conference in Edinburgh. I am sure you will be meeting her before long. Irina, Jackanapes further elucidates, is his bride-to-be, a Russian cardiothoracic surgeon nearly thirty years his junior who saved his life the previous year when he had his massive heart attack and whom, following the operation, he wooed successfully. They are to be married in June, and you will certainly be invited to the wedding. Of course you will.

The other three all nod at this. Have *you* ever been married? he asks you. Once, you say; you can't remember much about it, you add. But you are transfixed by the portrait, its beautiful and captivating eyes; at one point later in the evening when you excuse yourself to go the toilet you are convinced those eyes follow you across the room.

The conversation drifts onto the question of the lease-holders' position in this block of flats you inhabit; you have difficulty following the drift. Jackanapes says that, advised by the man in the suit (who nods, smiling), he is conducting a counter-campaign against the Freeholder, a shadowy figure you will have observed from time to time, flitting in and out of the building, always dressed in a sober dark coat, whose strategy over many years has been to buy up as many of the leaseholds as possible, leaseholds whose individual value is diminishing as the years go by, with the aim of eventually acquiring a majority of them, at which point he will have control over all the decisions pertaining to the flats. You will remember Mrs Somebody, over the landing from you, says Jackanapes – yes, of course you do, you agree – well, she was persuaded just before her recent sad passing to sell up to the Freeholder – "very bad, very bad deal," interjects the legal adviser in the dark suit, shaking his head – so that flat's also gone. But we are pursuing our plan to stop him, continues Jackanapes, we are building up our portfolio of leases to prevent him getting his majority. I am being assisted in this regard by our legal friend here, he repeats (he mentions the name of the suited man again, but, despite your straining to hear, the name is still garbled and disappears from memory as soon as it is uttered). You understand – oh by the way, I see you've finished your wine, would you like a refill? Of course, of course – will you refill the glasses, my friend? he says, turning to the man in the hoodie and white trainers, who assents wordlessly and collects the glasses for a refill from the kitchen. You understand, he resumes ... where was I? yes, English law on freehold and leasehold is very peculiar (the suited man nods eagerly); you cannot actually own a flat according to English law, because the supposition is that you can only own *land*, and a flat is not necessarily grounded in land, so what you have, essentially, when you buy a flat is a leasehold for x number of years on a parcel of air, you have the right for that amount of time to occupy that parcel of air – crusted around with bricks and mortar maybe, but you don't own those bricks and that mortar, they remain in the possession of the freeholder or *landlord*, as he is known, and as the years go by your hold on that parcel of air becomes weaker while the freeholder becomes stronger because he knows that he will soon regain the right to occupy that parcel – isn't that right? says Jackanapes, turning to his legal adviser, who says "correct".

And you are an expert on English law, then, you enquire of the suited man, despite being, I think you said, Italian?

No no, I not Italian, laughs the man, I am (and you think he says "Iranian" or maybe "Arabian", you can't hear properly).

And, you turn back to Jackanapes, you have the money to do all this? Oh, yes, says Jackanapes, oh, yes, I made my money in fish.

Fish?

Yes, we come from a well-established family in Grimsby, we built our estate on the fishing industry, didn't we, mother?

His aged mother confirms this with a pleasant nod.

Jackanapes has no trace of a Northern accent; he is what you would doubtless call well-spoken. We have an extensive portfolio built over many generations, he continues. In addition to the seven leases we already own in this block, including this flat, obviously – do you know the seafood restaurant in Lordship Lane? (You struggle to recall which one he means.) Well, never mind, I own that, you go in there any time, just mention my name, say I'll take care of it, you will get a free meal. I guarantee you that. Anyway, as I was saying we own seven leases, the Freeholder has got his hands on eleven so far, but we are catching up fast. You know how many flats there are in all the blocks altogether? (You cannot recall.) Thirty-two. We have to stop the Freeholder getting a majority, you see. So we have to go for it to make sure. Sixteen will get you fifty per cent, one more an unassailable majority. At that point, we can set policy. We can force the Freeholder to extend all the leaseholds, from the paltry few decades they have run down to, to nine hundred and ninety-nine years for every single leaseholder. Everyone will benefit. Win-win!

But your brain is spinning now, oscillating like crazy. You struggle but remain unable to assert yourself sufficiently to ask any further questions, or indeed even to formulate them in your mind. You cannot recall whether Jackanapes made an offer to buy up your own lease, or, if he did, what he was offering, and what your answer was. The second and third glasses of white wine have now been drained. By the way, Jackanapes leans forward, by the way, you wouldn't happen to want to rent out your spare room temporarily? Only my friend here (he indicates the suited Iranian or Arabian lawyer) is temporarily looking for lodgings. (The lawyer beams broadly.) Well, I'll let him talk to you about that. He's prepared to pay you a decent rent, ha ha. I would accommodate him myself, but of course my wedding to Irina is impending, and in the first instance she will be moving in here with me, while we look for somewhere more suitable. So I have no spare space. Speaking of which, did I invite you to the wedding? You did, dear, pipes up his mother, in a rare intervention. Of course I did, well, you would be very welcome, Jackanapes tells you. It's in June, he says. You will be getting a proper invitation. There's this great band we are hiring – you like music? oh, you play, do you? (Piano, you say, you used to play jazz piano years ago, but not any more – you don't even possess an instrument any longer.) Oh, fantastic, fantastic, maybe you would like to take a solo spot! (No, no, you demur, you're very out of practice.) Anyway, a fantastic band, they're a bunch of niggers, like you guys.

A what? Did he really say that? Was it meant as banter? The black man in the hoodie and white trainers continues with his poker face, the lawyer grins wanly. You look from their respective faces, which give little away, to Jackanapes' watery eyes, freckled forehead and trimmed beard with the traces of ginger and grey, to his mother, who seems to have fallen asleep in her armchair, to Irina's enigmatic dark eyes in the photo. You start to feel sick; you make your excuses, you get up and start walking towards the door.

Day 6

So WHAT HAPPENED next, do you remember? No answer. No? What happens is that there's a knock on your front door the following morning; you open it, and there's this dapper chap with a goatee beard, in a raincoat. Hello, [FORENAME], he says (in a foreign accent, extending his right hand in greeting), sorry if is inconvenient, but I just want to check about that room you have to let. You don't know where he got that idea from, or him from Adam, even though amazingly he has your name right, and he, noticing your confusion, adds: Remember last night, upstairs, your neighbour, he say you have spare room to let. My name is [name incomprehensible], we met last night?

Ah, you have some recollection now. Jackanapes. Jackanapes' lawyer. Sorry, you say, I couldn't place you for a minute, please come in. I'm sorry, you repeat as you lead him into your living room, where there is just one space to sit, on the sofa, which you indicate, in between the piles of books and other stuff you have not got round to sorting, I'm sorry, I didn't catch your name last night?

He has taken off the raincoat, revealing a dark suit but no tie, a white shirt worn open-necked.

You cannot pronounce it, he says. Everybody call me BJ.

BJ?

Yeah, the letters Bee, Jay, you know.

I see, you say. BJ.

Yeah. Sorry if I intrude. I have code for street door, you see, I come straight up.

You are about to formulate some polite way to get rid of him, but as it happens you think, why not, make a few bob. You don't need the spare room, and he seems pleasant enough. So BJ goes on to explain he needs a room for a few weeks, until he's fixed himself up properly, and you find yourself agreeing to some kind of deal.

These flats is nice, BJ exclaims, looking around him, beaming broadly. I would not mind one myself, maybe one day. Yes, they are nice flats, you agree, need a bit of doing up though. For sure, for sure, he says, but look – he indicates the bay window overlooking the park – ah! Yes, lovely outlook, that's the best part, you reply, though it's not looking at its best right now. Ah, no, he agrees, lousy weather. (Rain starts to patter against the panes.) Lousy weather in this country, yeah? And he laughs.

You just go with it, you can't do anything about it, you say.

You born here? he asks suddenly.

I beg your pardon?

You born in this country?

No, you say, as a matter of fact I was not.

You have been here long time?

Yes. I was born on a little island – quite far away – I don't remember it much. I came here as a small child. This is my home, anyway, I've been here – London – many years. More years than I can remember. And what about you, where do you come from, are you Arabian, I think you said?

Arabian! Ha ha ha! he laughs. No, I not Arabian. No, my friend. I come from Anatolia.

Anatolia?

Yeah, the eastern part of Anatolia, near border with Armenia. Actually, I am partly Armenian, I was born there. I study here in this country, I study law. You have no family?

All my people are dead, you explain.

Ah. Very sad, very sad. How much you want for rent?

You are taken by surprise. Well, you say, I hadn't really thought about it.

He suggests a weekly sum which you think is immense. You blink. Well, that sounds – about right, you say. About right. You haven't seen the room, though.

Is same as your neighbour's spare room? Your neighbour upstairs?

My neighbour? You mean Jackanapes – him upstairs? Jackanapes? he says, puzzled. That's what I call him, Jackanapes, you say, yes, I think so, I think the room's the same. They're all the same layout, these flats. There's a put-you-up bed, but I haven't had it out for a long time. I only use that room for storage, you see.

Very good, my friend. I give you four weeks in advance, OK? He takes his wallet out of his jacket pocket, extracts a copious wad of banknotes and counts the money out. Here you are, my friend. I am sorry you have no family left. I miss my family too.

I'm quite used to it now, you assure him. You don't tell him – because he wouldn't understand – that sometimes you still see your people. Suddenly they are in the flat, milling around, eating and drinking and talking as if it were quite natural. It happens spontaneously, from time to time. Some are in the kitchen, some in the living room, or even out on the fire escape at the back. And then again, all of a sudden they disappear, they're gone, they've left you, with no trace. But you know they'll be back. It leaves you distracted, though. It leaves you out of sorts. You walk through the flat from room to room, repeatedly switching on all the lights, then switching them all off again. It is hard to process all this these days. Thoughts that used to run at high speed through your brain now stumble pitifully, sometimes stopping and retracing their paths. You make an effort to tell BJ some of this, but your voice sticks in your windpipe. It's no use.

Will they come back? You can't say.

You can't say anything, you are mute. That's a foretaste of what's to come, that is to say the present day, the sixth of your immersion in the new ecosystem, which is building nicely.

But let's leave that, let's get back to BJ; you suddenly worry, with the bundle of banknotes he handed over now deposited in the drawer under the kitchen table, which is where you keep your valuables, what he will make of life in this flat, with its attendant hazards: the mutant mice, for example, you haven't mentioned them yet. At times, when the noise of the day subsides, you can hear their scurrying about behind the skirting boards, first at one end of the flat then the other, as though they have moved between regions with unimaginable speed, defying both physics and logic. You can hear the skittering, the grunting and ululating, if you listen carefully. At other times, when the lights are out, you have – on rare occasions, admittedly – actually caught sight of them, these rodents that have morphed into highly intelligent tiny organisms with their own secret society in the tunnels and labyrinths behind the walls, whose rules are impenetrable to your understanding, rodents nominally, but shape-shifting within a moment into other expressions of existence. For example, once you watched one of these creatures on the kitchen floor, who, noticing a crumb or two that remained on the table top, the same table in whose drawer your four weeks' rental proceeds will soon be placed, reached to fetch it, not by, as you would imagine, scurrying up the table leg but by standing on its hind legs on the lino-leum and extending its neck bit by bit, grotesquely, resem-bling at first a miniature giraffe with a mouse's face and then a kind of serpent with the mouse's body at one end and little rodent jaws at the other that snapped at the crumbs when they came within reach on the table top. Horrified, you stood in the doorway; then, at the very instant the creature noticed you, its neck contracted immediately, telescoping back into the tiny body that turned and scampered into a hole in the skirting board. But you don't mention any of this to BJ, best not, lest he be put off. Instead, you say: Well, any problems you have, just let me know.

OK, he says, OK my friend. You have key you can give me?

Key? Oh, sorry. I don't think I have a spare key at the moment, but I can get one cut. There's still a cobbler on the high street that does that. In the meantime, I always keep my key under the doormat outside my door, so you're welcome to use that. Oh, really? he says, that is not very safe, you know. Well, that's what I do, you say, because I've locked myself out before now when I've banged the door shut and the key is still inside, you see, I was always doing that, so I've got in the habit now of putting it under the mat when I go out. Well, is not safe, he says, is not recommended, but is your decision, one hundred per cent. I respect your decision. Anyway, I know the code for outside door and if you leave key under mat, that's OK with me – anyway (rising and putting his raincoat back on), I come back Monday with my stuff, yeah?

He shakes you vigorously by the hand.

He's gone, and so you wander into the spare room, which is gloomy because the curtains are drawn, so you draw them back to invite some wintry light onto the dusty bits of furniture and boxes that have a kind of half-existence there. You pull out that small sofa and spend the next hour or two figuring how it converts into a single bed – it takes a bit of remembering and then doing, with much huffing and creaking, but you finally manage it – and then you realise it will need some bedding – pillows, sheets and blankets – so you will have to hunt for all that in the cupboard. But there is plenty of time before BJ returns.

Doorbell goes again. A woman's voice on the crackly intercom. The nurse, or the care assistant, or whichever it is today. You press the door release.

Here she is. Bright smile. Mr [SURNAME]? She is uncommonly well dressed, in a skirt and heels, immaculate makeup, and carries a clipboard. Not wearing your uniform today? you enquire. Beg pardon? Not in uniform? Who did you think I was, Mr [SURNAME]? The nurse? you venture. Oh, no, ha ha ha, no, I'm not a nurse, I'm from Water Treatment, she says, we're doing a survey on hardness and impurities in the water in this area. Is that a government thing? you ask, but she just continues, Would you mind filling out a short questionnaire about the quality of the water that comes out of your tap? I do apologise for taking up your time, but it won't take very long, Mr [SURNAME]. So you show the young lady into the living room. She starts rattling off some questions: your name, your age, your marital status, how long you have been living in the property, whether you are a tenant or a leaseholder or a freeholder, whether you use your tap water for drinking, for washing clothes, for showering or bathing. You answer each one, and she writes down the answers on the form clamped to her clipboard.

One of the questions is whether you or anyone in your household suffers from eczema or other skin complaints. Well, of course, you do, this being one of your many afflictions: itchy rashes on various parts of your body, the insides of your knees, your wrists, your armpits, the crack of your anus, you name it, so you become very interested at that point. She says science has shown that many such complaints can be traced to the quality of the water coming through the taps. You never knew that, did you? The good news is that she has now assessed you to have qualified for a *completely free*, no obligation, comprehensive testing of your tap water, which should provide some answers, and, if you like, an appointment can be made right away for this, Monday being free if you are available. She is a very friendly lady. Very lovely. She assures you that the man who is to come round will identify himself with a badge, so you are not to worry, and it will not take long.

All of this is nevertheless most exhausting, so once she has departed you peer out to see if the weather has relented. It seems to have improved a bit, so you decide to shake off the tyranny this flat is beginning to exercise over you again, and go for a walk. It takes a great effort to crank up for this, the limbs do not wish to work as they once did, there's the pain in the right ankle and the pain in the left knee and the stiff-ness of the lower torso, and the general reluctance to articu-late and to propel, but even so those were the days, were they not, when you could actually move, you could definitely start from one location and end up in another, and then return to the first location at will, despite the pain involved, despite ... but let us not get into that, your present state forms no kind of comparison, no matter, the important thing is you sally forth as you always did in those days, if sally is the right word or not, who cares, you put on your coat, open your front door, shut it behind you, deposit the key under the mat, descend the stairs with care, holding on to the banister, observe the same stains on the same walls, smell the same scents, open the street door, and there you are. Fresh air. Not very fresh, but still. The fear of it, that's the thing. The outsideness of it all. People coming and going. Red buses passing, other traffic, sounds Doppler-shifting. Decisions to make. Across to the park, or veer right towards the high street? So many people, each their own consciousness, each a world in itself, how can that be, how can there be so many of them? One overlapping with the next, or alternatively, there being no contact whatsoever, the individual worlds sailing past each other, obliviously. And then each to be snuffed out one day, and that world gone. But the clash of worlds, the immensity of that. You marvel at it, you fear it. You become acutely conscious of your embedment in it, the it that all these worlds collectively produce, and this in turn produces fear and awe. (The recalling of this consciousness sets up a feedback loop.) What is the source of your fear, anyway? You proceed towards the high street. When you started out, you had the idea of getting a spare key cut so that BJ will not have to depend on the one snugly hidden beneath the mat, but of course you forgot to bring *that* key with you, you did indeed hide it under the mat as usual, so that can't happen, and in any case by the time you've reached the corner where the traffic lights are and beyond which the high street bends towards the left you have entirely forgotten this errand anyway. All you can remember is a vague fear. Is your fear that of your embedment itself in that world, the world of the many-headed beast, those worlds, or is it of potentially becoming disembedded? But disembedment is an impossibility, it can't happen unless consciousness itself vanishes, thus you cannot experience that, so why fear it? The worst that you fear, in other words, can't occur to you. These thoughts race in your brain, where the curves of your past meet the curves of your future, without always being recognised, as you mooch along the shop fronts for a bit and then turn and move back towards the park. You think you would like a nice walk in the park after all, but heavens, the weather has had yet another thought, and beads of moisture begin to appear in the air, and pretty soon it is unequivocal that it has started to rain once more; one or two passers-by unfurl their umbrellas, others hurry along with just that bit of greater urgency. And as you return homeward, walking past the arrowhead railings encircling the park, in that circle of everlasting rain, a glaze of water shimmers over a dog and its owner up ahead who appear to be making for the park gate, moving in your direction, the man holding the great dog back, a powerfully built bull-like creature that strains at its leash with great optimism and great will to match. The nails of the dog click smartly on the paving stones. You hang back here. The dog glowers at you for a moment, its clawed hands and feet pattering on the pavement before veering, push-pulled by the man, who is equally powerful of build, with a granite pate surmounting a black, greasy beard, into the park and thankfully away from your path. You cross the road, just to be on the safe side, as soon as the traffic allows.

In the park, the man and the dog are playing a game. The man encourages his creature to leap ever higher, pursuing a lure. The man shouts, the dog roars. Now the dog is leaping to catch an overhanging tree branch in its teeth; at the second or third attempt it succeeds in clamping its great jaws onto the branch, and there it hangs, many feet off the grass, swaying, suspended from the branch only by its teeth, while the man barks it on; then it falls to the ground, but leaps up again immediately to grasp the branch and disgustingly dangles there once more. The man is repeatedly calling the dog's name. You can't catch it. Is that 'Itler? You think you hear him bark, approvingly now, 'Itler! 'Itler! But he is a white man and it is a white dog. And as you look, it is the man's head itself that grasps the branch in his jaws and the dog that eggs him on; for you now see that the shaven head and the black, greasy beard of the dog matches the same features of the man; they are the identical head surmounting two separate bodies.

Day 7

THAT'LL BE THE doorbell again, Monday morning bright and early. You've not had a good night. It sounded like Jack-anapes was moving furniture around again upstairs during the night: numerous bumps and scraping sounds. You didn't get a great deal of sleep. So your brain is not in great shape, but you have a scribbled note blu-tacked to the back of the door, which says BJ COMING TODAY. Good thinking to do that to remind yourself – you go to pick up the inter-com, Hello, is that BJ? you say.

Am I speaking to Mr [FORENAME] [SURNAME]?

Yes, you answer, who is this?

It's (crackle)(crackle).

Who?

Ah, (crackle) Water Treatment (crackle).

Water Treatment! Of course. You'd forgotten about the appointment. The absolutely free of charge water test. You press the buzzer to let them in.

There are two of them. In identical pastel polo shirts. The younger, taller one identifies himself by waving an ID card on a lanyard in front of your face. He's an awkward customer. He has a twitch, a sort of swallow of the throat in between sentences, and his voice clucks like a chicken at the beginning of each sentence. I hope you don't mind, Mr [SUR-NAME], he says by way of introduction, I'm accompanied today by my colleague (nodding towards his elderly com-panion, who nods back at you), he's on a training course. Well, you think to yourself, the trainee had better hurry up and learn the trade pretty quickly, because he looks as if he's due for retirement soon.

So then the younger one asks to be shown to where the mains water pipe comes into your flat, and you show him into the kitchen, where they get down to work. They extract a whole paraphernalia of tubes and taps and connectors from the large bag they have brought with them – the older one handing items one by one, when requested, to the younger, who sets to fixing a complicated apparatus to the cold water tap through which the water is to be filtered. The next half hour is devoted to doing tests on the water. The result, says the young man in his peculiar chicken voice, fixing you with a ghastly smile, is conclusive. Your tap water is pretty bad. No wonder you suffer from all the health complaints you put down on the form. The man demonstrates: he obtains a sample of water unfiltered, straight from the tap, in a small phial. Next, he obtains a similar sample, but this time filtered through his apparatus. He adds a small quantity of testing chemical to each. The unfiltered sample goes a horrible murky colour. The filtered water remains pure and brilliant: he hold it up to the light so that you can see it sparkle.

By now you are all sitting in your living room. The younger man begins a lecture on the chemistry entailed, illustrated with photographs from various brochures to which he draws your attention from time to time. Meanwhile, his elderly trainee sidekick appears to be taking notes in a lined A4 notepad, while fiddling with his keyring. But when you happen to look more closely, you see that all he is actually doing is doodling. His keyring fob is in the shape of a swanky sports car, and he is tracing the outline of this vehicle repeatedly, then filling in the windows, adding shading and other details, while his younger colleague drones on.

After an hour has gone by, the doorbell goes again. You excuse yourself and get up to head for the intercom, but by the time you get there your front door has already opened and in walks BJ. Evidently he found the key under the mat. He has a backpack on and is also trailing a wheelie bag. Everybody takes a break while you show him to the spare room. You have tidied up there a bit, and you even found the hoover at the weekend, which miraculously still works, and have removed the more egregious samplings of dust.

While BJ is settling himself down, the lecture resumes. The young man explains that if you purchase one of his company's systems you problems will be solved. You will have good, clean water with no unpleasant taste or odour, and no risk of tummy upsets from impurities and bacteria. Chlorine and many other chemical compounds will be removed. Chlorine can be a problem particularly in the bathroom, he says: when your water is heated, when you're taking a bath or shower for example, the chlorine in it vaporises and you could be inhaling up to fifty times more chlorine than there is in a glass of cold water. And repetitive exposure to chlorine may contribute to psoriasis and eczema. So it makes sense to install a comprehensive system that treats *all* the water in your flat, not just in the kitchen. And the system also removes scum and scale from kettles; your washing machine or dishwasher will require less detergent, your boiler will work more efficiently and will be less likely to fail, and heating bills will decrease.

In short: this amazing system will give you peace of mind.

That is undoubtedly what you want.

I have a feeling, suddenly pipes up BJ, who has quietly re-entered the room and is sitting on a chair in the corner, I have a bee-eeg feeling that very soon you are going to be asking Mr [SURNAME] for a lot of money. He grins broadly at the young man, who scowls back. Am I correct? asks BJ. Not at all, says the young man, not at all. He gulps, his Adam's apple visibly moving up and down. What we are proposing is very good value and could in fact *save* Mr [SURNAME] money. Why, he says, expanding on this, you could go to a hardware store, B&Q or Wickes for example, or go online, and buy a portable water treatment apparatus off the shelf. You could spend anything up to eight hundred pounds on one. But what you would get for that would be very poor. Inadequate. You would be wasting your money. On the other hand, one of our bespoke systems, tailored exactly to your needs (he swings back to face you), tailored to *your* specific needs, Mr [SURNAME], would represent a cost saving in the long run, when you factor in all the improvements to your health and savings on your running costs, as I mentioned before. How much do you think such a comprehensive system, which would solve all your problems, would cost in the first instance? he challenges you directly. (You say you have no idea.) Well, normally, he says, normally it would be in the region of three thousand pounds. But as it happens, he continues, his firm has a special offer going, available only this week, which is a special promotional week, valid only in this particular neighbourhood which they are targeting. Just two thousand three hundred pounds, a saving of no less than seven hundred pounds, plus VAT, plus a renewal pack to be purchased annually at a cost of only seventy pounds plus VAT. Installation would be *absolutely free* and would take no more than half a day. The system would be installed in the space under your kitchen sink –in fact, the floor of the sink unit would have to be taken out to accommodate it, but the work would all be completely included in the price. Would it take up *all* of the space below the sink, then, you ask? Yes, it would. But that is where you keep the bucket and all the cleaning stuff, you object. Well, then, he can suggest an alternative, which would be to run a pipe all the way round the wall behind the kitchen units and the cooker (which would all have to be adapted) to the outside wall. How about that?

Can I think about it? you ask.

Well, you can, says the young man, but unfortunately the decision will have to be taken today, otherwise the special offer will expire. Seven hundred pounds-worth of savings, don't forget.

The older man, evidently bored with designing automobiles, appears to have nodded off.

Here BJ, suddenly taking on his role of legal adviser, intervenes again. Mr [SURNAME] will think about it, sir, he says brightly.

By now, the young man's earlier friendliness is beginning to wane. He exchanges glances with his colleague, who has suddenly woken with a start. Well, it's your decision, sir, he tells you.

Mr [SURNAME] will think about it, repeats BJ.

When they have packed up their equipment and gone, he says: That was close escape, no? and he laughs, a stuttering, succinct laugh.

You thank him for intervening on your behalf. You didn't know how you were going to get out of it. In fact, you had lost the plot well before the end.

These people, says BJ, they take advantage. You know what I mean?

You know very well what he means. A good guy, BJ, it seems, very polite always, no trouble to be around. Albanian, is he? You keep forgetting. Been to college, anyway, knows the law. He offers to make you a cup of tea, very nice of him. It's a good day after all, it has been harvested from what started out as a bad day. You are now anxious not to alienate him, to make him feel welcome: you show him the bathroom, you show him the kitchen, which he has already seen. Of course he has. You ask him to excuse your forgetfulness. You hope he will be comfortable. Anything he needs, he just has to ask, you assure him. You don't say anything about the problems you're having. Hope the vermin stay out of his way; don't mention the mutant mice. You do mention that he might hear you shouting out during the night; you apologise in advance for this, but he is not to be alarmed, you simply have bad dreams. You mention also that a care worker or a nurse will call round at regular intervals. You mention that you have to have injections. Also on a Thursday the ambulance has been coming round to take you to the day centre, but you're thinking of jacking that in. None of this need concern him.

I appreciate that, I appreciate all this, he says, nodding eagerly. You notice he has quite protruding front teeth, his jaw is pointy, and when he moves his head to look at something, distracted by a noise from the street maybe, you also notice that a small bald patch is beginning to form at the apex of his scalp. His eyes are bright and a very pale blue or grey in his dark face. He says that he in his turn will try to make the least trouble for you. His needs are minimal, he assures you, a bed to sleep in, a cup of coffee first thing in the morning, then he is usually off early, he has to go to college, he has some business to attend to, he is very busy.

You have business to do with Jackanapes, don't you? you enquire.

Jackanapes?

You point at the ceiling.

Ah yes, ha ha, your neighbour, you call him Jackanapes, ha ha. Yeah. I have some business with him, with his property dealings. (He makes a gesture to indicate confidentiality.) He have many good ideas, a lot of energy, you know? Sometimes I have to hold him back.

Do you indeed?

Yeah, I tell you another time about Jackanapes.

He has fancy ideas?

Ah. He is a dreamer. He dream the impossible dream!

You tell him: I didn't like what he said, when I was up there the other evening.

What he say?

He said what they now call the N-word. You remember?

I know what you mean. He say that. Is not good. He mean it like a joke, he think it funny. All good blokes together. He no mean any harm. But is not good, I agree. Hamza, he speak to him about it.

Hamza?

You know him, he was there.

The one with the white trainers?

Yeah, that one.

Who is he?

He your neighbour's bodyguard.

Jackanapes has a bodyguard?

Yeah, he paranoid about his enemies, says BJ with some relish. You know your Freeholder? He make some threat to your neighbour, stay out of my business, he say, or there will be consequences, that's what he say, consequences. We know him from before. He have someone beat up, we know that happen. The Freeholder, has he offered to buy your lease?

You confess that you are so confused these days about what is going on that you cannot remember whether this has happened or not. You do remember seeing the Freeholder prowling around from time to time, on the stairs or in the grounds at the back: like a great raven in his black overcoat. I can't keep up, you tell BJ, and he sympathises. Is confusing times, he says. You mention again, because you forgot you already did, that there will be people coming in and out of the flat, nurses, care assistants, social workers, and that he is not to take any notice of any of them. They have to remind him to have his injections, but only the nurse can actually administer medication. He keeps the insulin in the fridge, in case BJ was wondering. BJ understands. You want to be careful with these people, he says. They no right to tell you what to do.

They want me out of here, you say.

Well, if you want to stay here, you tell them.

They ask have you thought about sheltered accommodation? Well, you say, I have my own shelter here. Even if it leaks a bit.

They think you are At Risk?

Yes, you say, that's it, they don't think I can cope.

You don't wanna be At Risk. Is bad news.

They suggest sheltered accommodation, or, if I get worse, a care home.

You no want care home.

I have my rights, don't I?

Depends, he says, depends. You have rights as citizen. But if they think you At Risk, it changes the situation, you understand? And if you not born in this country, worse – they send you to Holding Pen.

The Holding Pen, I've heard of that, you say – although in truth you are not at all sure what he is talking about.

Is bad, says BJ. Holding Pen, they call it, but you never get out.

I'll tell them, you say, I can fend for myself.

Good for you, sir. Ah, what kind of world we live in, eh? What kind of world?

Day 8

HE WHO WITHOUT being dead enters the kingdom of the dead, with its walls of iron protected by deep waters, must look out for himself, for nobody else will. This place is inhabited by some recognisable (they say iconic) characters: the Easter Bunny, Sherlock Holmes, a trio of male French maids, Harry Potter, a wrestler (covered in the mud from which he arose), a Great White Shark and The Mask – all in rapid motion, squeaking and hollering, at times grotesquely distorted way out of their original shapes. A thumbed flicker book, a demonic montage. He descended. There is no credit left here, nothing to break the fall. No decisions can be taken. No lamentations are to be heard.

The arrowhead railings stand as sentinels before this realm.

In those days, before you were properly dead (it's been over a week now, and still no-one's discovered you!), your fantasies – of metamorphosis, of bodily deformation – recurred nightly, to the point where you no longer paid attention; they became the norm, the new benchmark, the measure of the metafictions created deep in the kernel of your brain and radiating way out in successive stages or layers or circles till they reached consciousness and began impacting on the world that lies outside, till you knew neither whence nor whither. The show must go on; it becomes the world. But to accommodate itself to this world, it seems your body itself must undergo change, metamorphosis, it must stretch and distort, find new shapes that fit the new consciousness, the new regime of total difference powered by unknown engines. It seems sometimes as though your skeleton is melting, the bones turning to primaeval soup within the chrysalis that is your being, running into new channels, hardening and reshaping into new configurations; and you wake from your dreams then in a great panic, rush to the bathroom mirror to witness the results, only they are inconclusive; your body is palpably there, but has it altered? you feel sure it has, the form of your breastbone is not as it was yesterday or last week or last year, nor the tilt of your shoulder, nor the articulation of your hand, but though it is difficult to hold in your head, your altered head, how precisely different all of this is, you know that things have changed, and not necessarily for the better.

Flashback. The phone rings.

You decide to let it ring. Because Father Fuck has lately taken to phoning you up, and you don't want to speak with him again. His pastoral visits having fallen pretty well on stony ground, he has now resorted to pep talks over the phone. You know what his message will always be. He has by now figured out that you are one of the lapsed. The perfunctory enquiries after your health being made, therefore, the essence of the pastoral message is that God secretly hates you and despises you, and moreover has prepared a special place for you in that regard. This is not what his literal words are, but you have developed the knack of reading the invisible subtitles as his lips move. "God hates you, Mr [SURNAME], and will hate you forever, unless of course you repent of being who you really are and return to the fold pretty quick, you damned black sheep – eschewing forever the multitudinous enemies of the Church and cleaving to the bosom of the one true and apostolic thingy." You have had the same phone call once too often; he always sounds so troubled by your plight, you can imagine his ruddy visage contorting, you can actually hear him perspiring on the other end of the line. OK, yes, he makes you feel guilty, that's the root of it, that's the problem there is no solution to, and even if you want to say "I haven't done nothing", well, that won't do either because of the Sin of Omission thing.

But this time for once it's not the priest. The outgoing message kicks in, a disembodied voice (for you have never figured out how to personalise it), and then ... the sepulchral tone, the studied syntax. It's inimitable. That is not Father Fuck, that is the Raven, you call him the Raven. Also known as the Freeholder. Ah, Mr [SURNAME] he always begins, as though in the role of Counsel for the Prosecution. Have you considered my offer, which you will recall I made this day last week? (You cannot recall this.) You will doubtless be aware, he continues, you will doubtless be aware that the value of the lease on your flat is inevitably decreasing year by year, indeed, day by day ... His voice sends a unique chill down your spine, yet you are agog for more: You will appreciate that the price I mentioned last week is therefore not one I can hold for very long, but I am willing as a favour to hold it for at least one week longer to give you time to consider this opportunity ...

Why do you call him the Raven? because in his infrequent appearances he resembles such a bird; you have observed him in the yard at the back of the flats, stalking the territory in his long, black lawyer's winter coat, inspecting this, inspecting that, his beaked nose turning back and forth.

... so if you will be kind enough to call back on this number my assistant will talk you through the procedures and we can get the business done fairly quickly. [Click, buzz ...]

You don't want to get on the wrong side of him, you

remark to BJ, who has just entered through the front door. Yeah, I heard the message, he says, grinning. What he say he say to many of the tenants. You know what he wants.

He wants us all to die, you say.

Yeah, but so long as you sell him your lease before. It happen with Mrs Somebody, you know.

I know, you say. Do you think he bumped her off?

I no saying that. No no, ha ha. But very convenient for him, eh, she sell him the lease, in return for a nominal rent, a nominal rent he call it, then a year later, less than a year, poof! she gone!

She went very quickly. She seemed in good health.

For a few thousand pound he has good return on invest-ment. Is good business. But more than that: when he get majority of tenancies under his control – then he can do anything.

He won't get nothing off me, you promise BJ.

That's good.

BJ has finished his work for the time being, he declares, and is free for the next few days, during which time he will, among other things, with your permission, make soup. The soup will remind him of his faraway homeland, and a taste of it, should you wish to avail yourself, will also give you a taste of that. Everything is trying to remind you, you con-clude, of what you may never have experienced. The world you have forgotten and the world you have never experi-enced, both are trying to speak to you, and it's difficult to distinguish between them. It's true to say that in the normal course of things BJ, during the past few weeks, has been undemonstrative, hardly to be noticed as he's gone about his work from day to day. There's that to be said about him. He fits in. From time to time he has gone upstairs to talk business with Jackanapes, and then you can hear faintly the murmur of their voices, sometimes for hours on end, only on one occasion becoming distinctly audible, when you had the impression they were arguing about something and had raised their voices – but BJ has never mentioned it subsequently, nor indeed talked about his dealings with Jackanapes very much or at all. You get the impression Jackanapes is often cantankerous, or flies into a mood, and that it is part of BJ's job to calm him down or convince him that the course of action he's set upon is futile or counter-productive or an illogical fantasy. One time, you answered a knock on your front door and there was Jackanapes himself, in his dressing gown, wisps of hair drifting across his pate: Is BJ in? No, you said, you hadn't seen him all evening, it was your impression he had gone to the pub (though he doesn't drink) to watch on satellite TV there a football match in which he was particularly interested. So Jackanapes asked you to tell him when he came in that he wanted to see him about something urgent that had come up; though when BJ returned and you told him he wrinkled his nose and said it could wait till the morning. That's about as much as you've had to do with Jackanapes' business affairs.

But now anyway BJ is off duty, has swapped his shirt and tie for a T-shirt with a mandala print on it, and his polished shoes for flip-flops, and busies himself, with your permission, in your kitchen, now his laboratory, where he has deposited a load of vegetables, arcane herbs and spices, rice and other ingredients he's shopped for down the high street in the various ethnic stores that have sprung up there. And before long scents of an exotic nature begin to waft into your living room where you are staring through the window at the park; something is coming into being, something attractive and nutritious whose particles begin to enter your sensory organs, to stimulate your salivatory glands for the first time in many years, it seems.

At last, BJ announces that his creation is complete. He

brings you a brimming bowl. You taste the soup. More like a stew, actually. It is thick, rich, hot, savoury and sour, with scents of herbs that seem to come from distant mountains. It is like delicious molten lava. At once primaeval and terribly sophisticated. It takes your taste buds down some winding lanes, familiar at first and then unfamiliar, in ways it would need the services and vocabulary of an experienced wine critic to do justice to. It is wonderful. You begin to gulp it down.

This is very good, BJ.

Thank you, my friend. Is typical of my native country.

BJ is meanwhile tucking into his own bowl with relish.

You should have been a cook.

If I were not a lawyer.

How's your business with Jackanapes (you indicate upstairs with your forefinger) coming along?

BJ doesn't answer at first, but continues, thoughtfully, spooning his creation into his mouth. Finally he speaks:

Ah, my friend, your neighbour I do not think will succeed in his project.

He won't?

He has fantastical ideas, yeah, but also has not the capital or ... well, what can I say ... and you know, the Freeholder, I fear he will, how you say *make mince*?

Make mincemeat of him?

That is so, yes. But we shall see. You are happy living here?

It's OK, you say, lovely outlook over the park. I have my things here all around me.

You have plenty books, BJ says admiringly, looking round at the bookshelves, you are, how they say, *a well read man*. You have read them all?

Not all. My eyes are not too good for reading now. I used to read a lot of books. That was the time when I flourished.

I was a bit of a self-taught intellectual, you declare – breaking off to laugh at this pretention, and BJ laughs with you – I used to read books about science and philosophy, also I liked to read poetry, also books about music.

I remember you said you play the piano, yeah?

Many years ago, you tell him. I haven't played for years.

But you have no piano here?

Oh, I sold my last piano years ago. I stopped playing it, you explain, and it needed a lot of work doing to it, plus the regular tuning, and I needed the money. Sometimes now I think I should get one of them electronic keyboards, you know? But even they are a lot of money.

You should play, my friend. What kind of music you play?

Jazz, mostly, you tell him. Jazz, I used to play a lot.

You play with band?

Sometimes, I used to get together with friends, sometimes we played clubs in Soho and other places, you know, a little quartet or whatever. I got paid for it in them days. People used to say I had a lilt to my playing, you know, a natural lilt. We called it swing then. Long time ago. I have a big span, you know, people used to comment on my span, how I could get them wide spaced chords, you know. (And you spread both your long, spidery hands, splaying the fingers to demonstrate your span.)

Ha ha, you should get together with your friends again maybe.

Oh they're mostly dead, you say. And the conversation also dies.

You like the soup?

The soup is the food of gods; you have not tasted better, or if you have then you've entirely forgotten that previously attained summit of deliciousness. This is what you try to convey to BJ.

You want more?
Just half a bowl, please.

Day 9

INTO YOUR SECOND week of lying in state now. Beginning to get your colour back? Have you been abroad? no of course not, you've not been anywhere in the past eight days except that bedroom of yours, have you? But you'd seemed so unnaturally ashen lately, and now ... well, anyone would think you've spent the past week on the Costa Brava or maybe in Eye-beetha. Or back in the Caribbean, perchance? But no, sadly, it is not the dusky honey of your natural complexion that has returned; your skin now is of a more reddish hue than that, a hue that suggests at first glance over-toasting, then at second, well, something else. It is not the result of overexposure to ultra-violet rays – far from it. It is a reddish tan with a hint of green in it, a discoloration that comes from within and is far from a sign of health and vigour.

This is what is happening: as your red blood cells start to burst, they release their haemoglobin load, which begins to diffuse through the walls of the blood vessels and to stain the surrounding tissues. And now they are undergoing chemical changes to form various derivatives, including sulph-haemoglobin which discolours the tissue to a greenish tinge. This discolouration is spreading quite naturally throughout the surface of your body, in a veinlike pattern. It glistens dully in the dusk of your room, faintly illuminated by the TV phantasmagoria. Large patches of epidermis here and there are already beginning to loosen and flake off, revealing a parchmentlike base. The smell is not good, and there's that fly still flitting about.

On the positive side: your nightmares have come to an end. There is no longer anything firing within that skull of yours, there is nothing to disturb you with incessant variations on archetypal patterns. The stage that was your brain is dark, it has been vacated, the actors or musicians that flitted on and off it having quit their dressing rooms and gone home; the performance is over, the audience long ago having filed out in silence into the night; they have gone home too. The house lights have dimmed for the last time. Peace reigns within. It's a pity you are no longer around to enjoy it. Assuming that you could put up with that wretched TV still going in the background, on and on.

But those nightmares. In the last days before it all unravelled, halcyon days you might judge them by comparison with what ensued, blue-kingfisher-flashing peaceful stay-of-execution days, you attempted to make sense of them by describing them to BJ – a sympathetic ear – when he came into your living room bearing two coffee mugs, one for you, towards the end of the day.

Bad dreams, you tell him, I said to the doctor I think sometimes they're getting better, but then they come again. And the worst of it, you say, is that I don't know what's dream and what's not.

You don't know where you are! exclaims BJ, sympathetically.

Yes, that's right. Did I shout last night, did you hear me?

I can't remember, he says. I sleep good.

I see my people, you say. They've come back, and they're in the flat. I see them all the time. But they're not there really. I know that. I'm not stupid.

What your people – you see your mother?

Yes, I see her, and my dead family. Sometimes I see them in the room, then they vanish, sometimes I hear them moving about and talking in the next room. I can hear children.

Sometimes playing and messing about, sometimes crying. Then I don't know if I'm awake or not. The other night ... I heard voices in the kitchen, I got up and went in there, I don't know if you heard me ...

No, I hear nothing.

... I saw three people I used to know, my brother-in-law and also my cousin and his wife, but I'll tell you something: I knew they were dead. I mean, I could see they were dead, their skin was very pale. I hadn't seen them in years. They were in the kitchen, they seemed to be chatting just normally. They looked at me, I don't know whether they recognised me. I went up to my cousin, I touched him on the arm, as if to say "Are you all right?" – only his arm was dead cold. I said "Why, you're really cold and clammy!" – just conversation, like. And he turned to me and said "Oh, really?", then he turned to his wife and touched *her* on the arm, just as I'd done to him, and said "You're right, we're all cold and clammy." But I got the feeling there wasn't anything there behind it. I mean, he was just like a, what do you call it, an automaton, and he was imitating me, my movements and my way of speaking, but he didn't have any consciousness at all, there was nothing there. He was not at all conscious, just, you know, instinctively following the mannerisms of a human being, and speech, what a human being would do and say. Like a zombie, you know what I mean? BJ, tell me something.

Yes, my friend?

Do I seem different in any way, I mean physically?

I don't know what you mean.

So you try to convey to him your deep conviction that your bones are melting during the night in order to be regenerated into new and unfamiliar structures; that you are convinced when you observe yourself in the mirror that your body is now distorted, its bones intersecting at new angles; that, in short, you are being metamorphosed into a new and unknown creature still bearing your name. And that therefore this change must be observable to others.

No. You the same, he asserts.

You apologise for your silliness, but you are most concerned about this, yet you feel unable to bring it to the attention of the stream of clinical practitioners who visit you, because you fear their scorn.

You the same as before, my friend! Nothing change!

But then BJ reflects, and adds: However.

However?

I have seen this before in a human being. A change of shape.

A change of shape, that's it. So who was that? you ask.

It was my wife. You had wife too, didn't you? he enquires. I think you told me that.

You mutter something in reply.

What was that?

Many years ago, is what you told him. It didn't work out.

I too, the same.

At that moment, the phone goes. You wanna answer it? says BJ politely. No, you say, let it be. The answering machine kicks in: Ah, good morning, Mr [SURNAME] ...

It's Father Fuck again, you exclaim with a groan. You recognise his monotonous, patient yet rasping delivery.

... I hope you are well this fine morning. I just wanted to find out whether you have had the chance to read that small text I left with you ...

Who? says BJ.

The priest. He wants to tell me I'm going to Hell.

Ah, yes, murmurs BJ philosophically, that is what they say, the priests. It is their job.

The priest finishes his message, and his electronic presence vanishes.

Is funny you say that. Because what you was saying about body change, and I say about my wife. Is coincidence.

What is?

Last time I saw my wife it was in Hell.

(You let this statement resonate for a moment or two.)

You last saw your wife in Hell?

Yeah.

You're joking?

No, is no joke. I visited Hell. The original Hell.

The original?

Yeah, the place believed to be where Hell was, in ancient times.

Where?

In my part of the world, says BJ, beginning to look uncomfortable. Is real place. Is no Disneyland or Disney World.

But you came back?

(No reply.)

You came back from Hell?

You never come back, says BJ, you never really return. From Hell, no, never. He is gazing out of the window now, at the darkening view over the park, where one or two shadows of people can be seen moving on the grass or on the diagonal pathway; now and again an illuminated double-decker bus passes slowly in the traffic in front of this, below and directly in front of the block of flats where you live, where you and he are talking; lights now begin to glow in the windows of the houses on the far side of the park. He turns to face you again. His face turns to void. You want I should tell you the story? he says.

Day 10

IT'S DIFFICULT FOR you to follow BJ's narrative, not because it is labyrinthine (it is, in parts) but because it repeats senselessly at times, each time making less sense than the last, perhaps due to his incomplete command of English compounded by his earnestness in trying to remedy this; and also because he shifts his ground continually, leaving you less and less clear as to where exactly and when the events in the narrative occurred, or whether they occurred at all, in this way or in any other way. So he bamboozles you, perhaps meaning to perhaps not, who can say, and it has to be admitted you are easily bamboozled these days. These were the days of your bamboozlement; you would have undoubtedly fared better in former times, in the period when you were flourishing.

He begins with this rambling introduction about his people and his former wife's people, giving the impression that his was originally a romance akin to that of Romeo and Juliet, doomed by a cavernous political rift that could never be bridged. He quotes popular songs from his homeland on this very theme, songs you are of course not familiar with, even though he hums one or two of them to you (and you remember how back in the day you used to be a "hum it and I'll play it for you" sort of musician, how you had that facility). But what exactly was that schism? Was it religious or national or racial or was it to do with social class? He tries to answer your rather fumbling question by veering off into a description of a great mountain, sacred to his people, but whose summit or even whose foothills his people are doomed never to attain; and yet the sacred mountain, a snow-clad peak wreathed in cloud, dominates the skyline beyond their great city. And this mountain, says BJ, is the repository of the Ark – "you know, the Ark from the Bible" he explains, although it's not clear whether it is Noah's Ark, whatever it is doing up a mountain, or the Ark of the Covenant itself as described in many a Hollywood blockbuster – but all this is beyond you.

Then he resumes his narrative about the shenanigans that ensued from or were entailed in his marriage, a tangled web of family feuds and vendettas, snubs, veiled threats and counter-threats; you get the strong impression that this romance was doomed from the start. His wife doesn't come out of it very well, anyway. But it is his narrative, after all. There is a strong hint that she was not entirely faithful during his absences from their native town while he was away studying at law school; on his return, there were inevitably rows and tears. Many arguments, my friend, many many arguments, he tells you, shaking his head sadly, I will not bore you with the details. And now his wife grew to be hypochondriacal, every day with a new ailment or imagined ailment, and all somehow to be blamed on him, he declares in sorrow. And that reminds him of the starting point, or one of the starting points, for this rambling narrative, your conviction that your body is morphing into new and unnatural shapes; well, that was the same with his wife, says BJ. Every morning, when he awoke, he would find she was no longer in bed alongside him, but in the bathroom, at the mirror, peering at herself anxiously. Do you not see it? she would howl at him, do you not see it? See what? I am changing before your eyes, she would say, and you see nothing! No, you are still beautiful, he would say, and she flung that back at him: Hypocrite! How can you say that? Sometimes it was her hips that were coming out of alignment, sometimes her breastbone or her collarbone, or the bones of her face; they were distorting, she was becoming a twisted caricature of herself. He paid for a doctor, but the doctor could find nothing wrong, and she then railed at the doctor too, called him a liar, so the doctor packed his black bag and said, regrettably, he was unable to treat her after all, thank you and good day.

It was an attempt at reconciliation that led to the final, tragic chapter of this story, continues BJ. He proposed to his wife that they take a holiday, just the two of them. They would drive into the mountains for a few days, towards the region that his wife's people came from, where the air was clear and there was cool green vegetation that would purify their minds. Apart from reconciliation, it would also celebrate his passing of final exams at law school. She agreed. So they packed the little car he had bought second-hand, although they did not have much money in those days as he had not yet started earning money as a lawyer. Off they went, leaving their town. Soon, all elements of civilisation were left behind. They passed from the arid desert beyond the suburbs of the town into a more moist region, flat, with marsh on either side exhaling a strange stench they had never encountered before. He wondered whether they had taken a wrong turn. But soon the road began to climb as they caught the first glimpses of the mountains ahead of them, a faint mist clinging to their shapes. BJ says that at this point he had felt sure the holiday would do them good, would at least begin to repair their failing relationship. They had the windows wound down in the car, both smoking cigarettes, just like the old days, and the scent of pine was strong on the breeze now, coming from the forest that was beginning to amass around them. Onward he drove. We did not know where we were going, he says; but he hints that they were crossing forbidden frontiers in the process, moving from the known to the unknown, from their familiar jurisdiction to a place that was governed by different laws, or was beyond the law altogether. These mountains they had arrived in, if not exactly sacred like the great mountain previously alluded to, were exotically tainted, harbouring thrilling secrets, it would seem. Some were observed at the horizon to be conical in shape, attesting to the volcanic nature of this immense range. BJ and his wife saw grey sheets of water below them, flocks of birds of some kind veering to and fro just above their surfaces. They saw and heard the tinkling of a long, snaking waterfall, glinting as it descended a steep gully. A raptor hovered in the blue-grey sky above. Once, they caught sight of a brown bear in the distance, making its way down to the lakeside, no doubt in search of food, perhaps after winter's hibernation in a high cave. BJ's wife, he says, was entranced by these sights (while BJ was concentrating on the perilously winding road), pointing them out to him; and for a brief while she forgot her ailments, or seemed to; at any rate, she had not alluded to them since they set out.

Now, however, they left the forest below them and were coming into a bleaker landscape. It seemed they had entered the clouds that were previously just wisps in a blue sky, and the sun was blotted out once more. The vegetation became more stunted, the slopes seemed harsher. They also started feeling hungry and thirsty, and although they had brought some provisions with them, BJ suggested to his wife that they look out for one of the roadside taverns or cafés that might be found in these parts – although, admittedly, he was not entirely sure where they had got to by now. And sure enough, as they rounded yet another bend they saw a building up ahead of them that might be a source of sustenance.

It promised less the closer they got to it. When they got really close, they saw it was a timber structure built onto the rock face – the road widening at this point to offer limited parking space in front. But there were no other vehicles there. A faded placard on a timber frame bore a message in several languages: BJ says he recognised Turkish, Armenian, Arabic, Farsi, Russian, German, French and English. And they all said the same thing: ABANDON ALL HOPE YOU WHO ENTER HERE.

I recognised what that was *immediately*, exclaims BJ excitedly, jolting you awake, because you have started to drift off at this point, lulled by the languid rhythms of his narrative. He says his father told him the story many years ago: that a cave had been discovered in these mountains by archaeologists, believed millennia ago to be the entrance to Hell itself. The legendary site of the ancient Garden of Eden had already been identified in that region, but this had escaped notice until nineteenth or early twentieth century explorers had chanced upon it and had done some excavations in very difficult conditions. There was little doubt, his father had told him, that this was the site; but further explorations were stymied by the advent of war, or rather, wars, both regional and worldwide, closing off this territory for another generation. There had been newspaper stories that it was to be opened up again – indeed, opened to the public – but continuing political difficulties, not to mention the relative inaccessibility of the location, got in the way of that, and people stopped speaking about it. Perhaps because there was nothing really to see there.

BJ continues: I said to my wife, I really want to see this. But she say, no, I don't wanna, we don't have time. She was anxious, you see, because we wanted to cross the mountains to the other side, to a town where we could get a hotel, and it was already the late afternoon.

Grudgingly, she agreed to stop for a few minutes. They parked, got out of the car, approached the entrance. Nobody else around. There was a window with a counter at the side of the main opening, staffed by an old woman in a headscarf who did not acknowledge their approach. When they came up to the counter she nodded and grunted. Both BJ and his wife spoke simultaneously:

How much is it to go in?

Have you anything to eat or drink?

The old woman shook her head at both simultaneous questions, indicating her non-comprehension. She did not seem to respond particularly favourably to any of the languages they tried. BJ's wife mimed the need for refreshments. The old woman indicated a cooler cabinet beneath the counter meagrely stocked with a few cans of Coca Cola and Fanta, and two unappetising-looking cheese rolls wrapped in clingfilm. That was all that was available. They could hear faintly the chugging of the generator that presumably supplied electricity here. When BJ proffered some banknotes, pointing at the entrance, she in turn pointed at a sign above her head, in the same several languages as the main sign. It said they were closing at five o'clock. It was now four. We have an hour, BJ told his wife. She sighed, said OK.

This was bad decision, BJ tells you sombrely. Worst decision of my life. He pauses, and continues.

They paid; the old woman accepted their currency without demur, gave them change, and generated from a machine two old-fashioned cardboard tickets on a roll, which she tore off and handed them. She pointed to the cavernous entrance, and again to the sign indicating closing time.

They were in a cool, dim, well proportioned entrance hall carved into the rock, with a faint smell of damp. No information visible at all, but a line of small lights was set in the concrete or stone floor, and they followed this into the darkness beyond. They came to the head of a wide flight of stairs winding gently downwards. More lighting, not very bright, was embedded in the handrails at the sides. So down they went, slowly, gingerly. I don't like this, said BJ's wife, and he promised: Well, we'll just take a quick look and come back up.

On the left side of the stairs was a series of illuminated placards in a descending pattern. It resembled, BJ comments, those advertising posters that accompany commuters on the escalators in London's tube stations. Each displayed a word (in some of the languages previously observed):

ABANDON
      ALL
           HOPE
              YOU
                    WHO
                          ENTER
                              HERE

It was a bit, how you say, *corny*? suggests BJ.

The versions in Hebrew, Arabic and Farsi were displayed, right to left, on the opposite side of the staircase.

As they descended, they felt a warm current from below beginning to temper the chill. At the foot of the stairs they emerged into another vast, cavernous space, its extremities too dark to make out. Tiny lights embedded in the floor seemed to guide them, and they passed through a doorway and onto a walkway that appeared to be suspended above an abyss from which the warm current emanated, perhaps indicating volcanic processes way below, the air now tinged with something new, or something old, rather, a sulphurous flavour to it. There also seemed to be a faint mist around them. They peered over the banister that flanked their bridge, could see nothing in the darkness, but heard a very faint burbling as from water flowing underground. Onward? BJ's wife began to register her discomfort: we've seen enough, she urged, that's it, let's go back now. But BJ persuaded her to continue, just to see what was on the far side of this bridge over the abyss, promising then they would return. It was another opening, another downward flight of steps, again with lights embedded in the handrails, so all they could see was their own feet on stone treads. And into yet another space, vaster still than anything they had seen so far, a cathedral in rock. The warmth and that sulphurous, damp smell pervaded it, and the faint mist. The floor lighting had now petered out; there was illumination of some limited kind hidden in the great folds of the walls, so they could make out mysterious shapes and shadows in the rock, but nothing else. They could barely see each other. Ha ha, BJ remembers saying, Hell is not so bad, there is nothing here. Worst thing I ever said, he tells you.

Then one of the shadows moved. BJ's wife uttered a shriek, clutched at BJ's arm.

A great dark shape moved over them, and BJ's wife's shriek was echoed, as though played back to them. And as their eyes were getting accustomed to the darkness, they saw a second shape moving above the first, and a third even further away, above that. And the shriek – it was no longer her shriek, it was an alien howl, it seemed as if the sound was generated by sampling hers and throwing it back at them – a repeated echo, again and again, ever more furiously. Three winged creatures, like gigantic bats, rushed back and forth above them, swooping, one almost brushing their heads. They could hear wings flapping. It was no longer possible to distinguish between BJ's wife's screaming and the echoing screams, almost catlike, emanating from these beings.

At this point I lost contact with my wife, says BJ, she let go of my hand and she ran, I think she was trying to go back to the entrance, and so I went after her.

He found himself in a space that was completely dark. He couldn't see a thing. He had by now starting yelling his wife's name, calling out to her again and again. The screams – his wife's and the creatures' – were now dying away. He called again. He didn't know where he was. Then he heard a whimpering, and he went towards it. He thought he could see the shape of his wife in the gloom. He called again. She answered with his name. He went up to the dark shape of his wife and held out his hand. He could hear her sobbing. And she was repeating something like: Don't look at me now, please don't look at me, don't say anything. If you say it, if you look, it will happen. That will be the end.

But he never understood this. There was a cigarette lighter in his pocket. He fumbled with it and flicked it on.

To his horror, BJ saw that this was indeed his wife; but she had utterly changed. Her hips were distorted, so that she stood there awkwardly splay-footed; her shoulder bones had become grotesquely enlarged, sending her arms out at a strange angle; her face, at first recognisable, was visibly changing in the flickering illumination of the cigarette lighter, flexing like a piece of rubber being squeezed; her hair, which had been luxuriantly dark, seemed in that inadequate light to be falling out in dry handfuls. She was becoming monstrous. He recoiled; she, or the shape that had been her, fled.

BJ spent what seemed like many hours stumbling about in the darkness, calling his wife's name over and over. There was now nothing but silence apart from the echo of his footsteps.

He had to get help. He tried to retrace his steps back

towards the entrance. But he could not find his way. He found openings that led only to tunnels that came to dead ends. He flicked his cigarette lighter on repeatedly until it gave out. It was only by chance that eventually he turned a corner and caught sight of the line of lights in the floor that told him he was going in the right direction. He passed through the cathedral-like space, ascended the stairs, crossed the bridge over the abyss, traversed the space on the far side of that, ascended the original staircase. He was back in the entrance hall, but there was no daylight ahead. A solid steel shutter barred his way.

He screamed and screamed. There was no reply. There was no-one there. He sat on the floor, panting, his back to the steel barrier.

Having retrieved his breath, he stood up again. He examined the shutter, feeling with his hands. He felt some kind of latch or bolt. He pushed and pulled at it. When it gave, he burst out weeping. There was a door within the shutter that opened. He stepped through.

There was still no daylight, because by now it was night. But the fresh air ...

This all happened a long time ago, before the use of mobile phones became widespread in his country. Even so, there would have been no signal here of any kind, BJ tells you.

He ran to his car, which was still parked where it had been. The old woman had evidently shut up shop and departed a long time ago.

Frantically, he got in, started the engine. He had to seek help. He drove like a man possessed. He would make for the nearest town, the one they had been hoping to reach on the other side of the mountains.

It was a beautiful night. A half-moon was half-hidden by drifting cloud. After he had been driving for twenty minutes or so, the road began to decline and the forest to return, its fragrant scent reaching his nostrils through the open window. It was a peaceful scene, but the sweat was pouring down his face as he traversed the downward, winding road.

He became aware of a kind of buzzing sound. Was it the engine? Please god, he thought, let the car complete its journey, please just let that happen.

Something flicked at his head. He put the brake on. The volume of buzzing increased exponentially. There was some kind of flying creature in the car. No, more than one. They were bees, or wasps, or more likely giant hornets. Two, no, three of them, buzzing around his head. He had never seen insects this size before, with angry black and yellow stripes, with faces, diving and swooping at him, making an unbearable, mad sound like supercharged motorbikes. He flung open the door, almost fell out onto the road.

After a while they went away. He didn't see them go.

It was an hour or so later, almost dawn, when he reached the town. He made enquiries, located the police station. He explained what had happened. The police did not seem to be as interested in that as they were in the fact that his papers were not in order. He was in a jurisdiction he was not entitled to be in. How had he come here? They snapped questions at him. Had he crossed the frontier? What frontier? He had not been aware of a frontier.

They did not believe me, my friend, BJ says sadly. I tell them everything, but they laugh at me. The police say, Hell, what do you mean, Hell? You say you have been to Hell, that your wife is still in Hell – ha ha, we have to go through Hell every day with people like you. I show them the tickets – they say these tickets could be from anywhere – it don't say Hell. So I persuade them at last to take me up the mountain, I said I will show you what I mean. But we never find the place. They say it does not exist.

You never found it, BJ?

No, my friend, we never. They say they have never heard of it. I was lucky they did not put me in prison.

So what happened?

Eventually ... eventually I went back to my home. I reported my wife missing. But she was never found again.

That's a terrible story, BJ.

What is worse, her family was very angry. They think that I do away with her, and I make up this story about Hell. So first they try to prosecute me, but nothing happen. Then her family, they like declare war.

They declare war?

Yeah. Her two brothers, I hear they are coming after me. I think they will kill me. I have to run away, I have to leave the country very quickly. I leave, I go to Greece, Switzerland, Germany. Eventually I come to this country. That is to cut a, to cut a story, how you say?

To cut a long story short?

That's it.

BJ seems to have come to the end of his narrative. Night has descended on the park outside your window, the lights are now all aglow in the windows of the houses on the far side, a sodium orange shimmer comes from the single street lamp visible to the right, and the lights of the traffic below your window move from right to left, from right to left, dreamily. BJ has fallen silent.

Is that the end of the story, then, BJ?

There is no end to my story, my friend.

BJ is illuminated by the standard lamp next to the sofa on which you sit. His face is close to yours: his neatly trimmed goatee beard, his slightly protruding front teeth, his mobile pointy face; you look into his eyes, which, once grey, now with the pupils fully dilated, are dark and inscrutable as night.

Day 11

THE CARE ASSISTANTS come and go. This one is Tanya. She is from Slovenia, she says in response to your polite enquiry – very merry she is, hums tunes to herself as she bustles about. Have you had your injection, [FORENAME]? Yes? that's good, my love. Well, I'll see you, cheerio. The one that comes next is Eileen, English, grumpy, in and out as quickly as possible. You don't care for her too much. Then Nadya, doesn't seem to speak a word of English, don't know where she's from, but she smiles briefly, she's OK. It's hard to keep up. Such a procession of cartoon mother-figures. You can't really hold all this information in your head for any length of time. Can't remember their names. True, the names are on their CARE-PLC badges, so there's no real need. But still. So anyway, the days go by in this fashion.

Another one knocks on your front door (they all have the code that enables them to enter the building). Hello, [FORE-NAME], I'm the nurse, my name is Sherry. (She is black – a lovely skin she has – but brisk, and wears a different uniform.)

Hello, Sherry.

We're going to do some tests today, do you mind?

Not at all.

Only the doctor is a bit concerned you may have memory issues, you know?

Ah yes, memory issues.

So let's settle down. Front room, or at the table in the kitchen?

Living room is nicer.

We start with this question, [FORENAME], says Nurse Sherry, arranging her paperwork in front of her while chewing on the end of a ballpoint pen. Are you ready?

Yes, nurse.

What is today's date?

That's a tough one. You make a stab at it: Well, I know it's not Thursday, because Thursdays the ambulance arrives to take me to that damned day centre ...

Never mind the day of the week, it doesn't matter. But the date and the month, any idea, roughly?

April, I think, you say, something like the fifteenth?

Nurse Sherry makes no comment on this, just smiles and writes something in the appropriate box on her form.

Now, next one. Who is the current Prime Minister?

Ah, you know that one. You can picture the face of that conniving, hypocritical harbourer of icy and entitled hatred, acclaimed by many, accursed by some, you've seen that face so often on the telly, it's so dreadfully familiar. Talking about cracking down hard on immigrants and all that. Talking about The British People. And the name is ... ah, it's gone. It'll come back in a minute.

No worries, take your time.

You take your time, but nothing comes, though you can picture that scoundrel.

OK, tell me something that happened in the news recently.

There's been a war. In the Middle East, I think. Oh yes, and there was a tennis match and the winner cried.

Can you tell me the names of twelve different animals?

Hmm. Cat, dog, horse. Cow. Bird, what kind of bird? Sparrow. Dog, no I said that, didn't I? Lion! Yes, lion, and elephant, and tiger. How many is that?

I make that eight.

Snake. I hate snakes, you add.

Any more?

(Long pause.) Polar bear. And penguin. Fish. Whale.

Well done, that's more than twelve.

Do insects count? Oh, and mice, of course. How could I forget?

That's all right, we've got the twelve. Next one, I need you to use a pen and paper, here you are. Draw the face of a clock and write in the numbers. Not the hands, just the numbers.

You are quite good at this sort of thing. You were always excellent at drawing. You draw a circle, then you put the number 12 at the top and go round, though by the time you get back to the 12 you are running out of space and having to squash the numbers somewhat.

That's good, thank you, says Nurse Sherry. It's now, what's the time, let me see, twenty-five past eleven. Can you draw in the hands of the clock, and position them for twenty-five past eleven?

You get a bit confused at this point. Twenty-five past eleven? you ask again, for confirmation. You have a stab at it, then you quickly realise you've done it wrong. Can I have another go?

Take your time, she says.

Your father used to wind the clock that was in the hall in the family home with a special key that he obtained from the cupboard below. That is practically all you remember of him. Oh, except for the music, of course. That was in another country, many years ago. The clock had Roman numerals. Ah, that would have been an idea, that would have impressed the nurse: draw the clock, but put in Roman numerals. You can probably remember how they are. XII at the top, then, oh, which way round do they go? I, II, III, that's it. It would have all come back, you're certain of it. The clock had a loud tick which seemed to mark the silence in the house when there was nobody there. It gave resonance to that silence. And it chimed on the hour. There was a whirring sound, as though it was clearing its throat, and then it chimed. They don't make clocks like that any more. What became of it? It was probably lost in the flood. The flood took everything, all memories, all was lost. That's why you don't remember much about the flood, the tidal wave, even though it was a catastrophe, even though it was the worst that could happen – it took away people's memories with it. And the fact that you were very young. Your father, he liked a drink, they said. Your mother always said that. He liked a drink. And he perished as a result. He drowned in it. He instilled in you his love of music. Even as a child you followed your art, and your art, so far as it could, followed nature. It was a sin of passion, which does not incur the same punishment as sins of deliberation. Wasn't the piano in the lobby, near the old clock? Did your father show you how to play boogie-woogie? You seem to remember that, and the way it took you, the way it grabbed you, a very fundamental way it was. The kid's got it, you remember him saying, telling your mother, the kid's got it, which made you feel very proud, of course. Because you knew what "it" was. He didn't have to tell you. But the smell of booze on his breath when he held you close, you remember that too. You didn't have the fear then, the fear of outsideness, that came much later. He's going to perish, said your mother, and said all the mother-figures in your family, one after another, echoing, and it will be his own fault. Where are they now? Gone in the flood, some of them, still talking to you in your head as they did once when you were a child; you will be an orphan, they said, poor thing, what will you do? It's all a bit mixed up in your head now, of course, bits and pieces all jostling to make some semblance of coherence. Nurse Sherry stands in for all the mother-figures in the family; just for the record, she's closing her files, are we done?

How did I do? you ask, and she smiles, That's fine, [FORE-NAME], we'll let you know the results.

Did you ask me the time?

I asked you (she pronounces it "arksed", that's nice) to draw a clock and I also asked (arksed) you today's date.

I believe it is the month of May, you say, I could have made a mistake there.

No worries, [FORENAME]. You have a nice day.

The nurse's paperwork looms before you, proclaims a message that is indecipherable. All that is the case looms before you, looms and fits. She is gone, there is peace once more in your flat. But no clock ticking, not ever again. Just the low rumble of the eternal traffic outside, travelling from womb to tomb, but you have no say in that, who has? The father within you, the father in your fingers, long and spiderlike but no longer performing, but crooked and distorted, the mothers surrounding you, but at a distance, things as they were but no longer quite as they were, but not at all as they were, that is, slipping from level to level, ah, the stories you could tell.

Day 12

AH, BUT THEN there is a mighty thump on the ceiling. Shakes your room, shakes you. The aftershocks seem to reverberate forever. And BJ, who has been in the kitchen, in the midst of preparing the thick, bitter Turkish coffee with which he kickstarts his day (yes, actually it's the start of another day, how quickly they come round), he's shaken too. He comes into the living room, his little coffee pot in his hand, with a puzzled and alarmed expression on his face. He's in a sloppy T-shirt and jogging pants, flip-flops on his narrow feet. He looks contemplatively at the ceiling.

A titan has fallen in heaven. The sparrows chirrup a commentary. The world pauses, continues.

Is that Jackanapes? you say. What happened?

It's silent as the grave up there.

I go up and see, mutters BJ, abandoning his coffee-making, I have key to his flat. Where is my phone? Here it is. He exits. You continue with whatever it was you were doing, which you've forgotten. What the hell was it?

Some sounds of movement above the ceiling. Some time passes.

BJ, in a great state of agitation – you have never seen this urbane fellow this way before, not even when he was telling that dreadful story – reappears, jabbering into his mobile phone, non-stop; you are profoundly alarmed.

What is it? Is it Jackanapes? What's wrong?

He stabs at his phone, looks up at you.

Yeah, my friend, your neighbour, emergency, yeah, his

heart stop I think his heart stop, is not good. I phone emergency, 999.

BJ paces up and down your room once, twice, then without another word disappears once more out of your front door; you can hear his steps rapidly ascending the stairs.

More time passes.

Blue flashing light. You look out. An ambulance has drawn up below, dazzling you. Not the friendly so-called ambulance that calls for you every Thursday to take you to the day centre, which is no more than a minibus really, though it wears the legend AMBULANCE on its side: no, a massive machine emblazoned with many logos and devices, in luminous, acidic livery. Some men get out. You can faintly hear the buzz of a front doorbell not your own, distantly an exchange of sorts, then the front door of the building opening, the sounds of someone coming through.

You are peering anxiously – your hand clamped on the handle – through the open front door of your flat, onto the landing. Up the stairs towards you climb three mythological figures, like warriors, three noble paramedics, half human half machine, bulked out with uniform appendages, carrying whatever it is they do not wear. Two males, one female by the appearance, but you cannot tell for certain. The one in the lead, reaching the head of the stairs, catches your eye – In here? he enquires, but you shake your head, point up the stairs, and meanwhile BJ's face appears over the banister, No, up here! he exclaims, and the three push past your landing; they seem perilously close to jovial in their eagerness, but also give the impression of almost equine power and presence, in their roles as divine mechanics, as perfect fusions of nature and artifice.

And more time passes, and once again you struggle to recall what it was you were doing before these thunderous events intervened and crashed your thought processes.

Events whose stage is your ceiling now, on the invisible side of it, the eternal life-and-death soap opera of the gods, a drama in which you play no part, in which you can't intervene – you can only think your thoughts now, which have no coherence, no sense of instrumentality, ah, it wasn't always so, they weren't so easily crashed, and besides you once had a sense of yourself as a man of action, a man of practicalities as well as aesthetics, but where were we? Never mind, make a cup of coffee, that's a thing to do. It is time for morning coffee, after all. Not BJ's undrinkable sludge, which never loses its bitterness no matter how many spoonfuls of sugar you ladle into it, but a mug of instant, with milk. So you go into your kitchen and occupy yourself for a while. And then bring your mug into the living room and stare through the window out at the park for a while. The scene – two dog-walkers, a woman in a pink anorak with a child in a buggy, under an almost white sky, blissfully unaware of any peril – is jerkily illuminated by the strobe-like effect of the light from the unseen ambulance below. You relapse into your thoughts, in which are mingled pleasant memories, but in which foreboding and dread are, as so often, never far away, and certainly never completely absent.

And then there are audible developments in the drama: urgent footsteps down and up the stairs outside, bumps as of large objects being manoeuvred. You return to your front door, open it cautiously.

The three magnificent horsemen/women are now carefully lowering a stretcher, step by step, upon which bundled a recumbent form, clearly the considerable person of Jackanapes himself, but he is unrecognisable, wired as he is to machines, his face completely obscured by a white plastic oxygen mask. The cortège arrives at your landing, and with much verbal coaxing gently urges its burden round the corner and onto the next flight down. Bringing up the rear is a distraught BJ, who excuses himself politely, pushes past you into your flat, disappears into his room, re-emerges in scarcely any time at all in his overcoat and good shoes, excuses himself once more.

I have to go, my friend, I have to go, I see you soon.

How is he? you enquire.

Is not good, is not good. I see you soon.

That was the last you ever saw of him in your flat. As a matter of fact. You didn't know that then, of course.

The cortège reaches the bottom, both wings of the front door are held open.

Within minutes a great wail is launched upon the air, as well as the revving up of a powerful engine. The ambulance siren reaches a peak and stays there, screaming now, wobbling up and down. You hear the vehicle pull away, and the wailing starts gradually to disappear into the distance. Before too long it has vanished into silence.

Peace returns.

Nothing for two days. No news at all. No sign of BJ.

You bump into the Christian window cleaner on the stairs. Oh, did you hear about your upstairs neighbour? he says, in passing, after the chit-chat. Yes, you say, your ears pricking, he was taken to hospital. Oh, apparently he passed away, says the Christian window cleaner mournfully through his crooked mouth. Did he really? Yes he did, he passed, God bless his soul. Mr Paul Jackson, that was his name, though you always called him Jackanapes – very sad.

And how on earth did the Christian window cleaner hear the news? Well, he goes into a long story about it, how he was in touch with the managing agent about the contract to clean all the windows in the block every twelve weeks approximately, and how that was all going to be tied up properly with legal effect, and so on and so forth, and the girl at the managing agent's office had just been talking on the phone to the Freeholder, who had all the information, Mr Jackson at number such-and-such, he has just passed away, she said. He was taken urgently to hospital at the weekend following a *myocardial infarction* (he pronounces the phrase with relish), and was then transferred to the finest hospital in the land for heart surgery, and had the best surgeons available attending, and yes (to answer your question), Irina, his beautiful Russian surgeon bride-to-be who, according to rumour, had saved his life on a previous occasion (that occasion famously precipitating their engagement), was of course summoned with urgent haste and flew to his side, but not even she could save him this time, and so, tragically, the wedding promised for June was off. And his aged mother, now in her ninety-first year (you remember her?), has been left without a son, not something you would wish on anyone let alone one of her age and fragility. Very sad, and may God have mercy on his soul, the Christian window cleaner repeats, giving the impression of a judge passing the ultimate sentence. But he has to add (and here he lowers his voice dramatically, with sideways glances lest anyone who might be lurking on the stairs should overhear his indiscretion – so you have to strain to listen) that he believes the feeling within the circles of the Freeholder and the managing agent is that the loss is not quite so painful to them, indeed more of a blessing, because Mr Jackson, or Jackanapes, was perceived as somewhat of a pain in the butt to all concerned with his endless threats of litigation re the various leaseholds in the building, but you are not to pass on this assessment, or if you do pass it on you are not to attribute it to him, he's just the humble window cleaner.

And what of BJ, you ask, have you heard from him? BJ? The Christian window cleaner frowns, he can't place him. Yes, BJ who was assisting your neighbour with his legal issues and who has been unofficially lodging with you. Ah yes, he remembers the fellow, he thinks, but has no news of him. Not that he can recall.

Well, you take your leave of the Christian window cleaner, and proceed on your way out the front door. You have made a resolution that life must return to normal, whatever that is. You will walk in the park once a day, crossing the frontier marked by the arrowhead railings, even if you don't feel like it, even if the open space strikes terror at first, because it's good for the soul and therefore for the body, because you believe there is no difference between the two and that this is a perfect truth (which is a subject you try to avoid both with the Christian window cleaner and with Father Fuck, who hasn't been around much lately). And you will ponder whether you have enough money accumulated in your bank account from your pension and BJ's rent to maybe acquire an electronic keyboard of sorts, not that you know what model to get, you are way out of touch, because it is true that it's a crime you are not playing, that you have not played for years.

But days go by, and you do nothing.

Oh, BJ did phone. You were not at home to receive the call, but his voice was unmistakable on the answering machine. Hey, my friend (crackle crackle), you OK? I have to tell you your neighbour is no more, he die in hospital, I have business to close his accounts, but I will return to get my things from your flat, only I don't have time right now, and I pay you the rent money what I owe you, I promise, I am very sorry. I am looking at maybe ...

And then the message cuts out – whether a glitch in your machine or the signal failing at his end, who knows? But he doesn't call back and you don't have his phone number and your machine does not store incoming phone numbers, so you will have to wait to hear again.

And you wait, and several more days go by, and nothing, and you forget.

Flash forward. The television blares out in your bedroom. We are living in a divided country, they say, we are living in times when presently all knowledge will be dead and the seas will be dead, and the good offices of nature will be fatally compromised, but on the other hand there is new entertainment to be had this spring season, coming very soon. If you had the power you would undoubtedly turn it off. Why watch that rubbish, why why.

Flash back. Peace returns.

But always intermingled with dread, is that not so?

Day 13

BJ NEVER RETURNED. Weeks have gone by. So far as you can tell, anyway. And his "things" – still in his room.

Those things. You get nervous about that, their presence, and his absence. No further phone call from him. You'd probably forget him altogether were it not for the things, which pull you up short from time to time, stop you doing any more than opening the door of the spare room – you dare not go any further. You stare into the room, which is gloomy because the floral-pattern curtains have been pulled together so only a desolate twilight comes through, and you stare at his dark suit hanging from a clothes hanger on the knob of the cupboard, and the bulky backpack propped against the wall, the wheelie case standing next to it with its retractable handle half up, the single sofa bed, opened up, with its bedding rumpled, his flip-flops on the floor beside it. Day after day. There it all remains.

So one day the Christian window cleaner calls, because he's come up with a plan to solve the longstanding problem of that leaking hot water tap in the bathroom, which you'd entirely forgotten about, and you take it into your head to ask him to intervene: You know BJ, the chap who was staying with me (ah yes, an associate of the late Mr Jackson, says the Christian window cleaner with a nod), well he's been away for a while now, and he's left all his things in my spare room.

Is that so? The Christian window cleaner nods again solemnly.

Well now, Chris, you go on to say, I'm a bit worried about this, can you do me a favour? Can you take a look in there?

Sure, says the window cleaner.

Only I don't like to, you see.

No problem, says the window cleaner, and he opens the door to the spare room. He enters. There ain't nothing much in here, he reports.

Can you see his two bags, well, can you have a look inside them? I just can't bring myself to do it.

The window cleaner grins back at you crookedly: You think he might be a terrorist? Might be bombs inside, or something?

No, no, but just for peace of mind.

No problem. The window cleaner goes over to the backpack and the wheelie bag while you stand anxiously in the doorway. He gets on his knees, unzips both, one after the other. They're not locked, he reports. He rummages around inside. First the one, then the other. After a while he speaks again. He says they're just full of clothes, nothing much more than that.

What do you want me to do? he asks you.

You're not sure. You just don't want them in the flat any longer.

Tell you what, says the window cleaner, there's a store cupboard on the ground floor of the block. You know it? Under the stairs?

That's right, you remember, under the stairs, on the left hand side as you come in the main door.

So the window cleaner proposes to gather up all BJ's things and take them downstairs and put them away in the store cupboard, where they will be out of your way but still available should BJ ever pop by out of the blue and ask for them back. This seems to you an admirable plan, and so you give the go-ahead and it is swiftly done.

I'm ever so grateful to you for that, Chris, you tell the window cleaner, and he smiles his crooked sweet smile. No problem, no problem.

Now you can breathe more easily again. Or can you?

You have difficulty sleeping. You leave the telly on while you try to drift off in the evening in your bed, for the programmes have a narcotic quality when they are not annoying you, and you can drift on the waves of repeated nonsense and sometimes achieve somnolence and even, eventually, unconsciousness, for a while at least, until something wakes you in the middle of the night; it is of course that blasted TV that has changed gear, making lamentations that can be heard as an echo, and has triggered you back to unwelcome consciousness again. So you reach for the remote at your bedside with your spider fingers and manage to switch it off and the room darkens and you are presented with your thoughts again, of which there is no end and no resolution. Voices eternally answering each other through a tangled forest of part-awareness, becoming solid, and you try to crush them but they bleed and complain and resume their discourse of nonsense and grief, of secrets unlocked ever so softly and allowed to roam from room to room, trying to find a way out and failing again.

Another night you abjure the television and try for rest unaided, with partial success, but once again you wake with a start in the middle of the night, at maybe three or four in the morning, the suicide hour, and a thought strikes you then for no reason: BJ, of course, BJ still knows where the key is. Under your front doormat, of course. So he could come in any time. He could enter now, and do whatever he pleases. You have a moment of panic. And you lie awake and fret over this while the wind blows in the dark trees outside, and you resolve in the morning to remove that key, but of course in the morning you forget this all over again.

And the next night that's when it happens: you wake in the early hours, again, and this time actually catch him inside your very room. Something wakes you, a noise that penetrates your fitful dream, is that the front door? Did you really hear the front door open? Are there footsteps? You wait in the dark, your heart palpitating, then you hear the creak as your bedroom door slowly opens, a shadow appears. So in a great fright you snatch up the empty mug that is on your bedside table – it's a lucky thing you didn't choose the tumbler in which your dentures reside – and throw it at him, at the shadow anyway, and it smashes on the wall, falls to the floor, makes a fearful noise, but the shadow doesn't say a word, just slips back out the door. You fling the duvet back, spring out of bed wildly with a spring that has not been seen in your body for many years, run to the door in that baggy old T-shirt you wear in bed. Dimly aware that this has happened before, perhaps many times before, you run out barefoot into the tiny hall, which is empty, fall upon the door of the spare room and hammer on it repeatedly. Hello? Hello? Is that BJ? What do you want? There is no reply. What do you want? You could just open the door, of course, but you don't dare to. You don't dare have your worst suspicions confirmed. But what are those suspicions? Those fears? That you may find him there? That he may not be there at all? Do you suspect BJ? Of what? But what if it isn't BJ? It must be the burglar, the burglar must have returned. Well, if so he's welcome to everything. He's welcome to all your possessions, you don't care any more, you don't want anything, just to be left in peace. That's what you will tell him, you don't care. And finally your breathing slows down: take a deep breath you tell yourself, one deep breath, and then another, take it in, and let it out. One after the other, that's right. Take it in, pause, let it out. There you are in the dark. Finally, you switch on your hall light.

Everything snaps to attention. The front door is shut. Solid. There is not a sound in the flat. (By this time you have already forgotten again about checking whether the key is still under the mat outside, about retrieving it.) You tentatively open the door of the spare room on which you have been banging and switch that light on. Nothing. An empty sofa bed, a cupboard, the floral-pattern curtains still drawn. No sign of the burglar. No sign of BJ or his things. And you sink to your knees and unexpectedly begin to sob quietly – you haven't wept for many years – because, why? because you know now that BJ won't ever return. Is that it? And because you are also aware that this moment you are now experiencing has happened before, perhaps many times, and will happen again, perhaps many times? And because there is nothing much that you can do about it?

Day 14

BACK TO THE present reality, then: which is, that you have lain for two weeks in your bedroom and nobody has yet discovered you. The multifarious events related in these pages, and which will continue to be related after this interlude – well, complex and varied though these may be, they are no more than an overture, an extended prequel to this. The present time. Or the palpable presence of the end of time. With the dread removed, it's fair to say, for you at least, though not for anyone who might contemplate entering your room.

It could be said, speaking metaphorically or metaphysically, that where *you* are now is actually the zero point, a zero location; that is, location unknown, where all activity has ceased. That is, the activity that bears your designation, your forename, your surname, the nicknames by which you are known, the soul, if you like (according to Father Fuck, for instance), the quality people used to discern in your distinctive mode of playing the piano, your manner of bearing, your voice, the memories you accumulated, the memories of you accumulated by others, all of that. But if the soul *is* the body, as you have many times asserted, at times in jest at others in all seriousness, then it's of course untrue to say that all activity has ceased; far from it, there's a lot going on, of great interest.

To elaborate. As mentioned, you've been here for a fortnight now. So far, nobody in the world has noticed. Even though you're a little bulked up. The build-up of gas, resulting from the intense activity of the multiplying bacteria, creates significant pressure within your body. This pressure inflates your body and forces fluids out of cells and blood vessels and into the body cavity.

If one or more of those flies that have previously been observed flitting across the room has managed successfully to lay eggs in your orifices or in that wound on your right arm, then the young maggots will by now be moving throughout your body, spreading bacteria, secreting digestive enzymes and tearing your tissues with their little mouth hooks. They move as a single mass benefiting from communal heat and shared digestive secretions. They are of course implacable.

They are like the studio audience, a many-headed collective organism that murmurs as one, laughs hysterically as one, applauds in short, well-coordinated bursts as the eternal fire descends. The flakes from the inferno dance in the master of ceremonies' jacket. He commands the studio and all its electronic devices. There is gold in his head, and his arms and shoulders are silver. But down in his groin dark substances pool – oh, he is full of such mischief. There have been rumours in the tabloids, to be fair. And the contestants are celebrities now, actors, models, comedians, reality TV stars of whom you have never heard in the first place, who have been dropping down the lists for the past few years so that they are now holding onto their places in the light for all they are worth (which is less and less as time goes by) and seeking desperately to squeeze a last few shekels from their dwindling fame before they disappear into the unrecorded realms of everyday life. In their desperation, they reveal more and more about themselves, or the selves they imagine themselves to be, or the selves that are imagined for them by savvy public relations firms. For the work of the imagination has to be done, you can't rely on the audience to work it out for *them*selves. (Or, it might be added, on yourself to do so – you are in no longer in a position to, after all.)

But then the show gets darker, the MC is no longer in gold lamé but in a dark suit with a dark blue open-collared shirt; his expression turns to a snarl, he stabs with his right forefinger at images on large screens at the back of the set, then points at the studio guest, a young man with tattooed arms sticking out of his polo shirt, a gold stud in his lip, a "whatever" expression on his face. What's the matter with you? shouts the MC, as he summons onto the set an over-weight young woman in glinty glasses with her blond hair scraped back, who slams herself down in an armchair with a cross of her legs, scowling and pointedly not looking at the young man, who is smirking now. We cut to the adverts. When we return, we have jumped forward. There is another argument flaring up between two other guests, monitored by the MC. A man barges onto the set, is immediately man-handled away by two burly men with SECURITY in white capitals on the back of their black shirts, and the audience whoops, cheers and applauds as the intruder is hauled backstage, a hand-held camera following them. One of the women involved makes scare quote signs with her fingers as she addresses a member of the audience, who are loving it.

But regardless of all this, the bacteria that have been living in your respiratory and gastrointestinal tracts throughout your life will now multiply without hindrance. No longer inhibited by your immune system, which is rapidly breaking down following the failure of your blood circulation, these micro-organisms are leaving their natural habitats and penetrating your mucosal layers, joyfully liberating enzymes that begin the work of breaking down your tissues into more digestible components. As the rate of decay increases, the smells and body fluids that begin to emanate from your body may soon attract more insects, some of them predators, feeding on the maggots themselves as well as on your decaying flesh.

Your complexion is definitely not great. Not so much a reddish tan now, as it might have been mistaken for just a few days ago: more tending towards the greenish. That end of the spectrum. Is not good, as BJ would have said. Not by any means peachy.

The piles of snowlike hailstones outside have all gone. It's a sunny morning, gold light on the tree trunks, dreamy sounds of traffic. Reawakened squirrels pounding the grass with their little feet. You might say it's a great day to be alive.

Your doorbell goes.

Oh, pardon, we are in the land of the living again, we're flashbacking to the prequel. It's maybe a week or two after the disappearance of BJ. Here goes.

Hello?

This is the police.

Have you got the right flat?

Police, open up, please, sir. We would like you to help us with our enquiries.

(Pause)

(Buzz)

They're at your front door in no time. A uniformed pair. These are not like the nice boys who arrived in response to Jackanapes' call when you were remonstrating about the water pouring through to your flat from his bathroom. All those weeks or months ago. If you can remember them, and their tolerant amusement. If you can remember that. No, these are two of the hard cases. No chit-chat, blank in the face. Mr [SURNAME]? the leading one blurts. May we come in? As if there's an option. You lead them into the living room, you offer the sofa. They ignore this, but have removed their headgear. The first one addresses you, the other, younger, taller, gazes around the room. Mr [SURNAME], we are following up an investigation into Mr Jackson, who we believe resided at these premises. Mr Jackson? Mr Paul Jackson. Ah, that would be Jackanapes. I think you're referring to my neighbour upstairs, you say. That's right, says the leading policeman – while the other has nipped out of the door without excusing himself – that's correct, he lived at flat number eight, we believe. He died, you offer politely. We are aware he is deceased, yes, says the policeman. Were you acquainted with Mr Jackson?

You ponder this a moment. He was a neighbour, you finally say. That's all. I met his mother once. By the way, where's your colleague gone?

The younger policeman reappears in the doorway.

You have to have a warrant if you want to search the flat, I think, you tell him. I believe you do. I believe that's the case.

Oh, so you know the law, do you? the young one sneers. And the older one adds quickly: Why do you assume we want to search your flat?

You start to say you're not assuming anything, you think better of it, you bite your lip.

The older policeman resumes: So we'd like you to accompany us to the station to answer a few questions. You are not obliged to and you are not being charged with anything.

What does "you are not obliged to" mean when they are looming over you like this?

Has Jackana- ... has Mr Jackson committed a crime?

They do not answer. And so you accompany them downstairs and outside, to a dark, unmarked saloon car parked at the kerbside opposite. You get in the back, they are both in the front seats. There is no further conversation. The car purrs away, the younger one driving, glancing sharply in his rear-view mirror, jumping through the traffic, making abrupt turns into the one-way system. Within five minutes it has drawn up outside the police station. You have passed this forbidding building many times, never seen inside. Well, this is your chance. The older policeman opens the passenger door for you, escorts you through the doorway, past reception, into a corridor, down some steps, through another strip-lit corridor. He shows you in to the interview room, which is windowless and completely empty apart from a Formica-topped table and two office chairs. A bare lightbulb hangs from the ceiling.

If you wouldn't mind waiting here, my colleague from the investigation department will be along in a minute.

He leaves you there by yourself, seated on one of the chairs. A minute goes by – then twenty more.

In comes a thin, drab, middle-aged man in a drab suit, tie loosened, glasses perched on his thin nose. He's carrying an untidy portfolio, which he dumps on the table. Sits in the other chair, across from you. Sorry to keep you waiting, Mr [SURNAME], this won't take long. Would you like a coffee or tea?

You decline the offer.

I just need to ask you some questions, and when we're finished one of my officers will drive you back home. Is that all right? He inclines his head sideways as he looks at you, a lock of colourless hair falling over his forehead. Now, Mr [SURNAME], if you would be kind enough to fill in the details on this form here: forename, surname, address. That's right, fill in those boxes, here's a pen – you live at flat number six, don't you? And the late Mr Jackson lived at number eight?

Why are you investigating him?

The detective does not reply, but pushes the glasses that

have slipped down his nose back into their proper place on the bridge as he studies his notes. He looks up at you again. Did you have a business relationship with Mr Jackson? he asks.

A business relationship? No, he was my neighbour.

That was all?

Yes, that's all I know.

The detective writes something down. Then he looks up again.

Mr [SURNAME], we are investigating one of Mr Jackson's associates. Are you acquainted with [INCOMPREHENSIBLE]?

What's that name again?

[INCOMPREHENSIBLE]. Do you recognise that name?

I don't ... I can't recall ... say it again –

Sometimes known to friends as BJ.

Ah, BJ, yes.

So you know him?

You become wary at this point. You haven't lost all of your marbles, not quite yet. Something – an ancient survival mechanism rooted deep in your reptile brain – tells you to go carefully. Don't reveal too much.

I think so. I think I may have met him. I'm not sure.

Did you provide any services of any kind to or have any business transactions with [INCOMPREHENSIBLE], who you know as BJ?

I didn't say I knew him. I don't think so.

Did you meet him in the company of Mr Jackson?

I ... I don't remember how I met him. If I did.

Were you aware that [INCOMPREHENSIBLE], who you know as BJ, was an illegal immigrant in this country?

I think I knew he was foreign, that's all I know.

You knew he was foreign?

Yes.

Did he tell you where he was from?

He was ... I'm trying to remember. Assyrian?

Assyrian?

No, that's not right, no, Albanian? ... not Albanian, wait, he said Armenian, I think. Armenian. Or something like that.

The detective writes this down.

Who knows what BJ was. Maybe Arcadian.

Day 15

THE DRAB DETECTIVE in the drab suit took his time over the interview, though never with any sense that he had a great deal of interest in it, or in you for that matter. He kept looking at the clock on the wall, the only other item furnishing that room, whose solemn ticking and tocking seemed to become more and more insistent and reverberant as time progressed. His face was grey, he kept pushing his spectacles up it. In a laborious hand, he wrote down what you said, or appeared to do so, except that, when he pushed the piece of paper over to you to sign and date, what you said had been translated into police talk: I believe I was acquainted with the male known as BJ, but I deny that I had a business relationship with him. I knew the late Mr Jackson as a neighbour for a period of several months, but I assert that I did not have a business relationship with this individual either.

The detective collected his things, and with not a further word departed the room. Another uniformed officer, not one of the original duo, appeared, and told you he was to drive you home. He didn't know the address, and you had to direct him.

So you have been released from the police station and are gratefully deposited back in your flat. You are not feeling very well, it's fair to say. You have lost your appetite, you are feeling fatigued, and you don't know what you should be doing next or what you would like to do next. You are fearful about the future. There is something, according to your intuition, which is not quite right about the future.

The doorbell goes.

Your heart misses a beat. But it's OK, it's, who is it this time?

It's, which one is it ... it's Janet from CARE-PLC.

Hello, [FORENAME], and how are you this morning?

You're depressed, you say, you are suffering from anxiety and depression, isn't that so? Very common, that, probably triggered by some trauma, such as daily life.

Oh, [FORENAME], I'm so sorry you're feeling miserable, says the care assistant. How can we cheer you up?

You smile wanly, make a mildly salacious suggestion.

Oh, [FORENAME], you're such a naughty boy, you shouldn't say such things. Have you had your injection this morning?

You cannot remember. It's been a disruptive morning.

You can't remember? You know it's important to have it every day. I'm not allowed to administer it, you know, I can only remind you.

You say that's all right, you're all right, you tell her it's just that you've had a bit of disruption, everything's got a bit mixed up, leading to the anxiety and depression and so on.

Can I make you a nice cheese sandwich? Or a cup of tea?

No thanks, I think I'm all right.

You sure?

I'm not hungry.

You sure?

Yes, I am. You know the nurse, she came to do some tests the other day? I remember that.

I don't know, [FORENAME].

How did I do?

I don't know anything about that, them tests. You'll have to speak to the nurse about that.

I would do, only I don't know how to contact her.

She nods sympathetically. Well, I have to be going now, she says. Her fifteen minutes is up. She reminds you to have your injection, then writes everything down in her book.

Will I see you tomorrow?

No, I'm off duty tomorrow, it'll be one of the other girls. Bye bye, [FORENAME], you take care now.

How the rest of the day plays out you can't remember. You intend to go out in the park for a walk, but when it comes down to it you're not feeling well enough, even though you know the walk would make you feel better, but if you're not up to it you're not up to it, and that is that. The desert is speaking to you again, in cluster-voices. In harmony? There is considerable dissonance. The hard margins are closing in. The imperfect functions that constitute your memory bring to mind, for no obvious reason, images of the guys you used to play with. The tenor sax player, what was his name now, a man with an eye for the girls, affectionate when he wanted to be, an agile beast, but a tyrant too, one thing you can't forget is his glare on you, mouthing "wrong chord!" and how you learned then, when you hadn't a clue what the change was, to do a rippling chromatic run that would more or less convince, until you got your bearings again. Hey, those were the days. You could go back to playing, even just on your own, but maybe you're not well enough, you couldn't cope with it, the mental strength is gone, even were you to regain the physical chops, the speediness, the ambidextrous facility in your spidery, semi-arthritic hands. Once it seemed those hands had little independent brains implanted in them to propel them confidently into new territories. But now? The vapours overwhelm you. And anyway, you do not own an instrument. That's the crucial thing. What was the tenor player's name, for heaven's sake? You were a sideman on his album, weren't you? the one with him looking all moody with a wistful girl in the background, who was the producer's girlfriend actually. What the hell was his name? Your brows pucker, no, you cannot call it to mind.

Let us say that another day goes by, and another. You are growing extra fingers, each one causing you agony as it buds, sprouts, comes uselessly through. There are armies of spiders massing in the corners of the room. Faint voices hum jazz standards from long ago in the flue behind the wall. You have seen the future, and it is not pretty. In the mirror. You are no longer the pilot of your soul. Your soul, which also doubles as your body, has taken unpredictable pathways, forking bewilderingly, mutating. The hairs come through, but there is no razor that is not blunt. The beard clinging to your jaws. Leave it, the stubble on your face, like a field permitted to go fallow. The walls fall in on you, they keep on falling, again and again. Come on, you make the effort, you go out into the world of winter, you view the teeming world, it's much as before, then you look again and it's a different place, one you don't recognise. Someone has scrawled a message in black aerosol paint across the front of the building: WE WANT OUR COUNTRY BACK. Which country would that be? Is it the one you inhabit? It's Buddha's birthday, you hear a passer-by saying. That kind of murmur. It's a young man in a hoodie. His girlfriend is talking into a mobile phone. Everything goes round in a circle, that's what they say. And the way back home is by way of a mountain, and wasteland beyond it. There is no public transport. Well, you get there somehow. Isn't it good to be home? Back in the flat, you point the remote control at the TV in your bedroom. There is chaos in parliament. The bomber's brother denied twenty-two counts of murder. Troops have entered the sumptuous presidential palace. The pound is down against the dollar.

That's when the burglar starts paying visits again, during the night; you know he's been, everything appears to be in its place in the morning but there's just something that's not quite right, it's just too perfect, as though someone, having disrupted everything, has taken the trouble to note the position of each object exactly and replace it where it was before, mapping the new configuration onto the old. But do you know what? just let him. Just let the burglar do his worst. He can take whatever he wants now, it's no longer any business of yours. He can come and go as he pleases. You just want peace of mind.

Hello, [FORENAME], and how are you this morning?

Hello, which one are you?

It's Sianette, [FORENAME].

Janet?

No, Janet's off today, it's Sianette, S-I-A-N-E-double-T-E. Are you sure you're OK?

I'm fine, thanks. It's Buddha's birthday.

Oh, yes? You look a little grey in the face, [FORENAME], you don't look well.

I'm suffering from anxiety.

Your complexion is not good. Did you do your injection this morning?

I ... think I did.

The nurse is going to come and see you again today. (She starts speaking slowly, articulating in an exaggerated manner, her voice slightly raised.) Later today. She'll be coming. You know that test they did?

But now the tables have turned, it is you who have forgotten. What test was that? you say.

The nurse was testing your memory, do you remember?

Ah, yes, I think I failed.

Oh, [FORENAME], don't say that, you didn't fail, it wasn't a question of failing.

I'm afraid I didn't make the grade.

No, that's not true, but the Management is a little concerned about you. About your ability to look after yourself.

I'm just a bit anxious and depressed. I'm suffering from anxiety. That's all. I can look after myself.

You say that, but not convincingly, and what is worse, at that very moment you start to feel that your legs may no longer support you in the timely fashion you're accustomed to, and you look around for a chair to sit down in, which you locate with difficulty, and having done so you are on it with a bump.

The Management believes you may be At Risk. [FORE-NAME]? [FORENAME]?

Sianette has one plump hand on your shoulder, while the other has whipped out her phone, upon which her thumb is a blur.

Just take deep breaths, [FORENAME]. Would you like to lie down?

Yes, please, you almost hear yourself mouthing.

Here, let's get you up, let's get you to the bed.

You are finally lying on the bed.

That's when the ambulance comes, the full monty again with all the bells and whistles, the flashing lights, the god-like half-machine paramedics whipping back and forth, all for you this time.

Day 16

YOU WAKE IN what seems to be an abandoned factory. Low lighting level. Silence. Or is there silence? Aren't there some very faint sounds? Is it early in the morning or is it evening? On the far wall of the space you appear to be in you can make out, dimly, some ducting of an immense complexity. But the details are obscure. It gives the impression of an unfathomable machine with pipework and tentacles connecting to the whole world, and you have this idea that it's dedicated to keeping you alive, but for what purpose? Nobody else about. Or is there? No, this is not silence. There are sounds of breathing, listen, you can hear them now. They are coming into focus in your ears. Coming from several directions, in different rhythms, at different dynamic levels, with different timbres: smooth and soothing, harsh and wavering, interrupted. How could you have missed this before? And how could you have missed the microtonal music, apparently from alien worlds, voiced by alien beings, a sublime dissonant harmony, interrupted now and then by low machine noises, mechanical grunts and low-level creaks, coming from everywhere. So not silent at all; or out of the apparent silence a universe of sound is emerging. And then you try to move, but it's difficult. It's not that you're restrained, but you are not free either. And your right arm does appear to be tethered in some way. It is, you make out, tethered to the machinery around you by a snaking tube joining you to it at the wrist. And above your head, as your eyes become accustomed to the low lighting, appears the word, in cool green sans serif capitals

SAFEGUARDING

and the breathing, the low-level machine noises, the ethereal music, weave themselves in counterpoint around this mantra, if that is what it is, this in-the-beginning *logos* that shimmers ever so slightly. You mouth the word, as though it is indeed a mantra

SAFEGUARDING

but no sound escapes your lips. You mouth other words, such as "where am I?" but no sound comes, and hence no answer. Then you get the idea that this may be some kind of gigantic spaceship escaping the doomed planet, and that the sounds of breathing you hear are those of the entire human race that is being transported, in a comatose state, to conditions of safety many light years away. The entire human race. Black, white, all nationalities in safe and loving harmony. This is huge. This is fantastic. Where am I? you mouth again; this time there's a slight croak, an infinitesimal utterance, the words have just about managed to escape your vocal apparatus and to establish a feeble presence in the soundworld that surrounds you. Upon which you have a vision. There's your mother, right there, beside the bed, for it seems to be a bed you are constrained by, and she says, There there, it's all right – just like you remember. There there. A sort of glow about her, as in visions before, but otherwise just as you remember her when you were a very small child. Is this, is this the day centre? you ask – the croak is a little stronger now. No, no, this is the assessment facility, says your mother kindly.

The what? The assessment facility. It's not the –? No, it's not. It's the assessment facility. How long have I been here? is your next question – it could be weeks, months, years for all you know. There is no answer. And your mother fades out of sight. You strain to see where she's gone, but even though the lighting level seems to be a little higher, you can't see much more. But there are more hints of activity. The breathing you can hear around you seems more broken now, interspersed with coughing and other human sounds; the music, if it ever existed outside your head, seems to have faded away, the machine noises are more insistent. And now you can discern other mother-figures, shadowy, flitting from position to position within the great space that is slowly coming into focus even as the sounds become more disruptive and dispersed. For there are others, other human beings, maybe thousands of them, millions, tethered to their respective beds or to their apparatuses, next to yours and then next to those and next to those, in rank and file, receding as far as you can see into the dismal distance, into (maybe) infinity.

You drift off to sleep.

Some time goes by.

You wake up.

One of the mother-figures suddenly appears at your bedside. She wears a pale uniform, and is pushing a machine of multiple devices that trundles on castors. She halts before you and switches on her smile.

Hello, my name is Magda (and indeed it says "Magda" on her badge, below the CARE-PLC logo).

She resembles a mannequin but appears to be real, and you have no option but to accept her as such. She looks up at something written above your bed.

Mr [SURNAME]?

Yes.

Have you moved your bowels this morning, Mr [SUR-NAME]?

Yes ... no.

Are you in pain?

Yes ... no.

The blood-pressure device constricts your arm. A device is thrust in your ear. Each reading comes up, and is noted.

Where, where am I?

The smile is switched on again: You are in the assessment facility.

The assessment facility. Ah.

Thank you, Mr [SURNAME].

The machine moves on.

You are untethered by other hands. You are invited to leave the bed. You find you are in a flimsy one-piece bed garment that just about preserves your modesty. You are shown the toilet. You are not sure how to act. You fear that you may have ended up in a cul-de-sac not of your own choosing. Others are certainly present. Not all remain in their beds. They are shadowy, they move slowly. Hither and thither shuffling. And back from thither to hither. But many just stay put. They seem very ancient, even more ancient than you, they don't acknowledge your greeting nod, they don't give their names. Worse than the ones in the day centre. Maybe torsos, with added bits, or not. Have you brushed what remains of your teeth? Yes ... no. You are handed a toothbrush. Your dentures also are handed to you – they have been preserved overnight, perhaps for many nights. There are shadows, and there is light. You have to sit in the armchair, right there, in front of the slatted window, while they make up your bed. Go to the light. How many days and nights have you been here? It seems an eternity and a half. But here you are. Make the best of it. It could be worse. The armchair is comfy. Here in full recline with the morning sunshine streaming through the slats, it's like being in a sanatorium. Not so bad after all. But it doesn't last.

Mr [SURNAME]? A disembodied female voice. It's time for your tests. The porter will take you.

You look all around you, but you cannot locate the origin of that voice, its owner, the putative mother-figure. Instead, the porter looms up, a big, uniformed man, a brother – yes, he's a brother! – in big black boots, with a telephone or something sticking out of his hip. His massive forearms are pushing a trolley bed, towards which he then gestures; you are to board this, with his surprisingly gentle help, to be taken to your next destination. You are in your standard issue dressing gown. Where you taking me? you ask him. Tests, bruv, he says. That's all I know.

Once you are settled to his satisfaction, with a sheet covering you, he wheels you out of that room and into a passageway, which leads to another passageway, illuminated by overhead strip lighting. He wheels you towards the doors of what turns out to be a service lift, stops, pushes the button, waits. He's gruff but seems well-meaning. Someone you can talk to. It's good to talk to your brethren.

What's it like outside? you ask.

Outside? He grins at you.

Out in the world?

The country is fucked, man, he says, still grinning. Excuse my language.

So you think I'm better off in here?

I wouldn't say that.

The lift doors slide open, he slides you in, presses another button. A shudder.

What you in for? he inquires.

I don't know, you confess.

Just keep them guessing. They might get tired of you. That's your best bet.

You really think so?

The door slides open again; evidently you are on another floor of this building, whatever it is. You traverse more fluorescent-lit corridors branching off corridors, each one the spitting image of the one before, their ceilings whizzing past you at speed. But in an alcove by a stairwell you suddenly spot, bizarrely, a pale wooden upright piano. I used to play one of them, you tell the porter, jabbing a finger as you are trundled by. Seriously? he says.

Yeah, I was quite good, people said. In my heyday.

What sort of music you play, bruv?

Jazz mostly, you say. That's what I loved.

Cool. You wanna play that piano, then?

Is that allowed?

Yeah, I think they got it to entertain the customers, but they couldn't find nobody to play it so it just sits in that place. I'll take you back there when you've finished with them tests.

You have arrived. The porter eases you off your trolley. See you later, he says. Another of the doll-like mother-figures awaits you. Mr [SURNAME]? Come this way. The porter and his trolley have vanished. You are taken into a waiting room where you sit. After a while she reappears, and you are ushered through the portal of an unknown machine. You are in the dark – again. Wait here. Take a seat. Put the headphones on, Mr [SURNAME]. A click-button is placed in your hand. Your brain tells you you are at the heart of another labyrinth; intelligent races live within its walls, you can sense them. But you can't see anything. Then the cool green sans serif capitals

SAFEGUARDING

appear in front of you. And disappear. You are alone in this universe. And then you hear the voice of the Lord God

Almighty in your ears: Please click whenever you hear the tone. You hear nothing. You wait in the dark. Vaguely, you are eventually aware of a tiny buzz, miles away. You click. The tiny sound happens in your left ear. You click. In your right ear. You click. A succession of images repeatedly flash up in front of you: a hand, a tree, a chair, a book, a cat. You are asked to identify each one. The voice of God instructs you to place your chin on the rest in front of you and stare straight ahead. In the dark, blood-red spots appear on your extreme right then switch to extreme left. Always on the periphery. God asks you to click when you see the spots. Sometimes they are sharper, sometimes duller. And finally you see the face of God Himself at the centre of his labyrinth; He comes monstrously close, peering first into the depth of your left eye then into your right, His features enormous. Please focus on the mirror image at the far end, He instructs, but what appears behind Him now is the white light of the void, the eternal sunshine that underlies everything, that is otherwise covered up by the day-to-day, here revealed in all its serene glory, and so you give yourself up to this, as those Buddhist muso mates of yours in times gone by used to tell you was advisable.

It's over. The doll-mother appears again. OK, Mr [SUR-NAME]? We'll send for you when we need to do more tests.

The porter appears again with the trolley bed.

How did you get on? he asks cheerfully, as he wheels you back through the corridors.

I saw God in there, you reply, although I still don't believe in Him.

Yeah?

I mean, He was unconvincing. But then I saw the light. I was enlightened.

What you been smoking in there, bruv? he says, laughing.

You tell him you have been off the weed for decades, not

touched it since you were playing the jazz clubs back whenever. You mention how you were a hit with the girls then. The strippers who used to come in from next door for a drink. Remember the one in the leopardskin skirt, who used to hang round the piano, who particular liked you. Did you get off with her in the end, or was that her sister?

Ah, you must have been in your pomp then, man, he says. You doing all right. You doing all right. Just don't let them send you to the Holding Pen.

Obviously the porter knows what's going on.

You think there's a chance of that?

Who knows?

What do they want from me? What are they trying to find out?

I don't know, bruv. They have their own agenda, you know what I mean? Here, you wanna have a go on the piano?

Ah yes, here it is again. You are seated at the keyboard in your official issue dressing gown. You flex your spidery hands. Oh dear, you don't know where to start. Your hands descend. A chord emerges. Of sorts. Is that E flat minor? It sure is. And then you go to, what is that, C minor seven with a flat five, then F minor seven similar, ah yes. Miraculously, your fingers still know how to make the shapes. That's familiar, that's "'Round Midnight". A few stumbles, but it's coming back. After all those years. Then B flat seven, and back to the root. Piano could do with tuning, though, especially up there in the treble.

The porter applauds.

You doodle about a bit more, your spider fingers each with a brain and a miniature memory of its own (just as the octopus is supposed to have in each of his eight limbs) walk up and down the keys at will, those impossibly tragic fingers of yours jumping with music that is pent up within them, that wants to come out; and now you're into another Monk tune, what the hell is the name of that one? You can't call it to mind, but you can play it. Everything else disappears, you're in a world of chords, with the little rippling arpeggios in the right hand.

And the next couple of days seem to pass cheerfully enough: the porter arrives to take you for more tests – scans and procedures of various kinds – and when you are finished he wheels you to the piano and you play until you are required elsewhere. This is not so bad.

But ...

Mr [SURNAME]? I had a job finding you. It's time for your interview.

She sounds rather brisk and annoyed. Where is the porter now? Gone.

You want to get this piano tuned, you know.

She makes no reply to this. She is also doll-like, if you like, or android-like. Another mother-figure? No, not really, of a higher echelon, but not so much of a mother anyway, more a Mother Superior, with a would-be wise expression on her face that in reality gives little away. Unlike the other mother-figures, she doesn't wear a uniform but a neatly tailored dark suit. She takes you to her office, or the office in which she is temporarily encamped.

Mr [SURNAME]? Please take a seat.

You perch yourself on the proffered chair, right next to the desk at which she sits, with all the clutter and the big computer screen that you can't quite see.

Now, your name is, let's see (she refers to her screen), [FORENAME] [SURNAME]. Is that correct?

You assert that it is.

And you live at, hmm, Flat Six, da-de-dah, London SE-duh-duh, yes that's all correct, everything is fine. Do you own that property or are you a tenant?

I own it, you declare. Leasehold.

Very good. She tap-taps on her keyboard with long-nailed, manicured fingers. Now, Mr [SURNAME], can you tell me: what are you hoping to achieve in this assessment?

You are flummoxed. Hoping?

Yes, what do you expect will be the desired outcome?

I ... don't know. I don't really known what you're talking about.

I'll put you down as N/A, then.

When can I –?

Your real question: Do I exist? But you don't formulate it as such, because it's only the beginnings of a question in the dim recesses of your brain, waiting forever for an opportunity to be recognised, let alone articulated. You are excused, it's a big question, and moreover one with no sensible answer.

– go home?

The Management will look after you for now. Mr [SURNAME], who is your next of kin?

Yes ... no.

Stupid answer. So she poses the question in a different way: Do you *have* a next of kin? Do you have a wife or partner? or siblings? children, grandchildren –?

I ... I used to be married. Long time ago.

And is your wife living?

Haven't seen her for years.

Have you any children?

I have ... I had a daughter?

And are you in touch with her?

She went to Australia, I think.

You think?

I'd like to go back home, you assert.

Safeguarding is in place, she says. Safeguarding has determined that you may pose a risk to yourself in your present circumstances. Therefore we will be holding you here until the assessment is complete.

I see. When will that be?

We can't give you a definite date right now.

When can you give me a definite date, then?

She ignores this. Now Mr [SURNAME], were you born in this country?

That came unexpectedly. You've got to give it to her, the way she bowls the googly. Can't read it at all. She floored you there once again, you look flabbergasted.

Yes ... no.

Where were you born, Mr [SURNAME]?

I've lived here seventy, more than seventy years.

What do you mean by here?

Not in this flat, I mean in this country.

You're not in your flat now, Mr [SURNAME].

I beg your pardon. Please remind me, where am I now, is this the day centre?

No, this is the assessment facility, Mr [SURNAME]. You are in the care of Safeguarding for now. But you were saying, you weren't actually born in this country?

I was a child when I first come here.

But you weren't born here?

No.

Where then?

You start to describe in a few words the island on which you came into the world, and your upbringing there, and the circumstances in which, as a child, you were transplanted to this country, but she cuts you short.

Mr [SURNAME], can you provide us with some evidence that you have the right to remain in this country?

Remain? What do you mean, remain?

It's just a formality for the record, so we know.

I ... I have a pension from the government. I have rights, I'm a citizen, you assert.

OK, we'll just leave that blank for now, we can come back to it later. That's all for now. Do you have any questions, Mr [SURNAME]?

When can I go home?

You feel as though you are at the edge of a pit, only you can't quite see over, you can't make out its dimensions or depth. If only you had a cord of some kind that you could pay out over the edge, bit by bit, you could measure the extent of it, fathom by fathom, but maybe that wouldn't do, you are consumed now with a fear that no cord would be long enough, not even that big ball of string you keep in your cupboard at home, you would come to the end of it before it touched bottom, you would be none the wiser and considerably more frightened.

Are you all right, Mr [SURNAME]?

I think so.

What do you mean by that?

I want to go home.

You'll be able to go home soon, Mr [SURNAME]. We just have to do some paperwork, that's all.

Day 17

YOU ARE BACK in your flat. At last. Though it looks different –
in what precise way is hard to put into words. It doesn't feel
an awful lot like home; it's open to the world in a way you
dislike, a way that makes you feel uncomfortable. It feels
more like a railway station, but with no trains. There are
moving displays on the walls, possibly train indicators, but
you can't make any sense of them. Sounds from outside
penetrate quite clearly in here, much more so than you
remember, even though the windows are all closed. You
keep checking the indicators. Nothing makes sense.

But it's good to find yourself back home, isn't it, or in a
place called home anyway, even though it seems rather dingy
compared to what you remember. It needs a clean-up and a
tidy-up. It's not at all how you remember it. Why is that?
The bathroom must be there, beyond that door, and the
bedroom, this is where you are, you believe, and the kitchen's right there, and the living room and the spare room
across the hall, well, they all look a bit jumbled up, but perhaps nothing a little sorting out won't fix. You are not sure
where everything is, where all your things are. They are in
different positions. You're home, but everything's changed.
It's odd how things change, and then change some more. A
moment ago it felt too open to the elements, too public, but
now you have a sudden rush of claustrophobia, you can't
breathe, the walls are hemming you in. The windows are all
tightly shut. There is not enough air, that's the problem. If
you could only open that window there, is that the one that

gives onto the park? Is that the one? Are you in your living room, then, after all? Not the bedroom? You would love to see the park again. Maybe the daffodils are out. Let's see if you can open the window. You can see nothing through it, the glass appears to be frosted up, or something. Give it a tug.

So you manage to get the window open, but to your horror, instead of the park being revealed in all its wonder, with the squirrels and crows and dog-walkers under the sky, there's only a huge sea of dark green, almost black, a flood of noxious water as far as your eye can see, brimming to the level of the windowsill, beginning to slop over into the room you are in, in just the same way as it brimmed in Jackanapes' bath; you try desperately to push the window shut again but you can't, and each ripple in that immense body of water that stretches to the horizon sends more splashes into the room. You need help, you need to make a phone call to get help, but your flat is now knee-deep in floodwater and debris, and you think you saw your phone among other objects submerged in there. You try to clear the muck, to no avail. There are people in the flat now, you can hear them moving about, are they your people, yes, you recognise some of them, but then you realise as always they are dead, or undead, they are only zombies posing as your people. Sometimes unsuccessfully: one resembles more a giant beaver with a scorpion's tail, who you realise will have the advantage of being able to continue to breathe even in the rancid water that is slowly filling up the flat. They are all chattering among themselves. They seem to be participants in a collective enchantment. Finally one of them, in a pale uniform pushing a machine, approaches you, and switches on a smile.

Hello, my name is Tracey. Have you moved your bowels this morning, Mr [SURNAME]?

(So you are not yet, after all, back in your flat. But patience.)

Yes ... no.

Was it normal?

Yes ... no.

Are you in pain?

Yes ... no.

On a scale of one to ten, in which one is no pain and ten is unbearable agony, how would you rate your pain?

No reply.

The machine moves on. You are sitting in the armchair in your dressing gown. Sunlight streams in through the slats. Is this the same place where you have awoken every morning for the past – well, that's the conundrum, for the past how long? Half a lifetime, it seems. You observe some of the other inmates. How slowly they shuffle from place to place, one or two of them using walking frames. Occasional mother-figures in their pastel uniforms skip lightly among them, then disappear. You wouldn't even think they were there at all. You start to dream ...

Mr [SURNAME]? [FORENAME] [SURNAME]?

You wake with a start.

It's time for your injection, says the new mother-figure brightly.

You go along with this.

Let's push up that sleeve, shall we?

You obey.

You used to do this yourself, didn't you, [FORENAME]? she exclaims with a sudden surfeit of attention, as she wields the needle.

I believe so, you say.

But you're having difficulty coping now, aren't you, dear?

You assert that you are not. Not in the least.

There you are, we're all done.

When she has gone, you resettle yourself in the armchair

and prepare for a nice dream, but it is not to be.

There are more interruptions. More tests of various kinds. Days may have gone by. Who knows?

Please come through, Mr [SURNAME].

It's another of the Mother Superiors. Or maybe the same one as before. It's hard to say. In a smart skirt and blouse, not a uniform. An identity tag with her photo on it dangling from her neck. She leads you into one of the many offices adjacent to the ward and closes the door. She indicates where you may sit.

First of all, have you any questions?

Excuse me, where am I exactly?

Let me see. She consults her screen. You have been moved out of Safeguarding, but you are not yet in Recovery.

Where am I then?

No reply.

Is this the Holding Pen?

No reply. She's looking at the screen intently, as though trying to make sense of something, and then is suddenly engrossed in a volley of typing at the keyboard – perhaps she didn't hear you. So you drift off. Although the door to this office cubicle is shut, you can still see, through a glass partition, the rest of that vast room of which it is an annexe. You can see the other inmates come and go. And you see clearly, at the other end of the room, that large man in the heavy uniform, with the powerful forearms, laughing and sharing a joke with one of the inmates as he attempts to load him onto a trolley bed. The jovial porter, of course.

A memory is triggered. Where's the piano?

I beg your pardon, Mr [SURNAME]? She transfers her gaze from the computer screen to you. What piano?

I was playing the piano, when was that? The other day, or the other week. I'm sure I was. I think the porter took me there.

Ah, that piano. Yes, you're quite right, Mr [SURNAME], there was a piano in the building. It was moved.

Moved where?

The Management felt it was disturbing some of the customers. There were complaints.

Who complained?

That I can't tell you. We take all complaints seriously, but confidentiality needs to be preserved. We need to provide a safe and caring environment for all the users in this facility, you understand.

I don't understand.

We are passionate about user safety.

But what about the –

Mr [SURNAME], we need to make progress. We need to ascertain your current status – can you provide us with some evidence that you have leave to remain in this country?

You have a distinct impression that you have been asked that question before.

I don't know what you mean. Leave to remain, sounds a bit odd? I have my rights.

Of course you have, Mr [SURNAME]. We just need some documentation, that's all, to complete this form.

If you let me go home I have some documents I think that will prove my rights. I worked for more than forty years, I paid all my taxes –

It's not safe for you to go home right now, Mr [SURNAME]. The Management believes you are At Risk. We feel, for example, that you are unable to undertake self-medication without supervision. As you know, you were going into a diabetic coma just before you were admitted here. So we need to come up with a care plan before you can go home.

I feel like I don't exist, you stutter – impolitely, but what the hell – like *you* don't know who I am. I mean ... who I am. You know?

She doesn't reply, just purses her lips slightly and looks away. It's as though you'd made a *faux pas*, an embarrassing breach of etiquette that is being tactfully ignored, for your own benefit. She looks at the computer screen again for a moment or two, taps something on the keyboard.

Do I exist? you ask yourself, because clearly you're not going to get an answer to this question from her. Ah, the penny has dropped now: yes, you exist, but only in the form of a vast array of numbers stored on the computer, numbers that change from day to day; and this state of flux represents, no, *is* your existence. It can be accessed by anyone who has the necessary security clearance, who knows the password. Anyone in this happy position then *knows who you are*, at least for the duration of the session, for this knowledge ceases upon log-out, and is revived on subsequent log-in, by whoever logs in. It is, you have to admit, a brilliantly elegant system.

So you exist because *the Management know who you are!* It's that simple.

You marvel once more at this. The results of all the tests have accumulated to build up an electronic simulacrum of you, which can be substituted for the real you in order to enable a read-out that contains all the necessary information. So if you are ever plagued with that old existential doubt that you are so prone to, well, that will restore everything. It has to be admitted that this is admirable.

As for your current status, in regard to leave to remain, whatever that is, which she has asked you to prove, that's just the missing part of the puzzle they need to fill in. They keep coming back to that. It's not personal. It's just a niggle, a box they can't tick. The system is not perfect, after all. Nothing is. This is just a glitch that needs fixing. So then, what's the nature of this status of yours? Can you tick the box for them? Your current status. You are, you think, in exile. That's it. But from what? And where?

I'd like to help you, you say, but ... please, can I go home soon?

The Management is deciding when you can go home, Mr [SURNAME]. When we think it's safe to do so.

And when do you think that will be?

Well, we have to manage that in stages. First, we would like to transfer you to a more appropriate unit, where you can have secure care until you are well enough to return home. But in order to do that, we need first to address a couple of issues. One is your current status as a resident of this country, which is being investigated. But also, I've just noticed, you made a statement that you owned your own property. Is that correct?

Yes, that's right, I do.

But my question is, did you make that statement? Is *that* correct?

I think I did.

Because it seems as though that statement itself is not quite correct. We have made inquiries, and it seems that you assigned the lease of your flat to a Mr Paul Jackson, now deceased. The deeds to your property appear to be lodged with the estate of Mr Paul Jackson.

What are you talking about, who is he?

Mr Paul Jackson late of flat number eight, a neighbour of yours.

Jackanapes? I had nothing to do with Jackanapes.

Did you or did you not transfer ownership of the lease-hold of your flat to the late Mr Jackson?

No, I didn't!

Because if you did so hoping to avoid liability for any care costs incurred, you must understand that this may be construed as a criminal offence.

I haven't committed any crime!

Please calm down, Mr [SURNAME], we are not saying you have, but you need to be aware that the law says you may not knowingly transfer assets with the intention of avoiding payment of due care costs. We are not necessarily saying you have done so –

But I didn't –

– nevertheless fraud is a serious crime, so you need to be aware of that.

But I never –

We will address all these issues in due course, she says. Look, I think the best thing to do is this: while you continue to recover and we devise a care plan going forward, and while we are continuing to investigate the issue with your property and also sorting out your current status in respect of your leave to remain, we shall be moving you to another unit for an interim period.

For an interim period?

The good news is that you will have your own secure room there.

Where is that exactly?

It's another facility, for an interim period only.

Will that be the Holding Pen?

That is not a term we use.

Day 18

THIS IS WHERE the fun begins, you hear someone say. Maybe heard yourself say that? Hard to tell the difference. There's an echo in here. Wherever it is you are now. It sends a chill through your bones. Your ancient and mutating bones. Even though it's really hot in here. But listen, you have your own room here – is that an improvement? – but is it actually what you would call a room, perhaps rather a nest, or a cell, though they don't call it that here, officially it's a *pod*, that's what you were told, you have been assigned to a *pod* in the edifice that surrounds you, of which you know little – and that's that. Next to the wall there's a bed, narrow, but not too uncomfortable, with a grey blanket, and a small table next to it, and a desk – your own desk! – made of cheapish laminate, its surface and its drawers empty of any paraphernalia, and on the third wall a cupboard in matching laminate in which you discover some clothes to wear: a dark blue tracksuit, which you find matches the one you are wearing now (how did that happen?) – so perhaps it's intended that it replaces the other one when that has to be laundered – and a small selection of socks and underwear that you don't recognise, stacked in short piles on a shelf, along with a couple of towels. Then next to that a small washbasin with a glass and your toothbrush in it, and a mirror above that, a little cracked and stained. And above the desk is a small window, without curtains, through which a pallid daylight flows, and the door on the opposite wall, which is shut, also has a tiny window in it, but, though there seems to be an electric light on all the time beyond that, you can't see much through it, just a cream wall. So you are sitting on the bed, your feet in their new socks resting on the floor, which is hard and shiny, looking at the window with the desk below it to your left and the door to your right and the cupboard and washbasin directly in front of you, and the thought occurs to you that you would like to look out of that window above the desk, to see what you can see of the world outside, but it's hard to reach it because the desk is in the way, so you have to partly climb on the desk with one knee, a major operation this, lean forward, see if you can grab that handle and wrench it back, with some success; whereupon you are shocked to behold a vast greenish sea out there, terrifyingly near, lapping just below the sill, so close in fact that you can see huge fronds of seaweed slowly undulating under the surface; and you fear you are about to plunge into this sea, so you half-fall half-climb down in haste. Are you in a building, then, or a boat? But it doesn't rock, it's perfectly still. A building, therefore, you get the impression of a huge building around and above and below you. How did you get here? And you remember now that you awoke in the night, it was already lightening outside, maybe just before dawn, feeling all melancholy hearing the unmistakable sounds of foxes screeching unseen out there, at least that it what it seemed to you, they used to be out in the park during the night back in those days when you had your own flat, didn't they, and then you were aware of your bowels all unsettled so had to go to the toilet; you'd been told the toilet was down the corridor, you are not locked in here, it's allowed, so you ventured beyond the door, the harsh strip lighting on in the corridor, which has many similar doors studding it, trudging along this passageway in the slip-on trainers you have been allocated, and you found the toilet, which is the last door before you can go no further, before you reach the heavy fire door secured by a keypad, and so you sat there on the toilet, which has a shower cubicle attached to it, with a feeling of futility, remembering now how, ah yes, you were transported here in a mini-van, observing through the windows people and animals and creatures of all kinds flying past outside, observing plastic bags and hungry ghosts moving about in the windy night in the city, observing a sex-hungry big cat dragging his engorged penis with a caressing motion along the pavement, and many other wonders and strangenesses.

You are not to know that the edifice that surrounds you is (probably) made of brutal concrete the colour of iron; that it could easily be mistaken for a budget hotel or else a hall where conferences or vast and solemn colloquia take place, and is structured (probably) with concentric rings of corridors, studded by those nests or pods, to one of which you have been assigned, with interlinking radial passages protected by security doors, those passages all converging and meeting in the centre, where the administrative and control units are located. But it has to be admitted that none of this is certain, and there are some obvious anomalies that are hard to reconcile with this putative ground plan. You do find out, because you are told by the attendants who instruct you from time to time – they wear a similar uniform to the porters in the previous establishment, but they are more surly, more predominantly white – that the heavy security door at the end of your corridor is unlocked at certain times of the day, and you can then wander a little further afield at these times. The first thing that confronts you when you pass through that security door is a large poster depicting happy-looking men and women of various ethnic origins, and even some children, disporting themselves against a sunny backdrop reminiscent of the depictions of the afterlife on those Jehovah's

Witnesses pamphlets that used to be delivered to your door; and the strapline

Interim Detention Facility
Passionate about your security

prominently displayed. There are also signs directing you to the "Restaurant" – where you are asked to queue up three times daily for your meals, alongside other inmates, also blue-tracksuited. They don't speak much; each keeps himself, or herself – for both sexes are represented – to him or herself. They are predominantly black or brown people. There's a group of two or three women who wear black hijabs over their tracksuits – they whisper among themselves and avoid your gaze. In this restaurant or canteen the queue moves very slowly, and the options are limited to: at breakfast, a mug of cereal, two pieces of limp toast with margarine and a choice of weak tea or coffee; at midday, a soup *du jour* and a roll followed by an apple or banana; and at six o'clock, variations on meat and two veg with a usually inedible pudding – all of this served up behind the counter by diminutive, mute young women of oriental appearance. You take your tray to a Formica-topped table and eat your meal there. Very little conversation occurs, and what there is is hushed and appears to be predominantly in languages other than English. Then at nine you are ushered back to the corridor that contains your pod, and the big security door is locked. And it's lights out abruptly at ten.

After this, there is darkness save for the illumination from the corridor visible through the little window in your room door, and there is nothing to do but sleep in your narrow bed, which is not easy. Not easy at all. What you'd thought was the sound of foxes rutting in the night outside (perhaps underwater) now bears an uncanny and increasingly unmistakeable resemblance to human cries – and they are much closer to home, or rather, to where you're located right now, which of course is not the same thing. The nights are long and hot. There are plenty of opportunities to analyse these utterances, which repeat themselves at irregular intervals throughout. To your left, a series of distant moans, rising at times to howls, then subsiding before the sequence repeats, never exactly. To your right, and a little closer, sometimes seeming to be almost in the same room, a man's voice calling out "Mummy!" at various times through the night. Sometimes in a wheedling tone, like a nagging toddler, sometimes as a command. Sometimes, in a variation, "Mummy Bear!" – repeating over and over, and then following up with "Come ON!" in the style of a professional tennis player berating himself when things are not going well on court. Occasionally you hear a door opening, and a brief, hushed, "Go to sleep!" and then the door clicking shut again, but the silence that follows doesn't last for long; within twenty minutes or so it's "Mummy!" again. With all this, there is not much opportunity for your own sleep; the upside for you being a respite from your more egregious dreams. And so it is a relief when that pale dirty daylight begins to seep through your window and you know the night is coming to an end.

You miss the mother-figures coming round every morning trundling their machines. Have you moved your bowels this morning, Mr [SURNAME]? Was it normal? Are you in pain? You miss all that. But every morning the nurse arrives – actually a different nurse each time – to give you your injection. She raps on your door, then enters regardless of whether you've called "Come in" or not. Sometimes, for a change, it's a solemn young man. It makes no difference. You get your jab anyway. Sets you up for the day. And the days go by. Sometimes you don't even notice them go by;

the uniformity of their routine is like a bucket of whitewash covering up the messy fragments of your emotions, rendering them invisible, undetectable even to yourself. You get used to it. The young Asian lad who barges in to your room every morning mopping the floor with controlled aggression, leaving behind a powerful scent of disinfectant that never completely dissipates. The burly attendants in their porter-like uniform poking their heads in and out barking instructions or reminders. One of these attendants, a white bullet-headed fellow who seems a little friendlier than the rest, looks at you quizzically. Without meaning to, you've indicated that you were beckoning to him.

Something wrong? he demands.

Sitting on your bed, you are taken aback by his attention, not sure what to say. Something comes into your head anyway.

Can you turn the sea off?

You what?

The flood water outside this room, is it real?

You got a flood here? he asks, perplexed, coming fully into the room, looking around him.

No, outside the window, you insist, jabbing a finger at it, but I don't know if I'm imagining it. It's like the sea.

You ain't by the seaside, mate, he says, laughing shortly, I can tell you that. He goes to the desk, leans over it and peers through the window. Nope – no sea, he reports. You sure? you ask anxiously. You wanna have a look? he demands. Effortlessly, he pushes the desk out of the way so that you can have unfettered access to the window.

You look out.

All you can see immediately is a wall opposite, and if you crane your neck and peer down there's some kind of a narrow yard visible, filled with junk. Daylight filters from above, but you can't quite see the sky.

A room with a view, eh, says the attendant, pushing the desk back.

Do you know why I'm here? you ask him.

No idea, mate. What you done?

Nothing, you say. I'm trying to get sent home.

Where's that?

London.

You're in London.

Well, nobody's told me anything.

They wouldn't, he says. He pauses. You're British, in't you?

Yeah.

Ah, you shouldn't be in here, then, among all them foreigners. I guess you're just one of the unlucky ones. The problem with you is, you got the wrong kind of skin. You know what I mean? Nothing that can be done about that.

Yeah, you say. I know.

Well, nothing *I* can do, mate. Way above my pay grade. Way, way above. Anyway, you'll get your review meeting in the next couple of days. Everybody has to have one. Maybe you'll be lucky in the end. Just don't do nothing silly.

Silly?

Some of the customers here, they end up self-harming. Just to draw attention to themselves. But it don't do them any good, in fact it makes things ten times worse.

What sort of things do they do?

For example, says the attendant, leaning against the doorpost with his big arms folded and warming quickly to his narrative, for example, last week the alarm goes, I'm called out to see about this chap, in the next corridor along from yours, I'm called out – which is always really annoying because you get so many false alarms and people trying it on – anyway, I'm called out to attend this customer who's cut himself. Nobody knows where he got the knife from. Big security breach, bad news. So I go into his pod, and he's sitting there on the bed just like you are now, bolt upright, looking in terrible condition, all pale, with a fucking great kitchen knife next to him on the bed stained with blood, and he has an eight-inch gash on his arm. Why'd you do that, I says to him. He doesn't say nothing. His arm is all swollen and discoloured, but there's very little blood. That must have bled a hell of a lot, I say, but he just shrugs. I washed it off, he says. Then he draws out a bucket from under the bed, don't know where he got that either, and it's filled to the brim with four pints of blood. Four fucking pints, half a gallon. That's the kind of thing we have to deal with here.

Your bones start to burn.

What's the matter with the bloke next door? you ask, after a pregnant pause.

Next door?

He calls out for his mummy all night long.

The attendant laughs. Ah, you mean Mummy Bear! That's Charlie, that is. Quite a character.

The attendant then tells you that Charlie, your unseen next-door neighbour, is recovering from a serious head injury, which resulted in his being in a coma for a while. It's very common in these cases, when they recover consciousness, he says authoritatively, to revert to repetitive early childhood language patterns. That's the stage Charlie is at. We've seen it before, oh, many times, he says. He adds that typically the next stage would be shouting out obscenities, and after that (We're used to everything here, but it can be disturbing to other customers, he says) obsessive masturbation.

How did he get his head injury?

Banged his head against the door. Several times. Well, can't stay around here chatting all day, I've got work to do. You'll get your first review meeting soon if you haven't had it, he says as a reassuring parting shot.

He disappears.

You are unsettled for the rest of the day.

Next morning, on returning to your room from the toilet, you are surprised to discover a strange woman there. She's pulling out the drawers of your desk – which are still completely empty of contents – and starts slightly when you enter; slams the last one shut and turns to face you. She is smartly dressed, in a two-piece grey suit and blouse, her hair severely cut. She is like the Mother Superiors in the previous establishment, you think, but not quite so glamorous – somewhat older, actually, with the appearance of one who has experienced what life has to offer and feels more than a little disgusted by it. She doesn't apologise for looking through those empty drawers of yours, in fact she brazens it out by looking at you intently, then consults the clipboard she is carrying in her left hand, adjusting her glasses to do so.

You're [FORENAME] [SURNAME], and this is Pod Eight Forty Two? she demands. Yes, you say, rooted to the spot.

I'm trying to get some information about why you've been referred to us.

I'd like to know that, you say, with all the passion you can muster.

Come with me, she orders.

And her order stirs in you a wonderful emotion all of a sudden – fear and apprehension are in the mix, certainly, but at the core there might even be hope. Just a smidgeon. She doesn't wait for you, but strides out clasping the clipboard in her left arm, and you hurry after her as best you can, lumpishly and heavily because you are not used to rapid movement after all this time, down the corridor to the security door where she briskly and nonchalantly taps in a four-digit code, hardly breaking her stride, the fingers of her right hand a mere blur, pushes the door open, and you follow. There's the poster with the Jehovah's Witnesses-style depiction of Paradise; she walks briskly past that, and you try to keep up, and past the door that leads to the canteen and on towards another security door straight ahead, access to which she also effects without effort, and through, and now you're in unknown territory.

Day 19

YOU ARE SITTING in what could be her office, though she doesn't say it is. You didn't catch the nameplate on the door, and though she wears an identity tag round her neck you can't make out her name there, you just see the word "Investigations". Where is this office? Is it at the heart of the building? You lost count of the number of security doors you were ushered through. Filing cabinets line one wall on your right side, on your left is a big window screened by vertical fabric blinds through which some outside light filters through milkishly. And the walls where exposed are painted a creamy-green, but there are very large pits in the wall ahead of you, behind the Mother Superior, as though this is a work in progress. The ambient temperature and general ambient conditions are rather more comfortable than those in your quarters: cooler, airier, less humid.

She is a being of a strange species, you think, whose skin is like parchment, whose hair is pulled as tautly as can be, whose fingers are nimble and agile; she would have made a good pianist, you determine, as you watch her sitting at her desk tapping rapidly at the keys of her computer, all the while glaring through her glasses at the screen.

That's funny, she says, stopping momentarily. I'm getting that you've been discharged. I don't understand.

You heart starts leaping rapidly and the pressure mounts in your skull, making your eyes hurt with excitement.

Something wrong. You shouldn't be here. It says discharged, date is two weeks ago.

You close your eyes to calm them. You start to say something, but you can't figure out what to say. So you remain silent, just sitting eagerly forward in your chair, in your navy regulation tracksuit.

I don't understand why you're still here, in fact, why they've referred you to us at all. This is exasperating. These cock-ups shouldn't still be happening.

She taps some more, screws her eyes up behind her glasses. Hang on. What's your date of birth?

You tell her.

Ah, wait a minute. I see what's happened.

You don't know what you should be feeling now.

I see what's happened, she repeats, we've got the wrong file, I mean the wrong person. You're [FORENAME] [SURNAME], right? Well, it says here [SURNAME1] instead of [SURNAME]. That's where the error was. So let's get *your* file up, here we are, [FORENAME] [SURNAME], is that correct?

And she swings the screen round so you can see it, for the first time. There's your name at the top, and your age, and your address. All present and correct. And then a huge mass of data you can't begin to make sense of, text and numbers, they become a blur. The numbers are churning all the time, perhaps updating. The evidence is slowing mounting up. Yes, you exist after all, you exist!

That seems to be me, you admit.

She turns the screen back to face her.

So let's see, why have they sent you here? She continues tapping and looking, tapping and looking, all the while muttering to herself: Uh-huh, uh-huh. You have a medical condition, it says.

Diabetes, you reply. And anxiety and depression, you add helpfully.

That's right, we have the nurse giving you daily injections. I'm going into the medical records. Well, that's all in order. Uh-huh, uh-huh, uh-huh (eyes flicking down the screen), so why the referral? Aha, yes. Yes. I see. Mr [SURNAME]?

Yes?

It appears there are a couple of small complications that need to be addressed. You were born outside this country, right?

Yes.

Well, we just need to be assured you are in this country legitimately.

Not that again. Your voice quavering, you intone: I've been in this country over seventy years, I keep telling you people.

No need to fly off the handle, Mr [SURNAME]. Do you have documentation for this? For instance, do you have a passport?

I did used to, you say, it expired, I think. Maybe I still have it somewhere.

Has to be currently valid, unfortunately. Otherwise ... well, were you employed for any part of that time you've been living here?

Well, of course I was employed, you point out, trying to moderate your emotions, otherwise I wouldn't be able to live. I worked as a musician. But that didn't keep me going, so I had to have a day job.

As a musician, you were working for cash in hand, were you?

Yeah, whatever the gig paid. But as I said –

That's a pity, that's not helpful. And what was this "day job", as you call it?

I worked for an engineering firm, in fact I worked for two engineering firms. I got a small pension from them now, and the old age pension too.

Well, it says here you're in receipt of state pension, but that in itself is not evidence –

I got evidence at home, you say (you can't eliminate the

bitterness from your voice, however hard you try), but nobody lets me go home.

And the other box to tick, if we may put it like that, she goes on, consulting the screen, seems to be that you were in receipt and continue to be in receipt of care on the basis of your home ownership, in other words that care costs would be recovered from your estate in the event of your demise, But there is evidence you have sold your flat –

And I keep telling you people that's a lie!

Nobody is lying to you, Mr [SURNAME].

I've also got evidence of that, if you'll let me go home, I'll prove it to you.

She sighs. It's a bit of a problem, then. We can't discharge you from this establishment until these issues are resolved, but on the other hand we seem to be at a bit of a stalemate here.

It's not right, you shout, it's not right!

Please keep your voice down, she says in a schoolmistressy tone. It's an unfortunate set of circumstances, but let's see what can be done. I'm trying to be helpful. But I don't think I can resolve this here and now. What I can do is discuss this with my boss.

Your boss?

Yes, Dr Thomas Hardy, he's Head of Investigations. We might need to arrange an interview for you with him.

Well, can I see him now?

You can't just have an appointment with Dr Hardy at a moment's notice! she exclaims, aghast at the very thought. He's an extremely busy man. The third most important person in his field in this country. We'll request an appointment. In the meantime, I'd better escort you back to the secure area for now, and we'll have to get back to you. There's nothing more I can do for you at the moment, Mr [SURNAME], I'm sorry.

By the time you are deposited back in the secure area that is now your home you have thought of a couple more questions to ask her. One that occurs to you is what that field was that Dr Hardy was third most important in – though she probably wouldn't have told you anyway. And the other.... There are other unanswered questions, of course, but in a very few minutes you have forgotten what they were.

A day goes by, and another night. Time is passing, and becomes past time. The daily ritual – lights out, noises and dreams, lights on, toilet, injection, breakfast, toilet, lunch, toilet, dinner, toilet, bed – almost anaesthetises you with its profound blankness, sedates you anyway, obscuring the free-floating anxiety you once had, or making it impossible, because there's nowhere any longer for it to float. So is that good? The feelings you once had, of anxiety, of dread, of sudden hope – in the other place, not to mention in your own place – seem to have been suppressed entirely now, and because you don't get enough of a sense of yourself here, well, that suppression in itself could function as the solution to a myriad problems. It could be the answer, in the long term. The night, paradoxically, is when you feel most alive, despite the heat and the closeness, hearing the sounds around you, sometimes a cry from afar, sometimes a whisper in your ear, and then sometimes that microtonal choral music you first heard in the other place, those otherworldly chants that come to you drifting down the light years, in other words hitting your aural membrane many years after they were first uttered in a remote part of the universe, an unimaginable elsewhere; all of this taking place in the dreamland to which you depart between the hours of ten at night and six in the morning – but then all of a sudden the light snaps on, and it's back, this thing called consciousness that you didn't invite and don't want.

After breakfast, wandering in the corridor outside the canteen, you notice for the first time a door marked LIBRARY. It's locked, but the opening times are typed on a card taped to the wall beside it: 6.30pm-9.30pm, Mondays to Saturdays, closed Sundays.

So after dinner, in that two-hour period before lights out, you cautiously push the door, and find it opens before you. The library is in fact quite a small room, without windows, brightly lit. There are no more than a couple of bookcases, a few chairs and tables scattered at random, and a desk at which sits a black man not much younger than yourself, in the same regulation dark blue tracksuit, wearing a glum expression. Pinned on his left breast is a round badge with the words PRIVILEGE: LIBRARIAN. There is nobody else in the room.

You the librarian? you ask.

Yeah, he says laconically, it says here (pointing at his badge).

Why does it say privilege?

I been here two years, bruv. It's my reward for good behaviour. Something like that.

Can I borrow books?

Yeah, that's the idea.

You start to browse the first bookcase. The choice is somewhat dispiriting. A shelf or two of romances and thrillers in well-worn paperback editions. A row of ancient cookbooks on a top shelf. Dictionaries (English, French, German, Spanish). A selection of self-help books, some in near mint condition. What Are You Doing With Your Life? is one. Also: Why We Do What We Do And How To Change, and How To Stop Doubting Your Greatness And Start Living An Awesome Life, and 100 Things Successful People Do.

Now a woman shuffles in and starts to browse the shelves, politely evading you as she does so. So you feel uncomfortable, you pick one of the battered thrillers off a shelf, take it to one of the tables to peruse. It will never do, you never read this sort of stuff. You wonder whether to take one of those dictionaries out; you always used to enjoy reading dictionaries. You can get a lot out of them, it's educational. So you get up abruptly, and collide accidentally with the woman, whom you didn't notice behind you. Oh, I'm sorry, you say, oh, I'm sorry, she replies. Dressed in the regulation navy tracksuit, she is of more than middle age perhaps, dark hair with silver in it, kindly, lustrous brown eyes. She smiles. It's the first smile you can remember seeing in a long while.

I beg your pardon, you say, with sudden boldness, but what are you in here for?

In the library? Her voice is mellow, soothing, speaking in a near whisper. So you lower your voice in sympathetic response.

No, I mean in this place, you say, with a gesture of your hand indicating spaces beyond these particular creamy-green walls, intending to denote the entire built environment that enfolds you.

Ah, she says, they review my case. But I am not so hopeful. Her eyes have sorrow in them now. You have now sat down again, and she sits in a chair near you. What is your name? she ventures.

You tell her your name. And you ask timidly: What's yours?

Suraya, I born in Afghanistan.

I can't hold on to information, you advise her.

I know what you mean, she says.

So I might have to ask you again, if you don't mind.

You finger the paperback thriller on the table in front of you, riffling the pages nervously.

I don't know what gonna happen, she says, interrupting the silence that has ensued.

Neither do I, you agree.

A big emotion is in me, all everywhere, you can even see it, the emotion is on my skin even. She shows you her pleasingly plump forearm, pinches it to indicate something, you know not what.

I understand, you say in a sympathetic voice.

I am here because I parted with my husband, you see? My husband, he leave me, and I have no, I have no, what they call, leave to remain.

Leave to remain, what does that even mean? I don't understand that.

What it mean, I can't live in this country no more. Because he leave me, I have no leave. I have no rights. I get a lawyer, but he can't do no more for me. It's the law. It's the English law, I got no human rights.

So what's going to happen?

They gonna deport me. They gonna send me back to Afghanistan. Is terrible, I fear it. My family there, they disown me, because I don't wear the veil. I cannot live there, I cannot.

That *is* terrible.

And you, she demands, where you born?

You tell her the name of the island that was your birthplace; you describe it in a few words, while she listens intently.

Well, maybe they deport you to that place.

Don't be silly, it's been seventy years or more, I was a child, I don't even have family there now.

They don't care. You have family, you don't have family. They don't care. Still they deport you.

I'm sure they won't, you say, though certainty is already draining from your voice, besides I'm going to have an appointment to sort the problem out with, what's his name? Doctor something.

She sits up suddenly. Is it Thomas Hardy?

Thomas Hardy, that's it.

You gonna see Dr Hardy? Wow! When?

Yeah, I'm hoping to get an appointment.

You gonna see Dr Hardy! Listen, I ask you a favour. Can you put in one word for me? Please, I beg you.

She has become animated now, edging closer to you in her chair, her eyes flicking anxiously in the direction of the privileged librarian, who is taking no notice of the conversation, engrossed as he is in a book of his own.

Well, I'd really like to help, but (you fluster, taken aback) – I don't know your case – I tell you what, I could ask him if he would make an appointment with you ...

I am told I cannot meet with him. Is not possible.

Have you ever seen him?

I saw him one time, Dr Hardy. I saw Dr Thomas Hardy, but I wasn't allowed to speak with him.

What's he like?

He is very polite English gentleman, very cultured, yes, but his face is red, you know, like there is fire under his skin. He wears dark suit, his suit smells of money. For sure. Why he is here, he is here for crimes committed outside.

What do you mean?

He was very important one time in the government, or something like that, but he do something bad. Something to do with finance, maybe. Then they punish him, they give him the job in charge here.

Is that so?

That is what people say. But Dr Hardy, he is the only one with the power to help. The only one. It would be my dream to see Dr Hardy. If you get an appointment, oh, I beg of you! Hey, listen, (she speaks your name sensuously)!

What?

She nudges you suggestively, with a side glance to see if

the librarian is paying any attention, which he isn't. I got a bottle of wine, she whispers. In my pod. You want some wine? Then we talk some more.

From then on, you cannot remember the sequence of events, if indeed there were any. You and Suraya are in a room. Is it her pod, or is it yours? It's hot and stuffy, but they are all hot and stuffy. You do remember sitting on the edge of a bed, her waving a wine bottle gently around in front of you, proudly showing you the label. Where did she get it from? She did tell you, but that information has vanished again.

We share, she says, but I got only one glass. She pours some red wine into her toothbrush tumbler for herself, and indicates that you are at liberty to swig from the bottle. Which you do. As far as you can remember. Which is not very far. Then you toast each other. I am so happy, she says, because you are going to see Dr Thomas Hardy, and maybe you put in a word or a few words, maybe he take pity, he is powerful man, Dr Hardy, she keeps repeating. He is the only one. She is so grateful for your attention. But you are sinking into a delirium by this time, you can't hear her voice very clearly. It seems you are at last free from the awful humid heat, free in the night air outside, you and she walking together by a railway track, it seems, though she walks awkwardly, you notice, as though crippled in some profound way, and the next thing is you are about to make love to her. You are lying together. On the track-bed. But the old blunt instrument isn't working too well these days. You remember seeing her flattened breasts beneath you. And then a cry penetrates from immeasurably far off: Mummy! and again: Mummy Bear! and that breaks the spell, because all of a sudden you notice her hair which has seemed so dense and dark is badly thinning at the back, in fact she is almost bald, and it's as though her hair were a wig imperfectly covering the ghastly aftermath of some major head operation, and there are grotesque growths on her otherwise beautiful body, and suddenly you are horrified and repelled. And the animals are now coming out of the walls, the creatures that dwell in the interstices of this institution have found a way out, and somebody screams: Mummy! I love you Mummy Bear! Fuck me! And the distinction between the inside and outside of your skull is now blurring repeatedly. You hear the sound of the door opening next door, and a gruff voice barking.

Stop it, Charlie!

Then the door slams shut and there is silence for a long period. There is no sign of Suraya, where is she? And where are *you*? The heat has closed in again. The darkness is profound. All you can hear is the panting which you soon identify as your own breath coming shallow and often, and a thudding which must be your racing heart. Suraya? you call. There's no response. Suraya?

Fuck me Mummy Bear! goes Charlie after a while.

And now you can hear another sound, softly at first, then increasingly distinct. A piano is being played in the middle of the night. You can almost identify the chords, your hands spontaneously go into their shapes. It's somewhere in the building. Not too far away. It dies. Maybe you imagined it. No, there it is again. What is that, so familiar? Maybe Debussy, you used to play a bit of Debussy as your party piece. But you cannot think now. It's intolerably hot.

Day 20

MORNING. AN INTERRUPTION. It's the attendant, the semi-friendly one. He enters the room without even bothering to knock. And behind him is a younger man with gelled hair, in overalls, carrying a tool bag.

You all right, mate? demands the attendant.

Yeah, you say, without thinking. You are sitting bolt upright on your bed.

We're fixing the heating, he tells you. This gentleman is going to have a look at the heater in your pod. OK, Jack, go ahead, he says to the other man without waiting for your reply. And Jack, without looking at you, gets on his knees beside the wall-mounted metal radiator that has been pumping out heat ceaselessly, opens his toolbar, produces a large crosshead screwdriver and sets to work.

The heat's driving me mad, you tell the attendant, who is watching Jack the repair man as though hoping to learn something of value. At night, especially, it's horrible.

Yeah, that's what they all say, he replies listlessly, not looking at you.

Also the noises in the night.

Charlie been bothering you?

I'm getting used to him. Actually, last night I heard a piano playing.

Did you now?

I wonder where that piano is. I was wondering if I could get to play it sometime.

You what?

Play the piano.

Piano? He looks at you now and roars with laughter. Are you fucking kidding me? He turns to Jack, who has got the cover off the heater and is peering inside: Hey, this customer wants to (puts on a mock-posh accent) *play the pyaahno!* Right, says the other guy and gives a brief guffaw without interrupting his work.

The attendant turns back to you, and resumes his normal voice: No, mate, there ain't no piano here. Anything else I can help with? he adds sarcastically.

No thanks.

The days go by.

Every day you look for Suraya in the canteen. At breakfast, at lunch, at dinner. Having taken your tray to a table, you sit and scan the people shuffling in the queue to be served: their heads down, not speaking, all in the regulation tracksuit, some of the women distinguished by hijabs, shuffling along and stopping, shuffling along and stopping, till they finally get to the counter. You go into the library after dinner and mooch about there until you are turfed out by the trustee at 9.30pm. But she never appears. You wonder whether you dreamt her. Soon you will forget her. It won't be long. Next day the same. At the breakfast queue, the endless shuffling. There's an influx of new people, ones you haven't seen before; they seem to have disabilities, some of them are twisted around, their bodies distorted, some almost seem to be facing backwards as they shuffle, or are bent over at nearly a right angle, it's horrible to watch. But wait. You recognise someone in the queue, almost certainly you do. A familiar face. That surely is, it's on the tip of your tongue. A slight, slim man, sharp face, little beard on his chin.

BJ! That's it, that must be BJ, it looks uncommonly like him. You crane your head, for the queue has moved on by now in the direction of the counter, but you've lost sight of him. You wait for him to come back in your direction with his breakfast tray, but he never does; maybe he's gone to another part of the canteen. Or maybe you were mistaken. Surely it could not be BJ. What would he be doing here? But then again, what are *you* doing here? You don't have an adequate answer to that, do you?

The sighting, or imagined sighting, troubles you for a while, and begins to displace in your mind the obsession with Suraya. It starts to haunt you, like all the other ghosts that flit into and out of that troubled mind. In the middle of the night, though, you wake with a start, with the new thought that has just popped in, out of nowhere: this could be the answer to your problems! Or at least *one* answer to *one* of the problems. If BJ can be located, he can tell the authorities definitively that you didn't sell your flat to Jack-anapes, that it was all a huge mistake; he can absolve you from that charge at least. It only remains to locate him, though. So that is another sub-routine in your aching brain, another tunnel for your thoughts to negotiate. It seems your mind-field is vast, and your fragile thoughts are tunnelling through it, hither and thither, trying for all their might to make connective passages linking one thing with the next which is a very long way away, and sometimes it also seems you are split up into components that you are trying like mad to bring together, as if one part of you, or one you, is boring a tunnel into this mind-stuff and the other you is boring one from the other side, wherever the other side may be, and the hope is that the two versions of you will eventually meet midway, that by a miracle the trajectories will converge and a passage will be opened up through which communication can take place, with much cheering, even if by then you've forgotten what it was you were trying to establish in the first place.

But the thought of BJ keeps coming back, at inopportune moments sometimes, but at other times in the canteen, or in the dismal library, and then you immediately scan the faces of whoever may be there passing through to see whether you can recognise among them his pointy face, his trim beard, though the objective of the exercise, that is to say, enlisting him as a witness on your behalf in the question of your financial liability, sometimes eludes your memory, so you're not quite sure why you're looking for him and what you would say to him if you did see him and caught his attention. But you don't see him. And then at other times the memory of having seen BJ fades, but that of Suraya comes to the fore, though you can no longer remember her name, and then you scan the faces of the women among the crowd, veiled and unveiled, as they pass by, and some of them look a bit like her but then you realise you are mistaken; at any event they don't return your would-be smile of recognition, indeed, usually turn their face away hastily, but not before it's been pretty well established that they are not her. And at yet other times you forget them both but have the nagging feeling that you ought to be looking for someone, someone who will be recognisable once they are located, but can't quite recall at this moment precisely why you are looking, although you trust that if and when you do see them, then all will be made clear, and so it's worth persisting in your search for you know not what or whom.

And, more often, the memory of either or both these individuals escapes you, and it's simpler to just follow the routines, day by day, without questioning them; there's a comfort in doing this, doubling down on apathy, that is not only beguiling but overwhelming. Yet you can never completely get rid of the feeling that there is unfinished business, that there's some agenda you vaguely remember, a meeting that has been set up, or might be set up, that will resolve your situation, but it's hard to focus on this. It keeps slipping into the wings. An appointment has been arranged, that's it. An appointment has been arranged with the top guy, to resolve this problem that you have, of not being able to prove your status. What the hell was his name? The top guy. That woman said, what did she say. That she would get back to you. When was that? And what was it you had to prove? That you are who you are, and you are where you are, and where you are is where you are supposed to be, and that your home is your home and has not been and cannot be taken from you. That sort of thing. But has an appointment been made? You feel it has, but you are not sure, and if it has you don't know when that was made and when it was made for.

In the middle of the night you are awakened yet again, perhaps by the animal noises, including Charlie next door wailing and moaning, but also by an exceptionally nasty dream – despair and horror, all the usual stuff features in it – and the picture of BJ pops once again, suddenly, into your head, BJ of course, and with it a revelation, of course he's the one to appeal to for definitive confirmation that you did *not* sell your flat to Jackanapes. Except, terrible thought, what if you did ... but you are sure you did not, but what if somehow it happened without your knowledge ...

Morning comes, there's the usual rap on your door; it's the nurse, for your daily injection. While she's busying herself sorting you out, you are still mulling over this business, whether you have an appointment to settle this once and for all, and if so when is that appointment for. How will you know?

Ask the nurse, why don't you?

She is one of the older ones, she looks a little tired.

You say, after she's jabbed you: Nurse, do you happen to

know whether I have an appointment with Doctor, Doctor, uh, I can't remember his name –

You don't have an appointment with the GP at the moment, so far as I know, she says.

No, no, he's not a medical doctor, he's the boss here, he's, wait a minute, it's Dr Thomas something –

You don't mean Dr Thomas Hardy?

Say that again.

You mean Dr Thomas Hardy, Head of Investigations?

That's the guy, you affirm.

I don't know anything about that, says the nurse primly. If *he* needs to see you, you'll be told in due course.

Thank you nurse, you say (she is already packing away her things and preparing to depart), but an unnamed sense, maybe of despair, is welling again.

Another day, and another night. The heat is unrelenting: the repairs to your radiator appear to have made no difference. And then another day.

And then night. With all its noises, from near and far, from inside and outside your skull.

There is a pounding on your door. Not your skull. It is your actual pod door. And a voice like thunder calling your name: [SURNAME]!

You hear the door opening in the dark, and a bright flashlight shines in your face as you raise your head from the pillow, even as your heart jumps into your mouth.

[SURNAME]?

Yes, you cry, in anguish.

What time is it? It's not yet morning, surely, not by a long chalk. The flashlight blinds you, but the darkness is all around.

You recognise the burly shape in the shadows, and the burly voice. It's one of the other attendants, not the semi-friendly one. The other one. Or one of the others. The one that looks like a tired bull elephant. Though they are all the same, really. But he wears the costume of a thief in the night. And you know your time has come.

Appointment with Dr Hardy, he says curtly.

Day 21

WHAT CAN I do for you?

The question takes you completely by surprise. It is uttered in a low, gentle croak. The utterer's face is lit by a desk lamp and by the ambient glow from the computer screen situated to one side of where he sits, behind a massive desk. It is a small face, reddish in hue and somewhat craggy. Written on it are the lineaments of eternal torment. The face is, you presume, owned by the legendary Dr Thomas Hardy, who has not actually introduced himself. His very first words were "Please sit down", but then he put on a pair of glasses and busied himself for some moments writing something in a notepad, and you were beginning to think he had forgotten about you until he eventually looked up, took off the spectacles and uttered that question.

He is tiny, and looks utterly weary. He wears a dark jacket and dark tie on a milk-white shirt. The rest of the room is in shadow. It feels like you are encircled – but he is the centre of that circle.

You were brought here by the elephant-shaped attendant, via corridors bridging the various concentric zones of this establishment, dark except for the low glow of emergency lighting, and via many security doors, through each of which he gained access by tapping laboriously a four-digit code, his torch illuminating the process. You stumbled behind his great, dark, pendulous shape and the bobbing light he wielded. You would appear to have penetrated even further into the heart of the building than before, perhaps even to its centre or near enough. The corridors started to mutate and shape-shift. A strange, greenish illumination began to manifest, and then you realised the walls were lined with glass from behind which an unearthly light emanated; and when you had given it more consideration you saw that this was a continuous aquarium, a tunnel of water within which from time to time odd shapes darted and undulated in what would seem a purposeful way. And then you found yourself here in this circular office, and the human pachyderm vanished.

No doubt he is sitting outside waiting for the meeting to conclude so that he can escort you back to your pod.

You flounder. I ... I want to go home. They said you could fix it.

They suffer from eternal optimism, says Dr Thomas Hardy, if indeed it is he. I apologise for the hour, I'm working rather late. Your name is, let's see, (replaces his spectacles) [FORENAME] [SURNAME]?

That's right.

Let's have a look. He turns his gaze to the computer screen, and is occupied with this for some moments. Mmm, mmm, he murmurs to himself. Yes, I see. I see.

You wait. While you are waiting, you cannot help but notice that the longitudinal aquarium filled with its greenish glowing water penetrates even here, occupying one wall of Dr Hardy's office. It seems to terminate in some kind of apparatus, which – the light is not good, you can't see properly – would appear to be connected to his computer. Perhaps it is some form of advanced messaging system. Anything is possible here, even likely. Those undulating shapes may be a species of electric eel or suchlike, carrying the ones and zeros of the information back and forth in the electrons they absorb and emit. Carrying impulses from the centre to all parts of the organisation and back again. This may be how it all works.

Dr Hardy speaks again.

OK, I see the reason for the referral. A classic case, if I may say so. I wish my students were here to take note of it. We need to assure ourselves firstly of your bona fide status, in terms of right of residence in this country, which in turn calls into question your right to receive care; and secondly, to assess the means you have to fund your care if it is indeed determined that you are entitled to it. Now, I take it you have no documentation to hand?

Not here, no.

But we cannot discharge you without that documentation, clearly.

The lady I saw said –

What she said is irrelevant, Mr [SURNAME]. You have been referred to me for a resolution of this issue. Now, I have a great deal of experience in this field, as you may know. I have helped frame policy, I've even advised prime ministers on occasion. And here I am, for my sins. I am Head of Investigations. But you must understand even I can't circumvent Management. I do not have the power to buck the system, if you will.

In a sudden flood of despair, you begin to expostulate; but, coldly and with a hint of contempt, he holds up a hand: Please go no further, Mr [SURNAME]. Calm down. We are all trying to do our job. Now, according to the notes here provided by my colleague, it seems you are asserting you may have at home some of the documentary evidence that we need, is that correct?

Yes, you plead, I've been saying that over and over –

Please listen. We cannot presently discharge you into the community. That would be in breach of the regulations. But I can see a case here for a Special Dispensation.

What's that?

This may be the reason you've been referred to me. A

Special Dispensation would enable us to take certain actions. For instance, what we term an Escorted Home Visit, or EHV. I may be able to trigger that under Management protocols that are available to me in special or unusual circumstances. It's not certain, but we may find that is appropriate.

What does that mean?

Dr Thomas Hardy takes a sip from a glass of some kind of amber liquor which you now see is on his desk beside him, and resumes:

It means you will be allowed home under strict security supervision for a limited period, typically no more than an hour or two, to enable you to put your affairs in order and produce any documentation that may assist you in putting your case.

Please, can you do that?

I can try. You will have to understand, however, that if the procedure turns out to be futile, that is to say, that it does not result in your being able to provide the necessary evidence, then the cost of that operation would fall to you, and would be added to your indebtedness. So you will need to sign a document saying you understand that.

I'll sign anything, you say.

I cannot promise that this would happen immediately, Mr [SURNAME]. We are operating under funding constraints currently. Severe constraints. In particular, a shortfall in staffing which certainly impacts on EHVs, among other procedures. And as I said, my powers, though considerable in some respects, are limited. But I can certainly put forward a strong recommendation that this should be fast-tracked. Now, is there anything else?

You start to panic. Multiple thoughts are jostling, crowding for space in your brain. Wait a minute, wait a minute, you say. And then the image of BJ manifests itself in your memory. Ah, yes. I know what I was going to say. That business about me selling the lease of my flat. There's somebody here who can tell you that's not true.

Is there indeed?

BJ, his name is BJ. He was helping Jackanapes, I mean Mr Jackson. I'm supposed to have sold my flat to him, but he can tell you I didn't.

You didn't sell your flat to this BJ?

No, I mean to Mr Jackson. BJ was his legal adviser.

So you maintain that you did not sell your property in an attempt to evade financial responsibility for your care?

No, no, BJ can vouch for me.

And this gentleman, BJ – the name does not ring a bell – is a *customer* here?

I saw him the other day! I saw him! BJ is what I call him. I can't pronounce his proper name.

Do you have any more detail about him?

He's Albanian. Or what, Arabian. Or no, that's rubbish, Armenian, that's it. Armenian. I think.

We have literally hundreds of people in this establishment alone at any one time. From memory, I cannot recall any Armenians currently being reviewed. But since you say he may be a material witness, I'll have a look on the system.

He turns again to the computer, glasses back on his nose, and frowns.

Let's see, let's see, search by country ... unfortunately, my PA, who is more adept at these IT systems than I, is unavailable for work at this hour of the morning ... Armenia, no, nothing. If you meet this gentleman again, please get his name and details and notify us if you think it might save some investigation time. Is that all?

Suraya now comes to mind. Her desperate plea to you.

Oh, there's somebody else.

Someone else who can vouch for you, as you put it?

No, she wanted *me* to put in a word for her. I promised her I would.

Who?

I can't remember her name. It starts with an S.

I'm sorry, Mr [SURNAME], I don't know who you mean.

She's from Afghanistan.

Very well, I'll search on the system once more. But then I'm afraid I have a hundred and one other things to attend to before morning. Let's see, Afghanistan, Afghanistan, yah, one or two matches here ... ah yes, there was a lady from Afghanistan recently, she may be the one you mean. We discharged her last week, apparently.

Discharged?

He takes off the glasses very deliberately and looks up at you. You fancy that his eyes are a watery pale blue, though you can't really see them properly.

Yes, she has been successfully repatriated to her country of origin. Anything else you wish to know?

A void is opening below you, and you blink; the void does not blink back, but remains implacably there. You fall into that watery pale blue, which is actually black, and incapable of further elucidation. It does not make complete sense, and therefore no sense at all. You sense nothing. That would be another way of putting it. Are you with me? Is anybody there? You inhabit no country, you have no hinterland, just for an instant you are bottomless; it isn't what you would wish. You know not your name even, what it begins with or what it ends with or the bit in the middle. You are pitched into exile, but from what, to where? You are any amount, between zero and totality, you are legion or you are nothing.

Mr [SURNAME]? Are you with me?

I'm sorry, you say, I'm sorry.

You start to shiver.

To sum up, announces Dr Thomas Hardy. To sum up. We will arrange for an application for an EHV under Special Dispensation. It will be done as soon as is practicable, and you will be informed if and when the procedure is due to take place. Thank you.

That is the end of the interview. You didn't see what he did, but he must have pressed a button or something, because right on cue the elephantine attendant looms behind you. You didn't even hear the door open. You know it's him without even looking because you can hear the peculiar grinding of the teeth that he does. And then you catch a brief glimpse of the folds of his face as he gives you a lugubrious eye before turning and leading you along the corridors of the forbidden zone again, through security door after security door. The elephantom; the elephantasm. This fascinates you.

Now something may happen. Even now Dr Hardy's instructions will be conveyed from his computer via the electric-eel-like organisms swimming through those fluid-filled aquarium tubes along the maze of corridors to the places where things might be made to happen.

You are back in your pod. How you got here you don't remember. Darkness, the usual noises. Mummy, mummy, fuck me, aaah! You hear the sound of your neighbour's door being opened, and a sharp voice, the attendant, or another attendant on night duty:

Charlie! Put it away, mate, you'll go blind.

And then the door clicks shut. And there is silence for a while.

Morning. The usual routine. Night. Morning.

One evening, while waiting in the dinner queue, a man just ahead of you, of Middle Eastern appearance, whom you vaguely recognise, suddenly turns, catches your eye and gives you a half-smile – very unusual here. How you doing?

he says politely. Not so bad, you say, I had an appointment. With, what's his name, Dr Hardy. Oh yeah? He looks suspicious. How you get that? I don't know, you say. But I've got what they call a Special Dispensation. Yeah, what's that? he asks, his mood having perceptibly darkened. That stumps you. You try hard to recall Dr Hardy's words on that occasion in the small hours of the morning which now seems an aeon away. Well, you say lamely, I can't remember the details now, but it might be the solution to my problem. Hey, you lucky, he says scornfully, you very lucky, some of us we still have problem. We still have big problem. And he turns his back on you as the solemn girl who is serving today prepares to fill his plate with his dinner, and that is the end of that conversation.

But then another thing happens.

You are now seated at your table in the canteen with your tray in front of you, contemplating your anonymous dinner with a mounting feeling of fatigue, as though it will be an effort even to lift the fork from your plate to your mouth, a feeling that starts to mutate into the symptoms of nausea – when something makes you look up, and there approaching among the bustle with his own tray held in front of him is – no it isn't, it can't be, but yes it is, it must be. He hasn't seen you, he has his head down; you half-stand, half-croak his name out loud:

BJ?

There can be no mistake, surely. The regulation blue uniform has replaced the familiar dark suit, the beard can no longer be described as a goatee, being untrimmed and verging on shaggy, but the narrow, chiselled features are so familiar, the domed forehead, the sharp nose, the uncanny light eyes in a dark face. He is very near. You reach out and touch him on the arm; he stops, looks round at you with a startled expression.

BJ?

Excuse me?

It is his voice too. But he looks blankly straight into your face.

It's BJ, isn't it? You remember me?

Excuse me, I don't know you.

BJ! It's me! You say your name, he remains perplexed, your eyes meet and are fixed in a mutual stare. You try again: You stayed with me, don't you remember?

Forgive me, when was that? he says, with an air of formality.

You were working with Jackanapes upstairs. You lodged with me in my flat.

He is now beginning to look very uncomfortable. He looks away.

I don't know what you talking about.

What are you doing here?

Now he starts to edge away. I am sorry, he says, I am sorry.

Don't you recognise me? Listen – you can help me, BJ. I'm in a terrible pickle, and you can help by vouching for me. I really need your help.

I am very sorry, he says, beginning to move again, I am very sorry, you are mistaken, it is somebody else you thinking of, OK?

But there is a flicker there, in his pale-blue eyes, a flicker that speaks contrary to his words, and there can be no doubt now. BJ who helped you, BJ who made wonderful soup, BJ who was searching for his lost wife in Hell, BJ who told you Jackanapes was dead, BJ whose belongings you asked the Christian window cleaner to put in storage when he did not return. There he is, in the flesh again. He knows you. But he doesn't want to know you.

Excuse me, he says, then does an about turn and walks

away with his tray, eventually being lost to sight among the throng at the far end of the busy canteen.

Day 22

FROM NOW ON things start to fall apart in every respect. This happens quite rapidly. The boundary formed by your skull is breached. The realm of uncertainty has expanded fourfold, or more. There's no longer any remaining, reliable measure as to what's the status quo and what the domain of phantasy; the messages are not getting through, or if they are, it's impossible to determine whether they are malicious spam generated by those phantom entities that have long resided in the furthermost recesses of your unconsciousness.

There is panic in the corridor. Alarm bells are ringing. All three toilets are occupied, but water is flowing from under the door of the third one along, and then starts to flow scarlet, pooling wider and wider. It's blood, shouts someone, look. That's when a posse of attendants assembles quickly, running in from all directions; they make their muster, one of them screaming "Everybody out of here!", others rapping on the doors of the other occupied toilets; the men within, emerging dazed and pulling their trousers up, are bundled out of the way. Ferocious banging on the third toilet door, no response, again, no response, then they break the door down. This takes little or no time. The word is they discover the man sitting on the toilet therein is dead; depending on who you talk to he has either had his throat cut or his stomach has been opened up, there is blood every-where, that's all you know, but quickly the whole area is sealed off, everyone is ordered back to their pod, maximum security protocols are now in place. Where did he get the knife, was it in the canteen kitchen, did he do himself in, or was he murdered, but wait a minute, how if so, who was he anyway, no questions allowed, you didn't hear anything, you didn't see anything. You especially didn't hear the body being trolleyed at high speed down the corridor outside your room, or if you did, you are to erase the memory.

The lockdown continues for the rest of the day, the toilets are strictly out of bounds, if you want to go you have to put in a request, you will be escorted under the emergency protocols to the other toilets outside your zone, you are to stand to attention, you are to stand at ease, then you can stand easy, you can go, but having gone you are escorted back promptly, there is to be no tarrying, no conversation, no colloquy, no fraternising whatsoever.

As you are being escorted back to your room, you notice that, for the first time you can remember, the door of Charlie's room, the one next to yours, is wide open. One of the attendants is standing outside, looking in. For the first time, you catch a fleeting glimpse of, presumably, Charlie himself. On the bed, dwarfing it, is a huge, bloated white body, resembling a beached beluga whale, completely naked, both fat hands grasping its groin. Another attendant is standing over him, trying to cajole him, but he is mumbling and moaning incoherently, rolling slightly from side to side. When the attendant at the door sees you looking, he immediately shuts the door – the show is over before it even began.

You are reminded of similar creatures that nest in the crevices and interstices of your brain, that you suspect inhabit the crevices and interstices of the building itself, only emerging at night, a whole army of them, crawling out, moaning and wailing throughout the night, before scuttling back to their hiding places as daylight begins to seep through the windows, returning to their daytime roosts.

Though another theory that you are beginning to formulate is that in fact they do not do so, that their strategy for concealment during the day in some cases is to impersonate the staff, the attendants, the cleaners, the clinical staff, and even sometimes to pretend to be other customers, so that you are never entirely sure who you are dealing with, such is the ingenious level of deception they attain, mutant giraffes and elephants and rodents and snakes and insects and unnameable hybrids impersonating staff and fellow customers, so that it's best to keep your mouth shut, to interact as little as possible in case you compromise yourself, in case you put yourself in a situation from which you cannot retreat. But this demands a fair degree of attention and concentration, which it's difficult to maintain, the opportunities for relaxing being extremely limited. For example, the toilet is no longer the refuge it was, because the huge, communal toilet you are now taken to cannot be secured, it's part of a completely open complex of rooms, including offices, where staff keep passing by despite your protestations that you are in full view; you beg them, while you are sitting there on the toilet seat, with your tracksuit trousers round your ankles, to please please desist until you've finished, but they take no notice, it's as if they don't even see you sitting there right in the middle of the thoroughfare in plain view as they come and go on their own daily business. Some of them are evidently junior executives, laughing and joshing with each other in groups as they come out of their meeting, or wherever they've been: the young men in dark blue or dark grey suits typically worn with tan shoes, their hair slicked back; the young women in high heels, in tailored skirt suits in sober colours and of elegant cut. Most are white, there is the occasional young person of mixed race. While you sit there on the toilet you listen to their banter as they flit past, little of which means anything to you: Did they do the business then? asks one, and another replies: Did they fuck! and there is a burst of laughter. And another goes: Like a frog in boiling water, he was. Which produces a burst of nodding, and another comments: They were all over the pitch, if you ask me, no fucking discipline. To which there is a clamour, seemingly of mixed approval and discontent, but without rancour, it's a game they are all enjoying. The group disperses, and you think you will be left alone on the toilet for a bit, you will have a chance to do *your* business, but just then another group of these junior managers appears from another adjoining door, arguing and bantering among themselves. But they are not all they seem: who are they? Who are they really? There are only two types of human being, after all, you hear one of them pontificate in a sententious manner, those that are going to die and those that are already dead! Which produces a huge laugh among this little group, one of the others repeating Very true, very true, and another chipping in with You're a proper fucking *sage!* and their laughter dies away as they disperse and disappear down different corridors. But then they are followed by a smaller group of older people, clearly members of senior Management, and you stand up now, your trousers still round your ankles, trying to discern their faces, looking anxiously in vain for Dr Thomas Hardy, hoping that if he were among them and saw you there, even with your trousers down, his memory would be triggered, he would be reminded to put in place for you the orders that would give you the opportunity to return home, if even for a short time, but it's no good, you can't recognise him. And as they too disappear to wherever they have to go, you sit down again, upon which you feel terrific pain in your buttocks, and it seems now that the toilet seat is covered in tiny spikes and barbs, and despite your urgent need you can't bear it any longer, you have to stand up, and with that you are assailed by a powerful vertigo, everything is spinning round you, the toilet, the open complex of which it is part, and beyond that the whole edifice of the institution, the building whose measure you are never able to apprehend, with its immense array of concentric rings of corridors, all very similar, bridged by great radial corridors, a ground plan that is beyond your comprehension, and intended to be beyond your comprehension.

It's night again. You are back in your pod. Can this be a refuge at last, can you finally attain a deep sleep unbroken by unwanted dreams – perhaps, perhaps, but no, you are woken by a commotion next door, muffled swearing, and then the door closing and a rumbling outside, the unmistakable sound of a person or body being wheeled past your room on a trolley. So now you are awake with your thoughts again, which is not what you wanted: but what if, but what if, but on the other hand what if.

But what if, but what if, no it couldn't possibly be.

But what if.

But what if you are mistaken, what if you have blanked out a huge thing that happened, what if you did do a deal and did sell your flat to Jackanapes? You search the wasteland that is encroaching day by day and night by night on your memory, and you find nothing. But that doesn't mean anything. Or what if, what if, no, that's too horrible to contemplate. What if BJ did, no he couldn't have, could he? What if BJ sold your flat to Jackanapes from under your nose, in a cruel deception, what if you were sold down the river by him, under the command of Jackanapes, and you knew nothing of it, what if they forged your signature, ah. Is that why he cringed from you when you confronted him, is that why, no, he couldn't have. You would know, but how would you know? What do you know? And for him to end up here now, in the same place as you, how could that happen?

What is BJ doing here, and why didn't he recognise you? But of course, he *did* recognise you, he just didn't want to know you. He didn't want to know you, that's clear. For one reason or another. And he backed off, frightened. But why is he here? The thought then comes: is BJ still looking for his wife? Is that why? Is he eternally compelled to search fruitlessly for his lost wife, and is this the place where he thinks he may find her at last?

But already you are beginning to forget about BJ, and about much else.

Day 23

A NEW COHORT of attendants is coming onstream, you can tell by the subtle difference in their uniforms, the subtle difference in their body language; and also, you notice, the nurse who arrives in the morning for your injection is completely unfamiliar; she does not wear the CARE-PLC name badge, in fact she wears no insignia whatsoever and has no conversation, she just does her job like an android.

Then it's breakfast, for which now you have to join the escorted party, you can't go on your own, for emergency security reasons. And then having breakfasted you are escorted back to your pod. But no sooner have you been deposited back here than one of the new breed of attendants pokes his head round your door, and shouts at you: Work!

What does he mean, work? Work! he repeats, come on, please look sharp, line up here. There's a whole platoon of customers already assembled, you have to be taken in a line through the corridors, attendants ahead of and behind you, to a large room you've never seen before, a sort of lecture theatre, packed with serried benches with little desks in front of them; your group files in one by one and when you are all seated more attendants, some of them women, come down the aisle steps to left and right doling out piles of blank lined school copybooks which are to be passed along, one to each customer, and also bunches of cheap ballpoint pens, one to each customer.

You hear one of the others, in the row behind you, complain, in an African accent: What's all this about? The answer comes crisply from one of the female attendants, speaking rapidly and with gleeful officiousness: under the emergency regulations now in place there isn't a leisure option any longer in the times between meals, there will from now on be compulsory paid work in those hours. Please sit down, she says, it will all be explained in a minute.

Compulsory work, that's slavery! shouts the African man, who is still standing in his place. You crane your neck to see him; he's familiar, you have seen him many times before in the canteen. He is always one of the more voluble ones. Please sit down, says the female attendant, this is paid work, this is not slavery. PLEASE sit down!

The ranked seats face a blond-wood podium, a lectern, a whiteboard.

When everybody is in place with their copybooks and pens in front of them, a young woman, fair hair pulled tightly back in a ponytail, looking very nervous, steps onto the podium. She is a research student, she explains. You are all being given the opportunity to participate in important scientific work. She mumbles, she cannot be heard above the general hubbub, one of the attendants roars: Silence, PLEASE! She begins again.

You are to write your name on the first page of your copybook, continues the student, and your pod and corridor number. If you cannot remember your pod and corridor number you must ask the nearest attendant, who will help you. As to the project you are being asked to participate in, you will see a series of numbers. These have been culled from samples of atmospheric noise. Atmospheric noise, she repeats mysteriously. You are to copy the numbers down in your book exactly as you see them. This task will take the rest of the morning. Your work will be paid for in the form of tokens that can be spent in the canteen to buy items of added value, such as individually wrapped puddings or sweets or crisps.

Onto the podium steps a middle-aged, squinting woman in the tracksuit that marks her out as a customer. She has a black felt-tip board marker in her right hand and a book in her left. Peering at the book, she starts to write out laboriously, beginning at the top left-hand corner of the whiteboard, a series of numbers grouped in fours, as follows: 4537 2381 3068 5335 9776…. She stops briefly, then continues in the same vein, transferring the numbers laboriously from her book onto the board.

Please start copying the numbers exactly as you see them, you and your fellow customers are told – and after a while each bends to his or her task. The sequence continues:

0973 2196 7678 9805 0765 7003 0903 5255 4715
5504 2285 5607 5056 6346 1690 1372 0634 5597 2310
6193 0429 4314 3548 7574 4640 1451 1441 3517 6175
5224 8872 5433 2179 6049 2608 8262 4968 7122 8486
3906 5724 5963 3537 2325 6234 …

And so on and so on.

There seems to be no pattern or purpose to the sequence. But you, like all the others, carefully copy it out, number by number, line by line.

Almost an hour has gone by, and the woman on the podium is reaching the bottom of the whiteboard, having filled it entirely with the integers. She looks round uncertainly. The research student tells her: That's all right, Olga, you can stop now. And the sequence of numbers is halted abruptly, and the woman steps down.

Now the student steps up. There is what turns out to be a damp cloth in her hand. Starting at the top, she begins to erase the numbers. She works her way downwards, but as she approaches two thirds of the way down, she provokes a cry from one part of the room: Wait a minute, I haven't got there yet! And from another part: I haven't finished! So she pauses, looks up again. After waiting a few minutes she recommences erasing the numbers. Eventually, she clearly observes that everyone has stopped writing, and so she wipes the last of the numbers off.

So, she says, now can everybody in row one, that is, the first row in front of me, pass their copybook to the person behind you in row two? Can you start doing that, please? And can everybody in row three, that is, the third row from the front, pass their book to the person behind them in row four. No, not you, you're in row two. I said row three. You should have two books. That's right. And the same with people in row five, please pass your books to people in the row behind you. Is that clear?

It is not at all clear to everybody, so there is much confusion, and some of the attendants, who have been watching over the process, intervene to sort it out. You are in one of the rows that retains two books. Now the people in rows left without books are ordered to leave quietly, one after another, filing out of the room under escort, apparently to complete another task in another room. And the student addresses those of you who remain: So you need to compare the two copybooks, your original one and the one you have been given. You are to go through the lines of numbers, compare them one by one and please mark any mistakes or deviations. Please do this by circling the mistake. Off you go then.

But what is the purpose of the experiment? asks a man at the back, in a heavy Eastern European accent. He is ignored. Everybody else eventually gets their head down, begins comparing, line by line, number by number. Another hour goes by.

You find it difficult to concentrate. The numbers swim around in front of you. Sometimes you forget whether you have checked all of them on a particular page and have to return to the top of the page. One difficulty is that the spacing in the copybook you have just been handed differs markedly from your own spacing – in fact, about halfway through, the person who handed you their book has evidently decided to abandon the groups of four and has copied the numbers in an unbroken series – and therefore it is easy to come adrift of the sequence and lose where you are in the comparison. Also the handwriting is erratic, and this makes it impossible sometimes to decipher whether a digit has been copied correctly.

When you have finished, announces the student, please write your own name and pod and corridor number at the end of the copybook you have been given, the one you are checking. Then please hand both books in, your original and the one you have been comparing. The attendants will collect them.

What will happen to the notebooks? asks someone. This is ignored.

Although some people are already handing books in, you are far from completing the task. You are tempted to skimp it, but then, if they find you have overlooked any mistakes, what will the consequences be?

What happens to the notebooks? Another man repeats the question to his neighbour, who shrugs.

I tell you what, interrupts the African man who earlier protested, they will be destroyed. I tell you that for a fact.

No! Why?

They are just random numbers. Random numbers! says the angry African.

What is the purpose? asks someone else.

They are messing with our minds! he shouts. That's all!

You decide you have no idea whether you have checked all the numbers or not, so to hell with it, you give up, put your name and identification down at the end of the book you've been given. The digits are swimming around in your mind-soup now, there is no chance of spotting any further errors. You hand in both books.

As you are queuing up to leave the room – it's lunchtime – you hear further mutterings among your fellow inmates.

Is getting really bad now, innit? says one.

Very bad, very bad, says his neighbour.

Another says there are rumours of a strike. What strike, are we on strike? asks someone. No, stupid, the staff, says the other, you notice for example, half of the staff have gone, where are they, we have new ones.

Yeah, we have new ones too, says another.

It's not just here, there is also civil unrest I heard, says the first.

Civil unrest? What you mean? Where?

Outside, says the first.

Outside?

Yeah, outside in the world, you remember?

I don't remember the world, where is that? says the second, provoking an outbreak of hollow laughter around you.

As you file out of the room, you are each handed a few plastic tokens – your wages – by an attendant who waits by the door. But when it's the angry African's turn he snatches the tokens and violently flings them back into room, where they scatter to all corners, bouncing off the floor and benches. Immediately, two of the larger attendants pounce on him, one grabbing each arm, and roughly haul him off, a third attendant holding doors open for them to manhandle him through. They are messing with our minds, people! he keeps shouting as he disappears. It sounds as though he is laughing, or possibly sobbing, it's not clear. Everybody else becomes very subdued all of a sudden. The African is not seen again.

You are taken to lunch in the canteen.

After lunch you are returned to the lecture theatre, and the same play is performed. This time there is no argument from any of the customers, no protests, not even questions; a resigned sullenness prevails, everybody head down copying number after number.

When dinner is over, the long process begins of shepherding you and all the other customers back to your individual pods. As you eventually near yours, you notice that once again Charlie's room door, next to yours, is wide open. But this time when you peek inside as you pass by, you see that the room is completely empty – the familiar scent of disinfectant emanating from it.

You are dissuaded from lingering. You are shown into your room.

When are things going to get back to normal? you ask the attendant who has been assigned to you, an older man you don't recognise.

There's no normal no more, says the attendant tersely.

Any idea when I'm going to be allowed home?

No idea, mate.

Only, they said I'd be allowed home to get some papers I need. (You hesitate. He doesn't respond.) I've been given what they call a Special Dispensation. (This is the only formula that sticks in your mind.)

What, for an Escorted Home Visit? Nobody gets those.

Yeah, that's what I've been promised.

You've got an EHV? he says scornfully. Who told you that?

I had a meeting, you say, I had a meeting with Doctor, what's his name?

Dr Thomas Hardy?

Yes, that's him. He promised me one of them home visits.

Much good will it do you now, says the attendant, laughing.

What do you mean?

He's gone, mate. Got the boot.

Your stomach, your whole digestive system, does a turn.

Dr Thomas Hardy has been sacked?

Yup. Gross incompetence, they said. This latest crisis was the last straw for the Management, they say. Got the boot, got the sack, he is no more, it's over – *finito*. And the attendant makes a gesture like the conductor of an orchestra bringing the symphony to a close.

But what –

The attendant is no longer there. He has wandered off, as though bored with the conversation; he's talking to one of the others now. They are a definitely different breed, these newcomers that have been brought in, perhaps as replacements, as strike-breakers, if indeed there has been a strike; they seem even harder, even less amenable to talking; you don't recognise any of them now, for example the semi-friendly bullet-headed one has not been seen for a while. They are jittery, even skittish you might say, they bark out random orders, they do not meet the eye. You can tell they are inexperienced, they are not used to it. Something is always bothering them; every little unexpected noise that occurs offstage is greeted by warning shouts, sometimes by swearing, either directed at each other or at customers. They are permanently in crisis mode. The latest crisis, he said. The last straw. That's what got Dr Hardy fired.

Crisis. What does that mean? Well, it's the turning point in a disease, the change that indicates impending recovery or death – one or the other. That's where you are right now. This is your situation. It's unsustainable. It simmers, but the flashpoints are beginning to merge, that's how it seems. Like a volcano that is about to blow, like a boil that is about to burst – the next few days, or hours, or minutes even, will be interesting. But you have no stake in this, have you?

You have to get out of here. That's all you know. But how?

Ten o'clock, and immediately the lights go out.

Darkness.

You can't sleep. Although it's unusually quiet. Nothing from Charlie. Charlie has gone. You miss him.

You have to get out of here.

Just beginning to get drowsy, and suddenly you are jolted awake again. A siren has started to wail. This is a noise you have never heard before. It starts quietly, but quickly crescendos to an unbearable level. A horrible electronic noise. You recognise the interval, a falling minor third, over and over again, endlessly, G flat to E flat, but what's particularly unbearable to you is that the G flat is not quite in tune, the interval is unstable. You put your hands to your ears as you lie there in the darkness, but it makes no difference. And then you start to hear shouting, from different parts of the building. You can hear someone distinctly shouting "Fire!" Can you smell anything? No. Everybody out, all customers out in the corridor please! you hear the call in the distance. What do you care? Let the fire consume you at last. You scramble out of bed, the noises are even louder, there are doors slamming now. In desperation and fright you get down on your hands and knees and scuttle under the bed. You lie there for some time, hoping desperately it will all go away. The sounds are more muffled now. It is almost peaceful here. There is a general hubbub, but it seems a long way away now. You drift off to sleep at last.

Day 24

You wake in what seems to be an abandoned factory. The pipework and ductwork is of an extraordinary beauty. There is no way out.

Actually, let us backtrack a little. What happened is that you awoke in darkness but with a hint of light coming from somewhere; thinking morning was approaching, you lifted your head, which immediately struck a hard surface. Ouch. You could not recall how you came to be here in this narrow place. Was this, at last, the grave?

Then you remembered you had got under the bed in fear, and had evidently stayed there all night.

You emerge slowly from under the bed. There is the beginning of a grey morning light, but details of your surroundings are still shrouded in mystery. You lie on your back on the floor. This brings into focus the pipework, the ductwork, all up the walls and on the ceiling, which you have never really noticed before: at first, in your present confused state, you thought those structures were the preserved exoskeletons of alien creatures that had once lived behind the walls and had emerged during the night, only to die as soon as they were exposed. But that must have happened aeons ago. They must be long dead. You lie there, contemplating in awe. And then, as the light strengthens, you begin to see. It is just pipework and ductwork. Of an extraordinary beauty, nevertheless.

You are naked. It's as though you have just been born.

You have been having bad dreams, but can't recall their details.

It's still very warm.

The door of your room is wide open. This is unusual. Far away you can hear some people shouting.

You get slowly to your feet.

You call out, HELLO? No answer. Perhaps you imagined it. There is no shouting now, anyway. Nobody around. It is eerily quiet.

You put on your dark blue uniform. You venture out into the corridor. Rows of pod doors, all open. At the far end, the security door. It's shut. You go up to it. Can you remember which ways the staff members' fingers went in order to tap in the four-digit code? No need, it's unlocked. You push the door, and it opens.

There's the familiar poster depicting happy families, and the legend:

Interim Detention Facility
Passionate about your security

From nowhere a river of rage torrents through you. You leap upon the poster like a wild predator, snatching at it in a frenzy with your overgrown fingernails. It is impossible to shred, being made of a tough plastic material, but you manage to rip it off the wall, and then stamp on it repeatedly as it lies on the floor, stamp on the stupidly happy faces. This makes you feel a whole lot better.

You turn left down the corridor, the well-trodden direction towards the canteen. All deserted. Rows of empty tables. The kitchen area shuttered. The rage starts boiling up again. Another burst of energy: you run up and down the canteen overturning tables as you go. One, two, three ... let's see how many you can tip over. A fearful clattering. Stop. Stop. This is stupid. Do you really want to draw attention to yourself? Pull yourself together. Take a few deep breaths.

There is no sound after the echo of the last overturned table.

You have to get out of here. That's the main objective. So don't be stupid.

Panting heavily, you trot back out of the canteen, and back up the corridor. The poster on the floor. You do a rudimentary little paradiddle with your feet on it. The security door of your corridor is on your right. You trot past it and continue along the main corridor, your breath still wheezing. There are long windows on either side through which dull pearly light swims, but high up, too high to see through. And at the far end another security door, which says over it: EXIT.

That door also turns out to be unlocked. It gives onto a staircase. You tumble down it, crazily, hanging onto the banister. Where to now? Gloomy corridor right and left, much dingier here. You pick right. No windows, but dim electric lighting from somewhere, the walls painted beige, the floor covered in battered linoleum of no particular colour. And at the far end there's another door, its cream paint flaking. Above it is the international sign indicating an emergency exit. A little stick-man, running away. That's you. So you push on the bar. It's stuck. You rattle it. What's that? Can you hear something? Are there faint voices to be heard coming from somewhere, or is this in your head as usual? And suddenly, after one almighty push, the door gives way and you fall through.

You are in the open air at last. Or are you? There is a hint of a breeze here, but overhead a strip of what may or may not be the sky is grey, inscrutable. You are in a narrow yard between dirty yellow concrete walls, the one you have just emerged from immeasurably high and studded with small windows from a storey up, the one in front of you not quite so high but windowless. And there is a strong smell of damp. As if this space had once been filled with water. The floor is concrete, multiply stained. Please advance cautiously here. Right or left? Left. There seem to be stacks of building materials ahead. Voices? Yes? no? Further on, this canyon-like yard is piled high with engine parts, window frames, piles of bricks, bags of cement and sand (some torn open and leaking their contents), lengths of plastic guttering and other detritus. There must be some way out. But on it goes, endlessly curving before you, promising something it never delivers; its long, empty sections punctuated by areas stacked with junk. You are starting to get very tired.

Wait a minute. A door in the wall to your left. This could be it.

You spend fruitless minutes trying to open it. But after a while the truth dawns slowly in your befuddled brain. Because you look around you, and ahead. The same stacks of building materials. This is *the same door*, the one you emerged from, what, half an hour ago? Longer than that?

You have gone round in a circle, you have circumnavigated a circular ruin.

Weary now, you shuffle forward.

The whole thing is spinning, that vertigo business again. You have to stop, lean against the wall of the building. What is that, you try to focus.

In the opposite wall is a black door you never noticed in your first perambulation. It is covered in hieroglyphic graffiti evidently executed a long time ago with an aerosol can of white paint. It doesn't make any sense to you. Try it.

This door opens easily with a squeak, and you walk through into darkness.

The voices can still be heard. Are they louder or further away? Or are you talking to yourself? Also, a whining sound that ebbs and flows. What is that? And then sudden pain. Your foot has hit an obstruction. You can't see a damned thing in this constricted space. Inch forward. A square of light ahead. Your eyes are becoming accustomed. There are piles of earth or sand in the way, and other invisible obstacles to be negotiated. Inch towards the light. Stumble. Curse. You get down on your hands and knees and continue to venture, to crawl through. Spiderwebs tickle your face. You are at the exit. There is vegetation to be hacked away. You emerge in yellowish daylight into a large compound smelling strongly of animal urine. Concrete at the back of you. Open air! The voices can no longer be heard, it seems – though you are not sure of this. Tufts of rough grass grow between the uneven contours of the terrain, and in front there is a perimeter of high chain-link fencing surmounted by barbed wire. Beyond the fence mist obscures the view. For all you know, there may be a crowd of spectators on the other side of the fence silently watching your movements. Look, Mummy, there's one of the animals! It's very warm and slightly humid. Clouds overhead are parting, a pale glow of sunshine emerging. You have not seen the sun in … what, weeks? months?

The animal smell is pretty strong. You fear there may be dangerous creatures lurking close by, but there is no sound of any.

You explore the perimeter fence, which curves round. The ground is rough under your feet. The fencing is broken at only one point, where there is a gate secured by two heavy bolts, giving access to a stairway that seems to lead up to a bridge that spans this space. You are able to slide these bolts. Through you go, and up the steel steps that echo your tread, chain-link on either side. You arrive at yet another enclosed corridor, windowless but with grimy skylights above allowing in some illumination. Is it worth proceeding? Will it take you beyond the fenced compound?

At the far end there's an open door revealing a room, an abandoned office it looks like, daylight coming in through a single, frosted-glass window. A brown carpet on the floor, a familiar smell of disinfectant. An office chair. A bare pedestal desk. Nothing in the drawers. A metal, brown-and-beige filing cabinet, also, on inspection, empty. Beside it a door, the only other exit. Locked. A keypad. PLEASE ENTER YOUR 4-DIGIT PIN is printed on a small plastic panel above it.

You think you can hear the voices again here. They are louder indoors.

You try all the zeros and press the button. No result. You try 9999. No result.

You sit on the chair. You notice there is a CCTV camera high up in a corner of the room. You wonder if it is working. You no longer care about being seen, you just want to get out of here. You stand on tiptoe to look at it.

HELLO? you go. HELLO?

You sit down.

You try some more four-digit numbers. 1234, 4321, 5678, 8765. No result.

You are not feeling at all well.

You have a sudden urgent need to go to the toilet. No toilet here. You run back out of the room, back down the skylit corridor. Down the steel stairway, through the gate, into the compound. Only just in time. You take down your tracksuit trousers. You defecate copiously on the rocky floor in the shelter of the chain-link fencing. It's tough going after days of constipation, and at one point you think you are going to pass out, but you make it. That feels much better. You find some dried leaves on the ground with which to wipe yourself. You leave your trousers on the ground. It's really getting very hot. On your way back up the steel stairs you also discard your tracksuit top. The sun is beginning to bake through now. You are in your underpants and regulation issue T-shirt.

Back in the abandoned office, you try more PINs. You stand and wave both hands at the CCTV camera. HELLO? HELLO?

Time goes by. Perhaps you've fallen asleep in the chair (for how long?). Then you awake again with a start. A cricked neck. That smell of disinfectant. The heat. You've had bad dreams, but can't remember them. Voices, louder. You can just discern one: Fuck you, fuck you! it seems to be shouting.

You try more PINs. No luck.

Back in that yard, wasn't there an axe among the building materials? Or a hammer? Could you smash your way through the door? But although you're feeling better now, and your brain is working far better than it has for months, the thought of returning all the way to the yard to fetch an implement is too much for you.

So you try the numbers at random, punching four digits, pressing the button, punching, pressing. You look up again at the CCTV camera. Is anyone watching? Or has it been disconnected?

More four-digit numbers. Then, suddenly, a click.

The door is ajar. You tremble. This door must never be allowed to close again, because you can't recall with any confidence the number you just punched in at random. And you might want to come back through. You open it as far as it will go, stretch out for the chair, drag it across, wedge it open with the chair.

You go through.

Another corridor. The same brown carpet. The voices are a little louder here. Where are they coming from? Also, the whining noise. On the left are doors, perhaps to other rooms; you try one after another, but they are all locked. On the right, windows with frosted glass let in the light. You contemplate smashing one, but you have nothing to smash it with. Your fist? But if you cut yourself? Perhaps the chair, back there. But it's holding open the door in case of enforced retreat. You think about it.

If only you had brought the axe with you. If there was one in that yard. Or the hammer, or a spade, there surely was a spade. A brick is all you would have needed. But you weren't to know.

It's too late for regrets.

You have made some poor decisions. That's all there is to it.

You decide to press on to the end of the corridor, where an open doorway leads to a junction. To left and right, short passages lead to further doors. Ahead is a downward flight of concrete stairs, with a steel banister on which green paint is flaking.

Down you go.

Still the muffled voices. Are they louder or quieter?

Another flight, no windows. It gets dark here. You can't see. Is there a light switch?

Very faintly now: Fuck you, fuck you. FUCK YOU!

Feel the walls, up and down; they are slightly damp. A button to press. A dim overhead light flickers on. You are in a small hallway; ahead is a door with that international emergency exit sign above it: the little stick-man, running away, the perfect image of you. There is another horizontal metal bar, which you push on. You push and push, but can't budge the door.

The light goes out; it was on a timer.

You feel your way back to the light switch and press it again. On comes the dim, yellow-toned light. Back to the door, push, nothing. Push. How can this be an emergency exit? This *is* an emergency, surely. Light goes out. Repeat the process.

Push. Was that some movement?

You are very tired.

Push. Light goes out. One big effort.

The door gives way suddenly, and you stagger into a bigger space, also dimly lit, partly artificially, partly from high fanlights. There is a mingled smell of damp and petroleum. The voices can't be heard so clearly here, but the high-pitched whine has increased in volume, dynamics wavering between unpleasant and unbearable and back again. You seem to be in a garage or underground car park; there are twelve numbered parking bays, marked out in yellow paint, arranged six on each side, huge pillars between them. But no vehicles. The exit is blocked by a great rolled steel shutter. No way through that. You look for implements, tools, anything, but there is nothing here.

HELLO? you shout during a lull, and your voice echoes. Then the whine increases in volume again.

You can't bear this any more. Exhausted, you squat on the concrete floor with your hands over your head. You remain there for some time.

Day 25

You look up. How long have you been asleep? Where are you? What awakened you, was it human voices? Is someone coming? Is the nurse arriving for your injection? You listen, huddled on the floor. Nothing. Just a whining sound. Where in hell are you? What is that gnawing feeling inside of you, what is that nasty feeling in your mouth and throat? You identify the feelings at last: you are very hungry and very thirsty.

You look up again. You are beginning to remember. You are escaping. What from? Where to? There are dark patches on the floor, spent oil perhaps. Where they catch the light from a fanlight they separate out into beautiful colours, forms like serpents that intertwine intricately. You are fascinated.

You try to take slow, deep breaths. You look around, and up. No way out from here apart from that steel-shuttered exit. Near the ceiling, the fanlights allow in a grey illumination that scarcely modifies the dim, artificial lighting, but they are far too high to reach, and there is no ladder or any other means of getting there.

Right next to the door you have emerged from (you remember that now) is a large paint can. You get up, walk over to it, pick it up. Its lid is encrusted with dried paint, it's quite heavy: perhaps half full. An idea comes to you: you could take it back with you, retrace your steps until you reach an accessible window, and use the can as an implement to smash it.

Could you retreat from here? A brief, cold thought: did that emergency exit door shut behind you? No, it's still ajar. Wedge it with the paint can for now.

So that's a plan. You *are* capable of learning lessons.

The whining comes and goes.

You think about it.

You pace around the perimeter of the garage. But hey, there *is* a door. You can't believe you missed it. Exactly behind one of the massive pillars, so it was hidden from view at first. It has a rusted lock, and the key is in it. You try this. It creaks, the handle turns and the door opens. You laugh out loud.

You're through, into the open air once more, a slight breeze in a space flooded by cold, bitter light. But it's not sunlight.

Evening must be coming on. The sky is grey. But four tall floodlights shine on a tennis court. The door you have just come out of is set in the featureless concrete wall of a tall building. The other three sides of the court are formed of a high chain-link fence.

Such a relief that the whining, the voices, have vanished.

You laugh.

What is that, at the side of the concrete wall? A tap! You fall upon it. Turn it. Have you enough strength left in your wrists, your fingers? It's stuck; then abruptly turns, and a stream of water gushes out onto the ground. You fall upon the water. You drink and drink avidly, you let the water pour over your face, run down your neck, pool on the ground.

You laugh.

Sitting on the ground, recovering, you see that the tennis court is in bad shape. The concrete surface is bumpy, cracked, with weeds beginning to push through; the markings have faded; there is a net in place but it's ragged, with large holes in it, perhaps having been chewed by animals. Every imperfection is harshly illuminated by the flood-lights.

The silence is broken by sudden birdsong.

A blackbird alights on a net-post, then swiftly hops onto the ground. It pecks and hops.

Tears well up in your eyes. This is the first non-human living creature you have seen.

It hops away, spreads its wings, flies high into the dusk and is seen no more.

Silence.

Silence, except for the faint rustling of branches. Outside the fence, some of their branches surmounting it and even beginning to hang over the enclosed space, are thick, entangled, dark trees. Nothing is to be seen beyond this.

Refreshed, you leap around the court, waving an imaginary racket, executing imaginary ground strokes just as you've seen people do, forehand, backhand, then, with a flourish, a volley, a winner. And then, miraculously, you have a real racket in your right hand, and a luminous yellow ball in your left. But nobody to play with. Here's what you do, you bat the ball high into the air, a huge lob, then race round the net just in time to receive it on the other side. The idea is to lob it up again, then nip back round the net again. See how long you can keep that up. Several attempts, partial success. You manage to do it twice in a row, then the third time, frantically, you get your racket beneath the ball but you put too much whack on it; it sails high, high into the air and over the chain-link fence, and that's the end of that. But did you actually have a racket? That seems to have disappeared too.

You laugh.

This sudden activity makes you tired, so you sit on the ground again for a bit.

You could try climbing the fence. You grasp the stout linked wires with your fingers. Impossible to do more than lift yourself momentarily off the ground. That's madness. Hang on, though. In the corner of the court to the left of the door you came out through is a gate. How can you miss such things? You are so stupid. So stupid. The bolt is rusted but slides open. Now you're in business.

This gate leads to a narrow path of broken, weed-ridden tarmac between high brick walls. It gets increasingly dark as you leave the floodlit court behind you.

Listen. The hoot of an owl. Or was it?

Silence.

HELLO? you shout.

Silence.

Creep slowly. You don't know what's ahead. The ground is rough under your feet. Night gathers. It's not as warm as it was. You wonder what happened to your tracksuit. You have a dim memory of having discarded it somewhere.

Where are you going?

You don't know.

You are in what seems to be an abandoned garden. It's too dark to see properly. It's wildly overgrown, and enclosed all round by a fence or hedge. You cannot go on much longer like this. You are a little chilled now. You trip over, suddenly you are on the ground, your fall broken by some bushes. It's comfortable here. You are asleep again.

And you sleep. Out like a light. No dreams.

There is a grey dawn. Birds chirruping.

You hear from afar what may be human voices. You long for them. You don't care about escaping any more, you have forgotten what you are escaping from and have no idea where you are making for. The voices appear to be coming from the grey brick house with shuttered windows that has appeared in front of you. Three steps up to a massive green door. On the right-hand door jamb is a grille with a button below it. You press the button. Nothing happens.

You press the button. HELLO? you shout into the grille.

There are definitely voices audible, apparently in conversation. Are they coming from the grille? It's hard to say.

HELLO? You press the button.

Voices continue.

You press the button.

It brings tears to your eyes to hear human voices again. You press the button. There is a buzzing noise. You push on the door, and it opens.

All at once, the voices become louder. You are in a hallway: polished floorboards shining in the illumination from the fanlight above the door; white, featureless walls.

The voices go: Fuck you, fuck you.

HELLO?

Fuck you, fuck you, fuck you. Just shut the fuck up. SHUT the fuck UP!

Where are they? You would give anything for human company of any kind. Your greatest desire is to join them. Perhaps your presence would have a calming effect on them. Are the voices coming from behind the door on the right? It's not clear. You rattle the doorknob, but this door is locked fast. Ahead, at the far end of the hall, facing the front door, is a carpeted staircase.

You ascend, step by step, stopping to listen at each step. It's not clear whether the voices are fading or returning.

A half-landing; and then at the top landing, a locked door on either side, and in front of you a pair of swing doors with glass panels. So you try them, and they push open easily onto a long passageway stretching before you, its end hard to make out, and flanked on either side by another series of frosted glass windows.

The voices seem to follow you into the passageway.

You are done with sensible escape strategies. All you want to do is break windows. The more you break, the freer you will be. Hey! Your memory has been rebooted and is working magnificently now. Here's what you could do: you could retrace your steps as far as the car park, retrieve the half-full paint can and use it to break the glass.

What an excellent plan.

Down the stairs you go. This is quite exciting. You have a purpose now. You open the front door. But will it remain open? It seems to have a tendency to close of its own accord. There is no guarantee that you will be let in again.

There, revealed in early the morning light, is the overgrown garden in front of you.

You experiment with the front door. If you are careful, it can remain just ajar without clicking shut. You just have to hope a slight puff of wind doesn't move it.

You leave it resting ajar while you tiptoe down the three steps to the garden. The voices are muffled out here. Past the undergrowth in which you slept. You re-enter the narrow pathway between the high brick walls. You come to the tennis court gate. You go through into the tennis court. Although there is now daylight, the four floodlights are still on. You pass along the concrete wall until you come to the door. So far so good. You pull open the door, and find yourself in the dim space of the car park. Here the voices again assail you, together with the wavering, high-pitched tone. Twelve parking bays, no vehicles. There is the paint can propping ajar the emergency door. Excitedly, you grab the can. Immediately, the emergency door clicks shut.

That was a mistake. Now that retreat option has been closed off.

You have made some poor decisions.

Never mind. All now depends on your present plan.

You carry the paint can across the floor of the car park

and out through the door. The voices and the whining sound are muffled. You carry it along the perimeter of the tennis court, through the gate, and along the path between the high brick walls. You enter the overgrown garden, and carry it up the steps to the door of the building, which you are relieved to be able to push open. You go through into the hall with the can, whose weight is beginning to hurt your fingers, and up the stairs.

The voices are again audible from somewhere within the building: No, fuck you. Shut up. Shut the fuck up. You recognise those voices, they are so familiar, but from where?

Quickly, you cross the landing and push open the doors to the long, windowed passageway. The voices follow you. You put the can down. There are two series of large, frosted glass panes, one on either side, sealed shut. You select one on the right. You lift the can, and swing it against the glass. It takes considerable effort, and you don't have much strength left. At the second attempt, the glass shatters. Large fragments fall out. You swing a third time. On this occasion, you lose control of the paint can as it hits another pane; it flies from your fingers, crashes through the glass and disappears. You expect to hear a thud as it hits the ground, but you don't.

There is a jagged, gaping hole where two panes of glass had been.

You look out. What you see is light-grey sky between two buildings. You look down; you behold a vertiginous canyon. Far below, perhaps forty or fifty feet beneath you, is a narrow yard between the two buildings that have been bridged by this passageway, and in the shadow at the bottom, between a group of wheelie bins, you can just see the paint can at rest in its final destination. It has burst open on impact with the ground and a star of paint, whose colour you can hardly discern, radiates from it.

You have made some poor decisions.

Day 26

DON'T TOUCH THE jagged edges of the glass. Keep away from them. What in hell were you trying to do there? Is your brain functioning in any meaningful way?

No, you seem to be disorientated.

You run to the far end of the passageway, followed all the way by those terribly familiar voices.

Here, there is another pair of swing doors with glass panels inset. You push them open. The voices are unbearable.

You run back along the passageway, past the shattered glass on your left-hand side, all the way back to the first pair of swing doors. Then you turn round and run all the way back, uttering little whoops and shrieks.

You do this several times. Back and forth, back and forth, along the raised passageway that links the two buildings, whooping and shrieking the while. There, you feel better again.

You stop at the shattered window and peer outside at the concrete floor far below, with the star of paint. Perhaps you could scramble through the jagged opening you have made and throw yourself down. That would be a convenient end to it all.

That would be a plan.

You move on slowly to the far swing doors, push them open and walk through.

The voices are unbearable: No, shut the fuck up. No, SHUT THE FUCK UP.

And the whining noise has also returned, ebbing and flowing.

This seems to be some kind of waiting room, with a padded bench on either side, fixed to the vinyl-clad floor, but no other furnishings or adornments. The smell here is a familiar one: disinfectant.

You sit down on one of the benches. Elbows on knees, you cradle your head in your hands.

The voices and the whining continue, interminably. The sound must be coming from behind the door you can see. A plain, white door, and a thread of light shining all around the rim.

You take your courage in your hands. You get up, stride over, turn the knob and open the door.

At once, the noise ceases.

You are looking at a brightly lit, windowless room, a medical facility of some kind, with two or three hospital-style trolley beds, their thin mattresses covered by sheets; cupboards lining the walls, some glass-fronted, displaying within them ranks of bottles and cartons; rows of drawers; and computer screens on shelves.

A middle-aged man in blue hospital scrubs has stopped in the act of wheeling a large steel contraption across the floor, and on one of the beds, legs crossed, sits an elegant young woman in a black knee-length cocktail dress and black court shoes, her blond hair swept up off her neck. They have both turned to stare at you in astonishment.

They do not move.

Hello? you stammer apologetically.

They stare at you. They seem frightened.

In a panic, you retreat, slamming the door behind you.

They were startled by your appearance, it's only natural. You are in your underclothes, after all, probably filthy too, you have appeared as if from nowhere.

All you have to do is explain. That's all you have to do.

But what can you say?

You compose yourself.

After a moment, you open the door again.

The room is exactly as it was, harshly revealed by fluorescent lighting – except that the cupboards and shelves are empty. And there is nobody in here.

You stumble around, looking everywhere, not sure what you are looking for, aimlessly opening cupboard after cupboard. The voices begin again, a murmur. You are scared. You make for a curtained opening, which leads to another, almost identical, brightly lit room: empty cupboards, empty drawers hanging open, and on the floor a litter of glass bottles and jars, hypodermic syringes, some broken. You pick your way through them.

HELLO?

Another abandoned room and yet another, a maze of them, desks, chairs, cupboards, and the voices getting louder again, nothing but obscenities, repeating and repeating, and the whine too, beginning to rise in pitch, you no longer have any sense of trajectory or orientation, corridors and rooms, rooms and corridors, glass partitions, curtains coming off their runners, the same vinyl flooring, the same muted colours everywhere, and then yet another shut door, or was that the first one you came to, it's all most confusing, behind which are yet more voices, or, to be more specific now, a harsh male voice going: SUCK ON THIS! SUCK ON THIS! and you open the door to behold a middle-aged man in blue hospital scrubs, the trousers down, the member erect, with a large shiny gun in his hand whose barrel he has thrust into the scarlet mouth of the young woman who is on her knees, the black cocktail dress crumpled on the floor beside her but still in her black court shoes, her eyes blank, wide open, whereupon he pulls the trigger ... and you slam the door shut in horror and keel over, dumbstruck, but when you come to, the door has swung open again and there is nobody in there; and then suddenly it comes to you like a monstrous insight, exactly why those voices are so familiar, because there is actually only one voice, there has only ever been one voice answering itself endlessly, it is none other than *your* voice, shouting SHUT THE FUCK UP SHUT THE FUCK UP SHUT THE FUCK UP, stop, you think, stop stop, the voices stop, you stop. At last, a bit of peace.

In one room you find an empty full-length cupboard, in which you try to hide, but the door won't shut properly.

In another room there is a steel trolley-bed with a plastic-covered mattress, on which you fling yourself and lie face down.

After a while, you discover that you can propel this trolley along by the expedient of dangling one leg down and pushing your foot against the floor.

You propel yourself in this fashion all the way out of the room and into a corridor flanked by glass partitions. It is quite hard to steer.

You push and push. The trolley trundles.

The corridor turns left at a right angle. You manoeuvre your vehicle round.

The corridor starts to slope down at a gentle gradient. You find that you only need an occasional light push with your foot to maintain the vehicle's momentum.

It is a very long corridor.

The trolley bed gains momentum. This is fun. You yell in delight.

Faster and faster rolls the trolley. You scream and whoop in delight. You whoop and shriek. You realise that you are completely out of control.

You are clinging on desperately.

The end is approaching. You put your right arm up to fend it off.

The trolley slams into a door at the end of the corridor.

You arm hits the door. You bounce off.

You are in pain.

There is pain.

Your right arm hurts very much. There is also blood. Perhaps you have broken it.

Somehow, you get to your feet. You open the door with your left hand.

It's dark here. You stumble forward, feeling your way.

It is as dark as a cellar. The voices and the ambient sound are absent, which is a great relief.

You can make out another door in front of you. Open it with your left hand.

Another corridor, terribly familiar though. Why?

And it's so hot in here.

You are in what seems to be an abandoned factory. The pipework and ductwork is of an extraordinary beauty. On the floor, beside the door is a discarded poster that has evidently been ripped from the wall. There are those happy-looking men, women and children of various ethnic origins. And the familiar words

Interim Detention Facility
Passionate about your security

Rage starts to well up in you once more. You trample the poster yet again, you point your head at the ceiling and roar like an aged lion. You rage against the ditch into which you have once more been pitched; you rage against the obscure machinery of management that has conspired to thieve your life; against the bleak country that seemed so welcoming in prospect, on whose shores you have been finally abandoned; against the talking fire that is humanity, scouring the world from end to end and leaving nothing but ashes; against life itself, a disgusting plague that infects the universe, and, since you're inescapably a part of that universe, that infects you too with its unavoidable contagion.

Your arm hurts very much. There is nobody about who can help you. There is nobody about at all.

Your arm hurts very much. There is superficial blood, but also it's beginning to swell and you've obviously sustained some internal injury. You can no longer put any weight on it.

You have made some poor decisions.

Day 27

IN THE MIDST of this long prequel, it may be time to return briefly to the present day. Are you still there? Are you still lying quietly in your bed, apparently in your own flat? Just checking. Yes, you are, as you have been for – well, nearly four weeks now. It still doesn't seem as though anyone has noticed. The world seems to have forgotten you. And look at the state you're in. It's not good news, on the face of it. You're not looking good. This is the stage of bacterial decay. Well, nothing to be done for now, let us return to the situation you found yourself in, four weeks ago: after all that business, nowhere but right back where you started.

To recap: you have made some poor decisions. Have you calmed down yet? No, not really – well, it's not surprising. But you have collected yourself enough to realise once again that this feeling of unwellness you've been perceiving within yourself for most of the past day is in fact a vast and profound hunger.

You stumble down the silent corridor in the direction you remember where the canteen could be found. There's the familiar door; you open it.

A scene of disorder presents itself to you: all the tables within your field of vision have been overturned, and the chairs are scattered to all corners of the room. Someone has been rampaging. Who has done this, and why? But never mind: can anything be found here?

The serving area is pristine, gleaming and denuded of food and food products. The kitchen area has been closed off. But if you nip round the counter you can find the cupboards where the confectionery is kept. You eyes light up. You fall upon piles of bags of crisps and other salt-based snacks, bars of chocolate and suchlike, the kind of things you could have bought with the plastic tokens earned from your hard work in that lecture theatre. You tear open bags and wrappers, you devour their contents one after the other. Next, you assuage your thirst by opening the sink tap, sticking your head in there and slurping it all up for a minute or two.

Now you are feeling nauseous. And exhausted, of course.

You stumble out of the canteen and towards the humid corridor you once called your home. All the doors are open. There it is: Pod Eight Forty Two. All yours. The bed is unbearably enticing. You tear off your filthy underclothes, kick off the regulation trainers that are beginning to fall to bits and fling yourself upon it. Seconds later you are dead to the world.

You sleep and sleep for hours. There are no dreams.

Awake suddenly. It's completely dark now. It must be the middle of the night. Or is it? What was that sound that awakened you?

Ah, that must be the nurse arriving to give you your morning injection. A bit early.

No, no. She doesn't appear. But there are definite, consistent sounds that were not there before. They appear to come from far away, but they are getting closer. Not the nurse, wait a minute, what's that?

What you don't realise is that there will never be another nurse, there will never be another injection.

You are not feeling very well at all, lying there in your bed sweating in the dark.

Suddenly you sit bolt upright. Fear has gripped you.

They're coming back!

What you can hear are bumps and scrapes, gradually getting louder, large items being manoeuvred perhaps, doors being opened and shut, and footsteps, lots of them, and with them a low hubbub of voices, also getting progressively louder, the occasional shout, perhaps someone giving an order, penetrating the general murmur. You fancy you can even recognise some of the voices, which belong to the attendants. They are coming out of everywhere, they and their avatars, perhaps exuding from the fabric of the building itself, wherein they have been banished by the emergency; they are taking form once again, regaining their old shapes, re-emerging into the world of the living.

They're coming back!

The horror you feel is indescribable. You leap out of bed, run to the door of your room. The noises are louder here.

In absolute terror and panic, you run out into the corridor. You run down the corridor to the security door. You are completely naked. The sounds of people returning seem to emanate from the direction of the canteen. Fear overrides your exhaustion. Blindly, you run in the opposite direction. Only dim security lights illuminate your way. The corridor seems to go on forever. But finally you reach the security door at the far end, the one labelled with an illuminated EXIT sign. Through that, and on to the staircase. The noises seem to be fainter behind you. Are you winning? You tumble down the stairs holding on to the banister for dear life. You have a vague memory of having done this before. At the bottom, there is a gloomy corridor to right and left. Some unimaginable instinct tells you to pick left. You picked right before, and it didn't work out in the end, but you won't remember that. The same walls painted beige, the same floor covered in battered linoleum of no particular colour, and then a door at the far end, above which is the international sign indicating an emergency exit, the little stick-man. Quick, push. It's stuck. The voices, the other ominous sounds, are starting to sound nearer again. Suddenly the door gives way and you fall through.

Last time, you found yourself in an enclosed yard. But now, well, it looks like you are in the open air, proper open air.

It's a street, quite deserted. You can make out buildings, mostly dark, and, where there is a gap, a line of corrugated iron fencing. A street lamp provides some orange illumination. It feels like a warm summer's night, very pleasant, almost balmy you might say. You can see a quarter moon in the sky, and also the tiny lights of an aircraft moving slowly above the horizon. You venture out onto the pavement, which is rough beneath your bare feet. Your breathing is laboured. You start to walk. There is nobody about. You continue to walk.

You find yourself on another street. Still nobody around. A zebra crossing, orange Belisha beacons alternately winking on and off. You hear the sound of a vehicle approaching. You retreat into the shadow.

It is a London double-decker bus, merrily ablaze with light. A night bus. And to your amazement you recognise the number and the destination. It is a route you have frequently taken. It goes past your home. Let that sink in: it goes past your home! Tears spring from your eyes.

Well, you can't actually catch the bus. You have nothing on you – literally. But if you could follow the route?

You set off. You walk and walk. The paving stones are warm beneath your naked feet.

The dark, fitfully illuminated streets go by peacefully.

It's a beautiful summer night, after all. But with the scent of dampness in the air. The metropolis is a sleeping beast. It makes its own music, which has travelled from deep within it; there are sounds in that ocean that no human has ever heard. There are noise clusters, there are chilling microtones and sweet harmonies in equal measure. The rain has held off. There are bridges to go under. There are intersections to cross. Rubbish has accumulated by the side of the street: a sad kitchen cabinet, crumbling, an old standard lamp, a burnt-out vacuum cleaner. A pile of bathroom fittings and other debris has been left on some shrubbery in a vacant lot. Lamplight reveals mysterious, hermetic messages scrawled in spray paint across the fencing. They mean what they are. Further on are grey, ultramarine and orange glass buildings, all of them empty, mirroring an empty world. They are superb palaces of artifice. They hold the light through the darkness: Lux Aeterna. These are sites of warring tribes that are now briefly at rest. The route passes a yard wherein three vans, in states of disrepair, are almost submerged in detritus of various kinds: bricks, planks, rusting tools, traffic cones, rubble. You walk under a dense vertical forest of scaffolding. An architecture of shadows. Unseen in a warm dark garden nearby, a cat betrays its presence by a faint tinkle from its collar bell, a familiar and comforting sound in the stillness. There are further gardens behind railings, where the great dim forms of plane trees move their limbs slowly, and beyond that you can hear the vixen scream. The sound of a piano somewhere, the hint of jazz chords. Shadows through steam. Even now, birdsong can be heard somewhere. Another cat scurries across the road, the only other living being to be seen. Tomorrow will of course be just another day. Tomorrow the beast will reawaken, the great masses will start to emerge, will busy themselves with their doing this and their doing that, their queuing, their immersion in their electronic devices, the stepping of their millions of feet onto moving vehicles, their faces lowered. Tomorrow morning there will be coffee to take away. Tomorrow morning brunch will be served in the executive lounge (steak, bacon, sausage, scrambled eggs, coffee and Bucks Fizz) before the main event of the day.

But if one were to venture out on that particular route within the metropolis, at the right point at the right time, which is anywhere between three and four in the morning, a relatively brief window when nobody is about, and if one were to make especially sure to look out for it, one would behold the sight of an elderly man, completely naked from head to toe, completely alone, walking resolutely through the streets, looking neither to right nor left.

Rapid crescendo of a siren. A police car approaches at speed, blue lights flashing madly. A screech of brakes as it reaches the junction, then after the briefest of pauses it veers sharply to the right and accelerates away into a side street, where its scream gradually fades into the distance.

It does not therefore encounter the naked man, who continues unconcerned, as though a halo of invincibility surrounds him.

He marches on briskly, not absolutely steadily – wavering a little in fact in his trajectory – but nevertheless with an overall sense of purpose, a manifest fixation on a given endpoint. Yes, he is poor, he is bare, he is forked. He seems to be dark-skinned, slight of build, with thinning, straggly grey hair, and if anyone were to get up close, which nobody does, it would be seen that sweat is running down his lean, denuded, crumpled torso and his spindly limbs right down to his skeletal, splayed toes pressing again and again on the tarmac, running down in miniature rivulets that shine under the street lamps, emitting a pungent but not altogether unpleasant odour; that his eyes are dark pools that cannot be fathomed, that there is a little froth on his lips; that he's unshaven and wears a kind of grimace on his face, like one who approaches the final stages of an urban marathon, but without companions, without the urging of a roadside crowd. If there are any witnesses at all they will have melted away into the night. Because anyone happening by chance to catch sight of him would likely be consumed by shock and fear, he will never be challenged; because he self-evidently has no means of concealing any wealth or trinkets or electronic devices about his person, he is completely unassailable. On he goes. There is a rumble behind him, and a second night bus passes him, the same route number as before, which must mean, since this is an hourly service, that he has been walking for about an hour now, but he pays absolutely no heed to it, continuing to stare fixedly ahead with the utmost concentration.

The naked black man is holding his right arm; he seems to be in some pain.

Now he is running, is he? Well, he is definitely starting to trot, and the trot is beginning to transform into a run. This is because he has recognised where he is. He has looked about him and spied some familiar landmarks. At first, he can't quite believe it, but as the elements of his neighbourhood begin to assemble themselves, he gains rapidly in confidence, and therefore in strength. And in pace.

He believes he's going home, he *is* going home, and suddenly, out of nowhere, he speaks – I'm coming home! shouts it, rather, but in a hoarse voice, not too loudly at first, then repeats with more volume, offering this insight to anyone who may be able to hear, which is no-one.

The strength he has gained is enough to counteract the unwellness that has been lurking within him for a while, the pain in his arm. And now, as he enters the familiar high street, the shops all shut and slumbering, of course, but all in the same places he remembers, he begins to sing, to the tune of a half-remembered football song:

I'm coming home, I'm coming home, I'm coming,

Hey! I'm coming home!

And there, in front and to the right, are the arrowhead railings that delineate the boundaries of the park whose diagonal path, the one he has traversed so often, lies within, shrouded in peaceful darkness.

I'm coming home, I'm coming home, I'm coming,
Whoa! I'm coming home!

He runs and runs. He doesn't care by now if anyone hears or sees him; the naked running man has been transported to a place of sanctuary made of dark shadows and yellow light, of industrial aromas and squeaky noises. He is nearing the end of his journey.

Day 28

YOU REACH THE front door of your building. There it is, the same as ever – as though you had never left. Another four-digit code is required to get into the building; but this is one you have in your muscle memory; you wouldn't even recall it if you were prompted, but nevertheless you know it as well as a C major chord, your fingers tap it out, and you're in.

The familiar hallway with the familiar smell, the familiar stairs. Push the time switch, the light comes on.

Up the stairs to your very own front door.

You have no key, of course. Look under the doormat, heart in your mouth. And there it nestles shining and undisturbed, where you have always left it.

You fit the key into your lock, and enter. The door needs a bit of a push. That, it turns out, is because a pile of junk mail has accumulated behind it. Apart from that, all is as before, all is as it was and as it should be.

And you got here completely unescorted.

You lean against the inside of your front door. You've been overcome, you haven't even had time to switch on the light. You have a feeling you are going to pass out, to collapse onto the floor. Emotions, or their physical manifestations, swim through your body, wave after wave. Minutes pass. It's so beautifully quiet. No sign of anybody in here, neither your people nor those other people (you shudder). A bit stuffy, but you don't mind that. You steady yourself. You're beginning to get over it now. You have survived the shock. In the darkness of your little entrance lobby all that can clearly be seen is the red pulse of your answerphone light. Eleven is the illuminated number, winking on and off endlessly. You have eleven messages to return.

You stumble to the bathroom, snap on the light. You look at your face in the mirror. You don't recognise it. A haunted, drained thing it is, covered in grey stubble. The eyes like windows into elsewhere. You turn on the hot tap in the basin. The water runs cold over your hands for some minutes, then gradually begins to warm up. So the boiler is still working. Supporting yourself with your good arm against the wall, you manage to get to the shower. You manage to get the shower going. It's warm. You step in. You drench yourself. It's very difficult doing everything with only your left arm and hand effectively functioning. You grab the towel that's still hanging there, try to dab yourself dry all over. This is exhausting.

The bedroom. You're still damp. Your puddly footmarks. On the floor beside the bed lies, crumpled, the baggy old T-shirt you wear in bed. With difficulty, you gather it, put it on. Your right arm is throbbing badly. You slide your feet into your slippers. You shuffle to the kitchen. Unbearable hunger. Open the fridge door, the light pours out from it. Not much in here. A slab of cheese still in its half-opened plastic packaging, a green bloom of mould on it. Manage to hold it down painfully with your right hand, scrape the greenery off with a knife in the other. Wolf down the residue, cramming chunks into your mouth. Fill the kettle at the sink, switch it on. While that's doing, look in the cupboard. Some tins. Baked beans, that'll do. It has a ring-pull, so you're able to get the tin open, wouldn't have fancied your chances one-handed with an opener. Set the small saucepan on the hob, pour in the beans, heat up. This is so good. Milk for the tea? No good, the carton in the fridge is clogged with sour-smelling sludge. Have to drink it black. Where are the tea bags? right here. While all this is doing, have a listen to the phone messages.

1. A bright young female voice: Ah, hello Mr [SURNAME], this is a courtesy call from Water Treatment, this is Tracy speaking. We came to see you the other day to discuss details of your treatment plan, I wonder whether you've had a chance to consider our estimate, if so, just give us a call on....

2. The voice of doom: Hello, Father Fuck here. Are you available to speak, Mr [SURNAME]? Are you there? No? Well, I just called to see how you were, as we hadn't met for a while, and to, er, invite you to one of our community services and coffee mornings here at the parish church next week ... but perhaps I had better call again, or maybe you would be so kind as to call back if you're interested. Thank you.

3. Another voice of doom – you recognise The Raven: Uh, Mr [SURNAME]? It's the Freeholder here. I wonder whether you've had the chance to consider our offer for your lease, which we outlined in a letter to you dated 18th February. You may be aware that another lessee is making spurious offers for leaseholds in this block and has also been making false statements about ourselves, so we would advise you to be very careful in this regard. Our offer is genuine, and, I think you will find, gives very advantageous terms. If you are interested, please respond by phone or email – the contact details are on our letterhead.

4. The bright young woman again: Hello Mr [SURNAME], this is a courtesy call from Water Treatment. We haven't yet had your response to our estimate for your water treatment

plan. We have some good news, there will be a further, exclusive ten per cent discount on the package you are considering, provided we have your response before the end of this week. So just give me a call back if you're interested. It's Tracy.

5. Male, Indian accent: Hello, I would like to speak to Mr [SURNAME]. Is regarding your internet.... [cut off]

6. Very bad line, almost indecipherable: [FORENAME]? Hello? ... [completely indecipherable] ... collect my belongings ... sorry ... *(Is that BJ? Is that BJ's voice? But it is cut off abruptly.)*

7. Father Fuck here: God hates you, [FORENAME] [SURNAME]! God damns you to everlasting torment! *(But this is your paraphrase of a long and convoluted message, almost indecipherable because of a bad line. Also perhaps Father Fuck has been at the communion wine, or more likely the whisky, for his delivery is considerably slurred.)*

8. Hi, is that [FORENAME] [SURNAME]? Mr [SURNAME], this is Water Treatment, we are giving you an opportunity to complete a short survey over the phone regarding the quality of the service you've received from our representatives. You will be asked to grade our performance on a scale between one and ten, to help us monitor how we are serving our customers' needs. And the good news is that if you take part you will be eligible to be entered into our prize draw to win some exclusive prizes. If you would like to respond, please call us back on....

9. The Raven again: Uh, good evening, Mr [SURNAME], this is the Freeholder. I understand that you may have sold the

leasehold of your flat to Mr Jackson, is that correct? I hope that is not the case, as we are of the opinion that this would be a very bad move. Please call us back or email to clarify the position, but if this is not the case please be assured that our own offer is still on the table.

10. The Raven, a third time: Good evening, Mr [SURNAME], the Freeholder here. We have now been given to understand that Mr Jackson, to whom you may or may not have been in the process of selling your leasehold, is recently deceased. I don't know whether you completed the sale or not, but obviously this complicates the position. Please contact us urgently to clarify. Thank you.

11. Hello, Father Fuck here, Mr [SURNAME]. Please ignore my last message. This was a misunderstanding. You are very welcome to our coffee morning, but I will speak to you again.

This is all very confusing and upsetting. But it's not worth worrying about. You are home. That's the main thing. You have now finished your tea without milk: hot, sweet and welcome. You are feeling a bit better, but very sleepy. Tomorrow will undoubtedly be another day. You'll be all right in the morning, you tell yourself.

Actually, according to your clock, it is now nearly four in the morning. You have only a vague idea what part of the year has been reached; but the indications are it will be light soon.

Wearing your baggy T-shirt of no colour, you retire to bed, but not before removing the dentures that have begun to feel uncomfortable in your mouth, and dunking them in the usual tumbler filled with water from the kitchen tap. From your supine position, head propped by the pillows, you grab the remote control and switch on the TV that sits in the corner of your bedroom. You stare at the coloured, moving lights that constitute the TV picture. Hard to make anything of this after all this time. You should have that right forearm seen to. It's no longer bleeding, the blood is now crusted. But it hurts. Maybe you've broken it. Do you have some paracetamol in the bathroom cupboard? You are too tired now to contemplate getting up again, going to the bathroom, pouring another glass of water. Also, it's a bit close – not as bad as the ... the place before ... but still ... could do with opening a window. Ah, never mind. The comfort of your bed trumps everything, including pain. So let it pass. You'll deal with it tomorrow. On the hour, a news bulletin interrupts the show. There seems to be some political crisis. The news is that the government has fallen. Which government was that? A pop star of whom you have never heard has died, and is mourned by millions. Millions more are starving. God is grinning and giggling in his lair.

Your eyelids can no longer support their own weight, and begin to droop: a fall from which there will now be no recovery. The TV still burbling away in the corner, you drift off to sleep.

Day 29

LITTLE BIRDS HUM and pipe, they hop and bob, they inhabit your peaceful head – if only they could come to greet you, to perch on your spidery fingers, partaking of titbits. That is what they used to do.

The island was full of noises. Where music came from.

Since your eyelids were first prised gummily open and began to take in what they saw you never stopped learning. You were taught the names. Warblers, flycatchers, finches, hummingbirds, swallows, woodpeckers, tanagers, orioles, nightjars, vireos, blackbirds, and also doves, parrots, cuckoos, owls, hawks, vultures, not to mention herons, pelicans, frigate birds, gulls and albatrosses. The hummingbird, the only bird that can fly backwards. Sapphire and emerald, flash of chrome. The warblers' songs bridging geographies. The mad cries of the gulls.

The island was full of crevices and hideouts of all kinds, where you spent most of your time, either on your own or with your cousins, who filled the spaces with their laughter and the drumming and dancing of their feet. The clock in the hall chimed the hour and the quarter-hour and the half-hour and the three-quarters-hour. The one your father used to wind, in the cool quiet of the house. And the smell of furniture polish on the piano. Your little hands used to dance on the keys, up and down, playing boogie-woogie, you had a knack for it, your father exclaimed, the kid's got it, he's got it. You picked it up and you took it away, you took off with it. What was *it*, you didn't have to ask. I can't teach him no more, your father said, delighted, but after a while he wasn't there anyway. Your mother cared for you. There was always someone. It was your Uncle Charlie who taught you to play cricket, on the beach with your other cousins, a trio of wooden stumps at one end of the sandy pitch, a single one at the other, a rubber ball he bowled at you, and you were slower picking that up, but one time when your cousin was bowling you whacked it, you really connected, and up it sailed into the blue sky, and Uncle Charlie, fielding at long off, that is to say, with his feet in the surf, had to plunge into the sea and swim out a short distance to retrieve it from where it bobbed on the waves.

And your father, before he vanished from your life, who had taught you the names of the birds, before he disappeared forever, promised to take you to see the seals on their island, because they were disappearing too, a vanquished tribe they were, who lived on the margin until they could live no more. You really wanted to see them; I'll take you one day, he said.

But the great storm surge swept all that away.

A five-barred gate, and through you went into England, into a pleasant grove of sweet chestnuts, where birds chattered, heavenly scents wafted, you needed to be careful not to lose the path, here was a stile and you were in open rolling countryside with the sun shining on it, a skylark twittered in its column of air, the distant thrum of a tractor, the thwack of willow on leather, butterflies danced, you followed the path but your footsteps became heavier and heavier, with each step you were expending great energy extricating each foot from heavy mud, then clouds came over and the atmosphere started to grow dismal; was that really birdsong or was it human voices shrieking, you became considerably confused, weights were pressing on your eyelids so that you could no longer see, however hard you tried.

There were long hard years when you were lost in a strange land. Be not afeared, your mother had said to you. Where was she now? Gone in the flood. You were an orphan searching for others to esteem you. The school was grim, you were well pleased to be through with it. Music, you thought, that was all that mattered. That which gives delight and hurts not.

What do you play?

Modern jazz.

The girl in the leopardskin skirt in the Soho club where you found yourself, who allowed you to buy her a drink, said she liked that.

Everybody revered the tenor player, a big man, a hushed man, a quiet man, except when he was playing, then he could be quite formidable. *Wrong chord,* he'd mouth at you, his eyes flashing from across the bandstand, *wrong chord!* and you had to get it right then and there. But he liked you. He hired you, after all. Night after night, until the wee hours, hardly any customers, hardly any money, how was it possible, but you learned fast. The years went by.

The big gig, you remember that – that was something. Not the usual club. You all had to wear suits for it, the leader insisted, dark suits white shirts dark ties. Look sharp.

The piano, a baby grand here, had been wheeled onto the platform for you. You'd checked it was in tune, of course. The customers were assembling, chatting at high volume, the tables filling up, the seats behind too. Africans were present. The world in all its many shapes seemed to be here. Someone was speaking what sounded like Norwegian played backwards. Tenor sax gleamed sexually on its stand; a double bass leant against the wall; a shining drum kit was being assembled. A hi-hat thwacked. People hurried into and out of doorways. Cymbals like suns. Your Buddhist mate winked at you, picked up the bass and was running his long slender fingers up and down a steep scale, stopping to adjust a peg. Someone was waving. This was how you wanted to remember the old days.

The quiet leader – he never used to say much about anything before the gig, let alone what you were going to play – picked up his instrument, went back into the side shadows, a reed held between his lips, looking to fix it in place on the mouthpiece. Saxophone arpeggios, spinning on a harmonic curve. He turned to you, nodded. And looked away again. Because of the clusters, voices. House lights went down. Almost by accident, there you were, four of you now assembled. You looked as dignified as ghosts in your suits.

Begin.

He counted you in, you knew which number it was now. Together, you ripped into the hush at a crisp lick, tenor sax, piano, bass and drums. The saxophone called you, and you responded with terse phrases, against the turmoil of the drums and the deep-throated underpinning of the bass. What does it mean when you say that music is fast? What is meant by speed? It signifies perhaps that there are many events within a short space of time, almost too many for anyone to comprehend; a torrent is what you might call it. The opposite might be when there is an amplitude of time and therefore a single note could expand to occupy all of it. You had experienced all of that too by now.

You dropped out, as rehearsed, for the tenor solo, a controlled yet agonising blurting, as though the leader was feeling his way: how much space do I have, he seemed to be asking, before finding, exploring it, a microcosm of all the possible spaces in the world, and you could almost feel the white and black keys grow cool under your own fingers as you waited, watchfully, to come back in; and then when you did it seemed as though you were outside yourself, contemplating those fingers of yours, now bunched, now splayed, cascading fourths and sixths against a rippling right-hand melody line, changing mode and changing mode, then your left hand going into a chopping motion as the chords punctuated more sharply again and again, and moving back into the rippling motion before the sax returned with the melody, and the rhythm section brought the number to an end. Wow, you thought, the band is really cooking tonight.

The saxophone player put down his instrument and for the first time smiled and nodded at you before walking quietly off the stage. And so you knew the next number would start without him, with the cadences of "On Green Dolphin Street" which you tried to make as sprightly as you could, that beautiful right-hand ripple now working to perfection, your mate on bass alongside trotting up and down the scale in his Zen way, brushes on the snare drum, the tune at first at a tiptoe, then working out at leisure, before eventually the saxophonist returned, singing in the upper register, and everyone was now really relaxed and into it.

That was undoubtedly the best gig you ever played. And it went down well too for sure. The buzz at the interval when the house lights went up was pretty fabulous. It seemed like everybody in the world was there in that Soho club that night. A group said to be from Athens, with the air of philosophers. Businessmen and policemen in their boots at the bar. Other musicians, of course, unusually generous with compliments. An Earth Mother. Bohemians. A band of dark strangers. A family of refugees. A Dante Alighieri lookalike. At a corner table, you could swear you saw local residents Mr William and Mrs Catherine Blake.

And the cute girl in the leopardskin skirt grinned sweetly at you, and you knew then you were going to spend your life with her. Or at least the next few years. How would that end? That is another story.

In the second set the tenor player was truly on fire. At

one point he seemed multiplied by three, suspended in air, accompanying himself: No 1 taking the high register, No 2 the middle and No 3 the bass part, weaving a polyphonic web out of those cadences that never actually resolved. And then you and the band came in out of nowhere playing a groove strung together like a row of beads, not one of them symmetrically constructed, none identical to any other, but following one another as though possessed by the spirit haunting the ancient reservoir of the blues and the melancholy house of the Negro Spiritual, yet venturing into the outer reaches of tonality, into unrepeatable areas, places visited for the first and last time. Beautiful, someone commented. But some of it was ugly. Deliberately so. A rumbling, as of distant thunder, like burglars licensed by the government battering at the doors. Every rimshot was the discharge of a firearm. Every cymbal clash signified the ruin of a culture. What a terrible world, and nothing of it was forgotten, but the pain could be overcome (this is what the music was saying), it could be vanquished. There was your mate the bass player strumming his instrument like a Spanish guitar, grinning like crazy, before returning to his stalking pattern; the drummer presiding over an array of glittering cauldrons each brewing up a different rhythm; and as for you, you felt at one with all the eighty-eight keys holding the measure of the thing. It was no longer modern jazz. At times it was not even music any longer, seeming to escape the very pull of gravitation.

So yes indeed, the joint was jumping! A lamb trotted across the floor; dolphins appeared leaping from the turquoise water; humpback whales sang in unison. Among the audience now were trilobites and polecats, and lost cousins come from afar. Everybody was welcome. The audience could no longer go home. And you knew you couldn't either, because all of that was gone before.

Then there was a great deal of after-hours drinking, which is what used to happen in those days.

You have experienced love, you have experienced grief. What else is there?

I'll take you to see the seals, said your father. The plan was to go in your Uncle Charlie's boat. And so one day you did: the boat tripped along over the waves, bumping hilariously in the sunshine, the breeze snapping sharply in your face.

You came to the place where the monk seals basked, the last of their kind. They lay on the wet rocks while the water lapped beneath them, some of them asleep, others raising their chubby, mournful faces to look at you. Dark, shiny shapes. We call them the sea wolves, said your father. Or was it your uncle? Did your father even go on that trip? Was he not away with the fairies by then? So it must have been your uncle. Sea wolves. Why? That's just the name we give them. The boat bobbed around the seals' island. You contemplated them. They lay and basked in the sunshine. Some were deep grey, others more brownish, their blubbery pelts lustrous but also as you got closer you noticed the greenish markings on them; it was like writing, like fine calligraphy, but whatever it was that was written on their skins, that in some cases covered their entire bodies, was indecipherable, even when you looked through your uncle's binoculars, and no matter how hard you tried to concentrate you could not read that inscrutable text, those elusive and mysterious messages.

Something had spooked them. Or perhaps it was just time to move on. They began to slither on the rocks, propelling themselves clumsily with their flippers. One by one, they slipped into the sea, transforming uncannily into creatures of grace and purpose, and soon were seen no more.

Day 30

AND ONCE AGAIN, for the final time, to the present. Thirty days have now gone by since you came home, that is, to the place where you have lived for many years, which you recognised with delight, which put a new spring to your step, having walked naked all night through the streets of London to get here. Thirty days have passed since you let yourself in with your own key, and found it all to your liking, were refreshed with some hot tea and scraps of food; thirty days since you listened to some confusing messages that you did not at all know what to make of but decided not to worry about. Thirty days since you found yourself back in your very own comfortable bed in your very own peaceful flat, and went into that lovely dream. Nobody can take that away from you now. Nobody.

Since then, however, you have not moved at all.

You have remained peacefully in your bed for a month, with only the monotonous sound of the TV to accompany you. Your eyes have remained closed. And you will of course remain there until you are found.

By now, sorry to say, your mortal form is in a state of advanced deterioration.

This is the stage of bacterial decay. The bacteria that once inhabited and indeed largely constituted your body – or the descendants of those bacteria – will eventually consume it even without the help of insects. But also several generations of maggots are present on your body and by now some will have become fully grown. Their instinct will be to migrate from your body and bury themselves in the soil in order to become pupae. But they have nowhere to go, so a mass death is continually occurring.

Predatory maggots, however, are also thriving, even as those pioneer flies witnessed previously cease to be attracted to your corpse. There may well also be predatory beetles ready to lay their eggs in your corpse and their larvae will hatch out and feed on your decaying flesh. If any parasitoid wasps were to be present (there is no sign of this), they would also be laying their eggs inside maggots and pupae.

Because your body will by now be anoxic, all metabolic activity taking place within it will be fermentative and will thus form various gases including methane, carbon dioxide, ammonia and hydrogen, as well as organic compounds such as butyric acid. This contributes to the unpleasant smell pervading the room, which attracts a new suite of corpse organisms.

Blisters are forming on your skin, of varying sizes, filled with dark fluids and putrid gases. Gas production begins to bloat your body, particularly in regions where the skin is loose. It is the most rapid in your intestines, where the majority of bacteria within your body are to be found. The gases formed cause your abdomen to distend and the pressure within to rise, perhaps forcing faeces out of your rectum and stomach contents through your nose and mouth. Gases cause your closed eyelids to become swollen, also your lips to swell and pout, your cheeks to puff out, and your tongue to protrude between your lips. Some blood-stained froth appears at your mouth and nostrils. The hair on your head and other parts of your body is becoming loose at the roots. Your fingernails and toenails and large areas of your skin are also becoming loose and easily detachable.

So it goes.

Were you to incline your head left towards your bedroom window, which of course you can't do, you would on at least one occasion have seen the top of the Christian window cleaner's extendable plastic broom, with its twin squirting jets of water, bobbing up and down and across the windowpanes, assiduously wiping them clean. You would not know from observing the merry bobbing that the window cleaner has had serious concerns about your absence. That he will be fretting, that he will soon be putting out an alarm. That he will already know, in his heart of hearts, that it's far too late, but that he could never have done anything about it, that he is not to blame, but that still he blames himself.

You will be oblivious to the life continuing elsewhere within this province, this corner of the universe that you once knew so well. Citizens walk their dogs in the park while the wind blows; the little streams flow into the pond at the far end, wherein unknown creatures dwell; boys play football and shout; at the back of the pub, a man strikes another in his paunch, which sounds like a drum, thereby unloading the sadness within him; and meanwhile, unconcerned and unknowing, others at the bar inside laugh and banter and quench their thirst. In the lower house of our parliament a goblin rises to speak at the dispatch box, assuming all the dignity that a goblin can muster, while the row of ill-born shades on the green benches behind mutter and nod their heads in unison. Their faces do not answer to their bellies, they hold their lips apart in malevolent sneers.

As evening comes on, the wind gets up, the trees in the park are swaying, there is a sudden crash in the garden behind the flats, but it's only a couple of metal chairs falling over.

You know nothing of all this, you are serene, you are in the middle of nowhere, a good place to be, some say. If only it weren't for that infernal TV, it would be admirably quiet and peaceful here. But you can't have everything. The sun has risen thirty times, visible or not from your theoretical point of view, brightening the window of your bedroom each time and setting off a flurry of jazz birdsong from the various denizens of London gardens you would have recognised as bluetits, great tits, chaffinches, sparrows, the occasional glossy starling, many pigeons – how they hum, how they pipe! – and it has set thirty times, on the far side of the park, where you couldn't see it from here anyway, but you would know that it had from the evidence of the dusk that has descended, sometimes with a reddish hue if the evening has been fine.

Left here much longer, your bloated body will reach a crisis point, marked by the abdominal cavity bursting open, but not before your organs have become discoloured and your tissues have liquefied, the eyeballs, stomach and intestines being the first to go, followed by the muscular organs. Small white plaques may form on the outer surface of your heart. That organ, which has served you well through more than eight decades, itself will become flabby and thin-walled. Your spleen and lungs will become friable, and gas formation will cause your liver and brain to develop honeycomb patterns, the brain turning to mush, your kidneys enduring for longer, turning into squashy bags filled with thick, turbid liquid, which will also in time rupture.

Eventually, your body will collapse to a flatter shape, with flesh of a creamy consistency, the exposed parts delivering a strong smell of decay. Body fluids will drain from you and seep into the surrounding bedclothes. Other insects and mites feed on all this. They and other creatures present, such as beetles (hatched from eggs laid by an earlier generation), will feed on and eventually consume the bulk of your skin, ligaments and flesh, and your body temperature will actually increase with all their activity. The surface of your body will become covered with mould as it ferments.

So it goes, from the discolouration of the organs to the liquefaction of the tissues. Your body fats are converted to oleic, palmitic and stearic acids, your proteins are ultimately broken down to amino acids, the original building blocks of protein molecules. Little by little, your body is being gently taken apart. Eventually, if you are not discovered, all your remaining flesh will be removed and your corpse will dry out. You are unconsciously striving, following the laws of nature, including the laws of thermodynamics, to reach equilibrium, to reach an accord with your environment, merging with the rest of the universe, or that portion of it that is local to you. Molecules that have accreted now disperse, molecules that have dispersed will henceforth accrete in new forms. Rest assured that nothing is lost, that you are being recycled.

So life occupies all the spaces, in your flat and beyond it, that it can. Mice grow into grotesque forms, at least in the imagination, which is a human by-product of all of this process, a faculty that leaves behind it only traces, as all forms do, a record of their passing through, and then even those traces themselves breaking down into their component parts, and then even the trail of that process itself....

Galleons shiver on the high seas, the wind blows them to shore, their planking breaks up, the fibres of the wood of which the planks are made being processed by the mouth-parts and digestive systems of mites, beetles and other creatures that themselves come to the end of their short lives....

Sepulchres continually give up their cargo within the necropolis at large. It's difficult to maintain the record-keeping, and the task may be seen as hopeless if one bears in mind that the records will themselves decay; if one bears in mind that mind will decay.

Day 31

But who in hell are you anyway? And are you out of it now? The two questions that matter: who and where. (We shall leave aside when and why.)

In other words, what is your status?

Now you have come to this. But then everything comes to this. Eventually. That's pretty banal. So what is the point?

Why the imperative that everything must have a point?

That is a good question.

But who were you? What are the elements of your history that add up to determining who you are? (That's called backstory, isn't it?) How can such elements be combined into a record that will be convincing and enlightening? Has enough been written by now?

And who is keeping the record? Is the record accurate? Is it truthful? Has every effort been made to render events faithfully, that is to say, in accordance with the facts, insofar as they can be ascertained, if indeed there are any facts to be had? And in accordance with the *spirit* of the thing, if we can use such terms? (Can we use such terms?) How plausible is the record? Will it adequately convince? How long will it endure before it, too, decays?

Of course, it may be objected, this is not a record, so much as an account. A bit more wobbly, one may say. No checks and balances. Too much room for manoeuvre. Potentially tendentious.

Who monitors all this?

Well, let's not get into any of that stuff. Let's get back to you. This narrative has striven to be fair to you. But it has not always been clear what your point of view has been in regard to it. What were you thinking all this time? And particularly towards the end. Was there any thought going on? Did you see the white light of the void? What do you mean, you missed it? Did you see the monsters? All the time, you say? Were those beings merely manufactured by your mind, as your Buddhist bass-player friend attested, or were they real? Did you hear a confusion of tongues, a babble? While you lay there in your improvised pyjamas? Were you offered a menu of options? Were you stung by a tongue? Did it tint your cheeks, did it offer you healing? Did you accept or reject what you were offered? Were you bamboozled by all this? In what ways does an actual death experience resemble a near death experience? Are there any lessons to be learnt? Who is to learn them? To what use are those lessons to be put?

What were the thoughts running through your mind at key moments? When, for example, 'Itler was being taken for a walk on his lead, his nails clacking on the pavement, his master confined at the very foundation of the universe, trapped by insuperable gravitational forces (that must be why his face was so squashy). OK, there you were, as a witness, it says so here. But there isn't much more.

There is a lot that can be said about you, however. For example, it is clear from all the evidence presented that you have a certain integrity of being, you cannot be bartered. You are not fungible. Nobody can assail you, and especially not when you run naked through the streets of London. You have certain powers. You are capable of hearing harmonies an infinite distance away, melodies that are constructed on no known principles. You can observe all the creatures that dwell within the margins of existence. You don't accumulate. You forget. You forget again.

It all comes back to you. You are all over the preceding matter. On practically every page. You are the anchor: whatever mazy runs, with shaking of tail feathers, the writing may embark on, you pull it back. That may be your most significant function. There you are again. That is to say, the second person, singular in this case, thou not ye.

But if there's a second person, who is the first?

The first person singular is I.

And who, then, am I? Never mind me – I'm just the teller of the tale. If there's a tale there has to be a teller. If there's an answer, there must be a question. That's all there is to it. That's all. It's better if the teller is an idiot, or nobody. The teller is a mere functionary, with no backstory, no prior or outstanding existence, at least not one that is pertinent to the tale.

But what, then, is or is not pertinent to the tale?

If the tale is full of sound and fury, does it follow that it really signifies nothing? Particularly if the teller is nobody?

Is the teller an angel, or an alien if you prefer, not a person? No body involved? Does this no body dispense hierarchies of illusion, all the way down to the fundament? Just as there is no musician performing, no instrument being played, no listener as a separate entity, just as, when it is really happening (really?), when the band is cooking, when it is at its zenith, there is *only* the music, so too can it be imagined that we may reach a stage where there is no I writing, no subject being addressed, no reader following the thread, where there is only writing? Once this state has been achieved, does it slip away into the flood and eventually disappear?

This teller has no correlate in the world that is the subject of the account. I is another, said a poet a long, long time ago. When you are addressed, does this happen only according to the rules of rhetoric, some of them made up on the spot? You are accounted for, but the teller is not held to account. The teller evades discovery, because the secret, that there is no teller, is unconscionable. If this were not the subterfuge, your story would not, could not then be told. But it is just a story, after all. It's not a corporate communication, for goodness' sake. There is no authority behind it. It confers no mandate, carries with it no responsibilities, is not put together within a framework of set policies, aims and objectives. Take it or leave it.

The only sure thing is that particles accrete, particles disperse.

How do we get out of here?

Nobody gets out of here. In a world where the bottom line is always paramount, that's the bottom bottom line.

I have another idea. Look: I can spin this out without you if need be; but I can *be* you in a trice, and you are then free to be whoever it is that means the most to you.

Shall we change places?

Day 32

(A CONVERSATION IS taking place somewhere nearby, outside my flat. It is said that hearing is the last sense to remain. Let's go with that, even though I am actually long gone, all my body fluids dispersing. The conversation can be heard clearly above the general low-level hubbub. They seem to be talking about me. One voice is almost certainly that of the window cleaner, Chris; the other, his interlocutor, is unknown.)

He told me he'd been married, that's all I know, says the voice of the window cleaner.

Ah, yes, says the other.

His wife died some years ago, apparently.

Do you know of any other next of kin?

He once mentioned a daughter who had gone to live in Australia, I think. But I don't know any more than that. He never said much about himself. Another time he mentioned he had arrived in this country as a child, an orphan, I believe. Said his family had perished in a hurricane or a tsunami, or something, and he was brought up by an aunt. But when I asked him a bit more about that, he clammed up. He obviously didn't want to talk about it.

Did you think he had something to hide?

No, not at all, he was just a shy man, I suppose. Reserved. I expect you probably know more than me.

We have no more information about his background. He was under investigation. Anything you can contribute would be helpful.

He seemed a nice enough chap.

Uh-huh.

Used to be a musician, he once told me.

Is that so?

Yes, he showed me an LP that had his name on it. He played jazz piano. But he said he had given up playing some time ago. All the musicians he used to play with were dead, he told me. He said he'd even stopped listening to music, which was quite sad.

Uh-huh.

Don't you think so? I think that's quite sad.

Yeah.

He was not a well man. He had diabetes, had to inject himself every day, he told me, but he started getting memory problems, I know that because he began to ask me all sorts of strange questions. Kept forgetting to do the injections, apparently. Do you think that's what's happened here?

I have no detailed data to hand on his medical record, or any medical issues he may have had. It'll be on the files, though.

Well, I know he was taken to hospital by ambulance, when was it, oh, many months ago, then I heard no more.

Yes, he was an emergency admission, then he was in Safeguarding for a while, before being transferred.

I heard on the grapevine he'd ended up in the Holding Pen.

That is not a name I recognise.

Because of some irregularities about his status, being originally from overseas. That's what I heard, anyway.

I can't comment on that.

But now you're telling me he escaped?

I can tell you there was a significant security breach. That's what we're investigating. And following that, a major failure in communication, which is clearly very disappointing.

He escaped from the Holding Pen! That's not possible. No-one escapes from the Holding Pen. That's what they say.

Is that so?

So what is this security breach that you're talking about?

I can't discuss that in detail. It followed industrial action and an unrelated fire incident in one of our IDSs.

IDSs?

Sorry, Interim Detention Facilities.

So what happened?

I can't comment, obviously. But something went wrong during routine evacuation procedures. Clearly, heads will roll over this.

The public need to know about it.

I don't think there's any necessity for that. The public understands the need for security at this time in our nation's –

Well, of course, nobody cares about the Holding Pen.

I beg your pardon?

Is that what you're saying?

I am neither asserting nor denying –

Well, you're probably right. Most people have no idea such places exist, and don't want to know, I suppose.

What do you mean by "such places"?

Maybe they don't exist, I don't know.

Can I go back to what you were saying earlier, you were saying you had no idea he had returned to his flat?

No. I clean the windows in this block, and occasionally I do other odd jobs. I would meet him from time to time. I remember the ambulance taking him away. So far as I knew, he was in hospital, or wherever it was he was.

I see. But you did not notice his return?

What's that?

You never noticed?

I did ... I noticed too late. I mean ... I blame myself, really.

Why?

Well, I did think he was back at first. I heard voices in the flat.

Voices?

I thought they were voices. I thought one was his. I don't know, I thought "That's funny".

What was funny?

Not funny. Strange. I let it go. I wish I hadn't. What I realise now of course is that it was the TV that had been left on. I mean, you can still hear it now, it's obvious once you know. But I didn't twig then, and so I didn't report it. I should have.

That would have helped. But it doesn't make any difference now. We have a situation.

What are we waiting for now, may I ask?

The police. As always. Nothing can be done without them. But as often as not nothing is achieved with them. And the local authority need to put in their oar as well, and Uncle Tom Cobbley and all.

Well, to go back to ... then after that I wasn't around for a long while. And when I returned, I thought, I wonder if he's in? And I was on the landing, I thought I heard the same voices. So I didn't like to knock, in case I was disturbing something –

Hang on, they're on their way. You were saying?

Nothing. I must admit I forgot about it again, though something was niggling me. But then the third time, oh my word ... I caught a whiff....

That's the clincher. I can smell it too.

I went all cold. I had a realisation ... I thought, oh my goodness, that's not ... that's the telly that's been left on ... for a moment I wondered about putting together the long ladder, trying to have a peep through the window, but I thought better of it ... so that's when I called the emergency services, and as soon as I gave the details I was put onto you guys. Who are you, by the way?

It doesn't matter who I am. Well, you mustn't blame yourself.

I do.

Seriously, it shouldn't have come to this. It's the fault of our systems. It's been a major cockup from the start. Not just the security breach with which it all started, but following that the failure to track him back to his home address. It seems to have originated in a glitch – systems not talking to each other properly, you understand. Artificial Intelligence, it's popularly known as, but if it's set up by idiots it's Artificial Stupidity. Well, there was a lot of administrative confusion at the time, for example the care providers had had their contract terminated for incompetence around that time, but the company that took over were not much better. Anyway, there was apparently some confusion about the address, whether he actually lived here, and if not, because we had evidence he had sold his flat, what was his proper address? And no means of resolving that issue. So now it's become serious. I'm as conflicted as anyone about this. Yes, thanks to yourself we've located him – unhappily, too late, as it almost certainly appears. But now can you imagine the huge amount of bureaucracy this is going to generate? I'm going to have to spend hours filling in online forms, there are going to be endless recriminations, people blaming each other, senior management doing their best to evade responsibility as per usual by passing it down the line, it's going to be a nightmare.

Well, you can't blame *him* for trying to get away, can you?

I beg your pardon?

I mean, he never deserved that.

Deserved what?

How he must have been treated.

Deserving doesn't come into it. It's not a question of deserving, is it?

Isn't it?

Our systems do not support notions such as deserving or not deserving. It's not a question of deserving, it's a question of whether the correct protocols have been followed.

(Here the conversation becomes blurred and confused. There are other voices coming in now, a veritable babble of them. Doors banging. A new cohort of people on-site. Their voices seem to come from the bottom of the universe, where all gravity converges. Sometimes sound like the croaking of benevolent frogs.)

We have a casualty?

Unconfirmed.

Any means of access?

I checked the windows, they all seem tight shut.

That's a pity. Worth breaking one open? No?

It must be pretty stifling in there.

Yeah, it won't be great.

No, I think it's best we go in through the door.

It's your shout.

Anybody checked the neighbours?

Nobody around. The one across the hall seems to be vacant, the one below likewise. Immediately above, it's unclear. No response, anyway.

Well, this is classed as an emergency, you understand.

We do this all the time, it's kind of routine, but, like, every one is different, you know what I mean?

Yeah.

Ah, you're ready? You looking a bit peaky, like.

Yeah ... did you catch the match last night?

I feel your pain.

Premier League season has only just started, and already this.

Fucking nonsense it was. No help from the ref, mind you.

Gawd help us.

Well, to work, guys. Wayne, where's Wayne, there you are. You're coming in with us, lad, you all right with that?

Yeah.

It's not going to be pretty, it's not going to be nice, you understand?

Yeah.

If you find it difficult to handle, nobody's going to blame you, OK? Eventually you get used to it.

(It seems they don't know, nobody knows, and nobody is going to think of it and find out that I've left the key under the doormat as usual, that it was there all this time, that they could simply have lifted the mat and found it and let themselves into my flat by using it, without all this performance – but that's the way it is.)

You got the hammer, right. Let's go. Let's go, mate.

(There is a momentary gap in the conversation, then the silence is broken by a mighty crash, and then another. Within three expert blows the door is breached and can be pushed open. They go through.)

Yeah, no doubt about it, it's a bad one.

(I have been discovered!)

Fuck me, where's he going?

(The boy Wayne, if it is indeed he, is withdrawing from the proceedings, he is trying to hold himself together at the threshold. Sorry, sorry, he's saying.)

It's OK, lad.

(He turns and runs, out of the door, down the stairs, flings open the street door. Observers may be able to watch him run across the road, choosing a gap in the traffic, vault into the park like an Olympic athlete. He might then be observed throwing up onto the grass.)

He'll learn.

(Minutes pass. The men go into their routines, wordlessly.

The boy returns.)

You all right, Wayne? You've lost your colour.

Yeah, OK. Sorry about that. Couldn't ... couldn't help it.

No worries, son.

(Another voice:) Sorry. It's as we feared. There isn't much of him left, actually.

(The voice of the window cleaner may be heard in the background. It is unclear what he is saying. Then silence intervenes once more. The men are working. They are setting about their allotted tasks with the minimum of fuss.)

Day 33

ALL CREDIT TO those who have been entrusted with the unpleasant task of removing my mortal remains. They have been charged with the need to observe proper decorum and respect, and this need they do their best to fulfill, with only the occasional lapse. Screens and barriers have been erected, the curious public has been told there is nothing of significance going on, there's nothing to worry about, all will be sorted in an hour or two, and then the flat will be sealed off, the heavy cleaners will be going in, the fumigators with their overalls, masks and gloves and sundry equipment, chatting almost normally, for by now the burden that was once mine, that I carried for more than eight decades, will have been lifted and removed elsewhere, only the traces remaining, of no more significance than the detritus in an alleyway, though there's still something hanging in the air, both metaphorically and actually, that causes voices to dip respectfully below a certain dynamic level as a matter of course.

I'm really sorry about all this, about the trouble I've caused. If I could, I'd thank them all in turn and apologise personally. If I could only give voice, in my own time, in my own way.

To be given my voice at last is a great thing, even though it's when I'm no longer alive, when the last physical traces of me have been eradicated. Even though that voice is only borrowed. Does it suit me? I don't know. Who cares, now.

Let's describe what I imagine may be happening. It's a

really beautiful summer's morning. The long shadows of the trees fall upon the golden spaces in the park. It's not what it was, but it's still pretty nice at this time of year. As I always say, this flat has a really good outlook, you have to agree. The ducks are beginning to make a hullabaloo in their pond on the far side. People are going about their business, ears stopped up by the buds of their electronic devices. Traffic hums peacefully.

In the neighbourhood church, Father Fuck is praying for me. He has remembered to include my memory in his early morning mass. It's rather lower in key than his Easter sermon, which had featured an at times verging on hysterical rant about the enemies of the Church being all around us. Some said that was an embarrassing performance, it turned a lot of people off. But now Father Fuck is in a more sober mood. His face is less purple. Father Fuck is holding the chalice aloft. He doesn't really enjoy wine. He has confided to the altar boy in the privacy of the sacristy that he wishes it were possible to transubstantiate malt whisky. But there you are, you have to work with what you're given. The three or four in the congregation, devout women of mature years, come up to the altar rail and kneel. Father Fuck is dispensing the magic biscuits.

At the end of the day the window cleaner too remembers me, with a jolt, though his memory is heavily contaminated with distress and guilt. He says his prayers silently in his head as he reclines in bed, the low-wattage bulb of his bedside lamp still burning, his wife beside him already beginning to breathe deeply and regularly, with a very gentle nasal whistling, as she drifts into the first shallows of sleep. He asks for forgiveness for not reading the signs in respect of my return after so many months away, for mistaking the voices heard within my flat for those of others who might be helping me, for not realising there was nobody to help me.

But hey, it's just one of those things. He wouldn't have been in time to intervene anyway, so it scarcely matters.

And so the days and nights go by in the world I have now left. That's OK with me – I've had enough, I'm out of it.

Someone somewhere is listening to an album by a jazz quartet led by a tenor sax player of some repute back in the nineteen sixties or thenabouts. It's on the original vinyl, purchased for an extortionate sum, on account of its rarity. Who's the pianist on this one? Don't know. Turns the record sleeve, scrutinises the credits. Piano is given as [FORENAME] [SURNAME]. Hadn't heard of him before. Nice solo on that track. Lovely. What happened to him? Early sixties, well, rock came along, the Beatles came along, jazz started to have a hard time, the clubs closed, there weren't the opportunities any more. No, I don't know what happened to that pianist.

They were giants in those days.

Today it's all computers, you can't believe it. Everything's simulated. It's all virtual, you don't need reality any more, away with it. The kids all have their devices. The real musicians are all dead. You will not see their like again, but nobody cares. Out there it's a dog toilet, or it's a beautiful sea of daffodils, who knows, but everyone's off in la-la land, having a wonderful time, waving their stupid flags. They have all had their memories amputated. It works better that way, they say.

I wish someone would turn the bloody TV off. Wait a minute. I think they have. What a relief.

How I know I'm dead is that I can't see the future any more. Whatever that amounts to. I remember the light, which darkness gave way to. I think the light used to come in on the left-hand side. There used to be differentiation. So that's a window, that's how the light comes in. How very interesting. It's strange that I seem to have a profound spiritual capacity for recognising fundamental realities like this, yet at the same time being paralysed so there's nothing much if at all I can do about it. But what country am I in? Does it have a name? Have I? Surely I must have a name? What day is it? Are these questions? Does time pass? I'm not aware of time passing. It may be passing, without my noticing it. I think it has passed, it is passing. There is no sure thing, but what I do remember almost for sure now is turning over in the bed – it is a bed! – turning onto my left side, facing the window, if there is a window, but I've lost it now. I can't turn over. I can't do any of that now.

Is that you?

Who are you?

Is it you?

Or is it the burglar, is he back? I don't have anything left, he's welcome to anything he can find. The TV, he can take that. He did it before. The key is under the mat, he's welcome to use it. Or is it the nurse, I'd like to see her again, to explain my problems. Complex medical problems. It's all condensing out of nowhere. Who was that chap who swindled me? I'm almost certain now he swindled me. Not BJ, surely he wouldn't have. Surely not. Or did he? All of this is coming back, it's imploding. All of my life: how I was a young man first, and then I became middle-aged and then I became an old man, and that was that. End of story, nothing more to say. Everything that was found is lost, or the other way round, it's hard to work out. All the light in the world's jammed together, pulled back by gravity. What country am I in? Have I asked that question before? What has happened to that country, was it ever my home, did it ever welcome me? That country they want back, the stupid flag-wavers, they're welcome to it. I don't think much to the country these days. But what is this place? The place where water is vertical? I don't know, I must be back in the Holding Pen, there's no escape from it, after all. The usual labyrinth. The usual ordeals to be faced. Endless travel, through corridors that become streets, in the strange city at night, in the usual realm of nowhere, with distant views of travelling cranes, and the people milling about somewhere but completely out of sight, my people, your people, nobody's people. All my people gone. Long gone. The nurse pats me on the hand. I'm in the Holding Pen, for sure. Distant howling of humans, or of animals, perhaps they're only urban foxes. They all have their needs. And I'm found wandering and told to stay in a strange room as a punishment. The orders come directly from Dr Hardy, I believe. Who was he? Punishment for what? They tell me all the evil in the world, which is the human world, because the non-human world hasn't yet heard about evil, all of it has been condensed and distilled and infused in me, without my consent I might protest, but that doesn't count for anything, and the monsters I see on my travels through that world are therefore products of my evil mind, and obviously that has to be dealt with. But then I think these people are play-acting – later, they try to convince me the episode that I reported never took place, that there was no strange room or punishment, that I had probably got muddled because of my condition. No, wait a minute, what am I talking about? Now I remember. Clear as crystal. I escaped from the Holding Pen. I did. I am out of the Holding Pen forever. That's my hope. I still have hope, that's good. But I can't speak. This is my voice. Well, OK, I borrowed it. And there is nothing behind it.

Nothing else exists.

Somebody else's voice: Are you kidding? *Nobody* escapes from the Holding Pen.

But the pain has gone. That's good. There is more detail. I just can't make it out. The world has been flooded, it has been overwhelmed, it will never be the same again. Nature will have its revenge on the human race, you understand, because the human race has forgotten it's part of it. Of nature, I mean. Of the world. I can't see the world now, admittedly, but I can hear something, you know, did I mention before that they say hearing is the last sense to fade? Well, I found that. Lots of things going on. The background hum of humans, it's unmistakeable. I don't care for them much, humans. At one point I even thought I didn't care much for life in general: a malign force introduced into the universe by god knows what: one part, the part that is stronger, forever and without compassion consuming the other, the part that is weaker, to what purpose? None whatever, none that I can see. But I've somewhat relented, I've changed my mind a bit, at least since I've been disintegrating these thirty-odd days, I realise now that I am not I, that we are a community, all of us, the flies, the beetles, the bacteria, the micro-organisms with their tiny mouth parts munching away, the cells consuming themselves, recycling, recycling, always recycling, they're all OK, and ... but humans? Hey, is that you? No? That you? There you are, you were kidding me all along. The world continues, for better or worse, that's what my mother always used to say, when we lived on the island – that was many years ago. Those were the days. And there is nothing better than listening to meaningless platitudes uttered by those you love.

The worst is over.

Also available from grand**IOTA**

Brian Marley: APROPOS JIMMY INKLING
978-1-874400-73-8 318pp

Ken Edwards: WILD METRICS
978-1-874400-74-5 244pp

Fanny Howe: BRONTE WILDE
978-1-874400-75-2 158pp

Ken Edwards: THE GREY AREA
978-1-874400-76-9 328pp

Alan Singer: PLAY, A NOVEL
978-1-874400-77-6 268pp

Brian Marley: THE SHENANIGANS
978-1-874400-78-3 220pp

Barbara Guest: SEEKING AIR
978-1-874400-79-0 218pp

Toby Olson: JOURNEYS ON A DIME
978-1-874400-80-6 300pp

Philip Terry: BONE
978-1-874400-81-3 150pp

James Russell: GREATER LONDON: A NOVEL
978-1-874400-82-2 276pp

Askold Melnyczuk: THE MAN WHO WOULD NOT BOW
978-1-874400-83-7 196pp

Andrew Key: ROSS HALL
978-1-874400-84-4 190pp

Edmond Caldwell: HUMAN WISHES/ENEMY COMBATANT
978-1-874400-85-1 298pp

Production of this book has been made possible with the help of the following individuals and organisations who subscribed in advance:

Tony Baker
Peter Barry
Christopher Beckett
Andy Benson
Thomas Bissinger
Paul Bream
Andrew Brewerton
Ian Brinton
Jasper Brinton
Peter Brown
John Cayley
Claire Crowther
Brian Docherty
Rachel DuPlessis
Michael Finnissy
Allen Fisher/Spanner
Jim Goar
Giles Goodland
Paul Green
Penny Grossi
Charles Hadfield
John Hall
Randolph Healy
Peter Hodgkiss
Christine Holloway
Richard Hull
Kristoffer Jacobson
Richy & Gill Johnson
Pierre Joris

Andrew Key
Sharon Kivland
Ian Land
Richard Makin
Michael Mann
Askold Melnyczuk
Peter Middleton
Linda Morris
Richie Nice
Paul Nightingale
Toby Olson
Irene Payne
Sean Pemberton
Dennis Phillips
Keith Rodway
David Rose
Lou Rowan
Emily Rubin
James Russell
Maurice Scully
Steven Seidenberg
Alan Singer
Aidan Semmens
Valerie Soar
Eileen Tabios
VISUAL ASSOCIATIONS
Keith Washington
Marie Whitehead
June Lovell-Wilkes

www.grandiota.co.uk

Lightning Source UK Ltd.
Milton Keynes UK
UKHW012314090822
407081UK00001B/73